Frost outside, Jacob Knight hot and hungry for her inside—it was everything she needed right now.

There was danger in both places, but this was the danger she chose.

Desire spiked through her, and she marveled that her heart didn't stop dead in her chest. But when he lifted his lips, she simply pulled him back down. "Don't stop."

Threads of thought were all she had left and, even with only half of her brain functioning, she managed to see his eyes go dark. And darker.

This wasn't a new thing between them, just an old spark that never quite had a chance to ignite. Merry Christmas...

JENNA RYAN

MISTLETOE AND MURDER

TORONTO • NEW YORK • LONDON
AMSTERDAM • PARIS • SYDNEY • HAMBURG
STOCKHOLM • ATHENS • TOKYO • MILAN • MADRID
PRAGUE • WARSAW • BUDAPEST • AUCKLAND

To Rick and Mary for making this
and other stories happen.

ISBN-13: 978-0-373-69294-1
ISBN-10:   0-373-69294-3

MISTLETOE AND MURDER

ABOUT THE AUTHOR

Jenna Ryan loves creating dark-haired heroes, strong heroines and good murder mysteries. Ever since she was young, she has had an extremely active imagination. She considered various careers over the years and dabbled in several of them, until the day her sister Kathy suggested she put her imagination to work and write a book. She enjoys working with intriguing characters and feels she is at her best writing romantic suspense. When people ask her how she writes, she tells them by instinct. Clearly it's worked, since she's received numerous awards from *Romantic Times BOOKreviews*. She lives in Canada and travels as much as she can when she's not writing.

Books by Jenna Ryan

Don't miss any of our special offers. Write to us at the following address for information on our newest releases.

Harlequin Reader Service
U.S.: 3010 Walden Ave., P.O. Box 1325, Buffalo, NY 14269
Canadian: P.O. Box 609, Fort Erie, Ont. L2A 5X3

CAST OF CHARACTERS

Romana Grey—Former Cincinnati police officer marked for death by Warren Critch.

Jacob Knight—Cincinnati police detective. Red Christmas cards from Critch mark him for death, as well.

Anna Fitzgerald—Romana's cousin. She has a police record and a nose for trouble.

Belinda Critch—Critch's wife. She was murdered seven Christmases ago.

Warren Critch—He believes Jacob Knight killed his wife.

Dylan Hoag—Belinda Critch's embittered brother. He and Romana attended the police academy together.

Michael "Mick" O'Keefe—Jacob's former partner knew Belinda in the past and is in love with Romana now.

Patrick North—Friend and confidant, he worked closely with Belinda.

James Barret—A corporate executive. He's enjoyed the company of many women, but was Belinda one of them?

Shera Barret—A jealous woman, she'll do anything to keep her husband from cheating on her.

Prologue

Lovely Romana…
I will think of you at Christmas
Until the day I'm free.
Will you stand beneath the mistletoe
And think as well of me?

Warren Critch wanted to write more, but he knew the card would be inspected before it left the facility.

Federal prison, that's where the judge had sent him. Twelve years inside for attempting to shoot a police officer. There'd been no mention as to why a high school chemistry teacher had been holding a gun on the officer in question and only a fleeting reference to the woman said officer had murdered.

Warren pictured his wife's face in death. Sweet Belinda. How beautiful she'd looked, even with a bullet hole the size of a pigeon's egg in her chest.

Oh, yes, they'd let him see her. Someone said there'd been mistletoe leaves scattered around her. The police had murmured the usual platitudes. They'd shuffled their cop feet and cleared their collective throats. But not one of them had made eye contact with him. Not in the morgue, not in his jail cell and certainly not in the courtroom.

Jacob Knight was one of their own; Warren Critch was not. As for Warren's wife, well, just because Jacob had been involved with Belinda once, had lunch with her two days before she'd died and argued with her in public, that didn't mean he'd killed her. Cops didn't shoot innocent people. Warren was wrong to believe that. Someone else had put that hole in her chest.

His lips thinned. Did they take him for a complete fool? Jacob Knight had threatened Belinda twice. Then he'd done the deed.

Warren could have stopped him, would have if Officer Romana Grey hadn't slipped into the alley and pressed her own gun to the base of his neck. She'd warned him to back off, and he had. Dammit, he had. Because of that, Belinda was dead.

Warren's fingers shook as he shoved the festive card into a bright red envelope. Red for Christmas; red for blood— Belinda's blood, the blood Jacob Knight had spilled one year ago this Christmas season. Knight had stolen Belinda's life, then had his own returned to him courtesy of Romana Grey. They would go on being cops while he moldered in prison and Belinda rotted in a coffin.

No justice there, Warren reflected. But there would be, in time. He would see to that.

He would be good, so very, very good. The years would pass, and he would trade these bars for freedom. Christmas would come again and again. And at length two more people would die.

Romana Grey first, then Jacob Knight. By the time their bodies were discovered, he'd be in South America, sequestered in the Amazon jungle, where he'd spent a large portion of his youth. An eye for an eye, the missionaries on the big river would say. A fitting Christmas present, was Warren Critch's more cynical judgment.

A grim smile flitted across his lips as he opened a second card. Time to offer Jacob the same Christmas wishes he'd bestowed upon Romana.

"Enjoy the holidays while you can," he whispered to them from a distance. "You have only a handful left."

Chapter One

"It's the perfect scent for you." The woman behind the department store perfume counter gave one of her test bottles a spritz. "Mysterious and exotic, with a hint of Eastern spice."

Romana Grey sniffed her wrist. "It's lovely, but I'm not shopping for me."

A finger in her spine preceded a cheerful, "Note to self, Ro, as females, we're always shopping for 'me,' even in December." Romana's cousin, Anna Fitzgerald, picked up another bottle and sprayed the already pungent air. "This smells expensive."

"Ten dollars a pump," the saleswoman confirmed, then excused herself to intercept a group of excited teenage girls.

Fitz set her forearms on the glass case. "So, who are you shopping for today? Mom, Grandma Grey or one of your si͏ sisters-in-law?"

"Five. Noah's divorced." Romana gave her wrist a shake͏ "This really is nice." Then she glanced at her watch. "Why͏ are you here at three in the afternoon?"

"Some wires fried in the main lab. The forensics team'͏ been evacuated until morning." Out of the corner of her eye͏ Romana saw Fitz finger a tiny bottle. "I was bagging a hai͏ sample when I smelled the smoke. Well, actually, Doc Patrick͏ smelled it. You know him—tall, sexy dude who never re- members to get a haircut and whose socks don't match."

Romana swatted her cousin's wandering fingers. "Stop doing that."

"I'm not going to steal it."

"And I'm supposed to know that? It's me, Fitz. I arrested you twice for shoplifting when I was a rookie."

"Then got me into rehab and back on the straight and narrow. I'm a respectable citizen these days, thanks to you, a kindly judge and a totally cool bunch of coworkers in foren- sics. Which brings me back to Patrick North. Unmarried, shy, in need of a female to match up his socks."

Romana knew where this conversation was headed. Her cousin's mind was a one-way street. "Patrick worked with Belinda Critch, Fitz. I hate the way it all circles back to that. It feels like everyone around me knows or has a connection to somebody who was involved in her death."

"Cops know people in forensics, Ro. It's the nature of the biz. Belinda analyzed body fluids. She got around. You knew her, I knew her, and, trust me, so did a whole lot of men."

"Including my ex." Romana toyed with a fat genie bottle. Her much-anticipated shopping trip was starting to suck. "I figure Connor slept with at least two of his female cowork- ers. Belinda was probably one of them."

"Connor was also taking bribes from Cincinnati drug lords." Fitz sniffed. "Don't sweat the loss of a creep."

"I never sweat my losses, but marrying Connor Hanson wasn't the smartest thing I've ever done."

"No, divorcing him was."

"Good point." Shoving her brief funk aside, Romana sprayed a cotton ball, frowned and wrinkled her nose. "This smells like jalapeño peppers."

"It smells like Belinda Critch."

It did, actually. Romana warded off another pang of guilt and dropped the ball into a silver waste receptacle. "Belinda's gone, Fitz. Life goes on."

"That's a fact. You traded cophood for a college degree. I got my head screwed on straight and managed to work myself up the forensics ladder to a great tech job. It's not your fault or mine that Belinda Critch is dead. Maybe it's Jacob Knight's fault, but no one could prove it, so one way or another, her killer's probably still out there."

"Not helping me here, Fitz."

"Sorry." A pause, then, "Do you think he did it?"

"No."

"That's it, just a flat no? Come on, Ro, someone put a bullet in her chest, and Jacob Knight was involved with her once."

"If a guy I dated in high school turned up dead tomorrow, would that put me at the top of the suspect list?"

"I think you're not sure about him, and that's why you get twitchy when the subject comes up. You saved Knight's life, and, bam, two days later, Belinda's dead. Critch said Knight threatened her, so he must have believed it. Although..." She drew an air line with her finger. "Knight's partner did stick up for him. Michael O'Keefe..." Her smile flashed quickly and dimpled. "Who am I to doubt the word of a fellow Irishman?"

"An Irishman you dated once as I remember."

"You remember very well. O'Keefe's cute. Okay, older than me, but I like an age gap."

"You like any gap when it comes to men."

"Guess I have something in common with Belinda, after all. Maybe two things. Her brother Dylan's kind of cool, don't you think?"

"Uh-huh. Tell me, Fitz, is there a man we both know that you don't like?"

"Yeah, Jacob Knight. Except I don't not like him, I'm just not sure of him. Critch was convinced that Knight killed his wife, so much so that he pulled a gun on him. But there you were, on the scene and duty-bound to jump in, with no idea who was wrong or right. Come on, Ro, a dilemma like that would give anyone twitches."

Romana erased the smell of peppers from her fingers with peach hand cream. She considered changing the subject but knew Fitz would only find a way back. With a sigh, she said, "It's guilt I'm feeling, okay? Not about helping Jacob in that alley—that's what cops do—but because I didn't listen to Critch when he said his wife's life had been threatened. He had no proof, there was nothing to go on. Someone—not Jacob—" she shot her cousin a warning look "—wanted Belinda dead. I didn't investigate the allegation after Critch was arrested, but I should have, because that's also what cops do."

"Well, yes…"

"Jacob said he didn't murder her. I believe him." Was determined to believe him. "Subject exhausted. I mean that," she said when her friend's mouth opened.

One long look, and it closed with a snap. "Tell you what." Fitz's eyes sparkled. "Why don't we go sit on Santa's knee? I hear he's a hottie under the white whiskers."

Glad for any reprieve, Romana went with the idea. She ticked off items on her fingers. "I want new ice skates, a mountain bike, scuba gear and a cool white Boxster. But I'm only telling that to the real Santa Claus."

"Your doting dad."

"He's playing Father Christmas at an outdoor festival in

Boston this year. Something to do with the barbershop quartet he sings with when he isn't whizzing around the globe producing travel shows for cable TV."

"Lucky him. My father's still upholstering sofas and chairs at Barret Brown. I think he's going to stuff a bright red recliner in my stocking this year."

"I'd love a new chair from Barret Brown."

Fitz's cheeks went pink. "I'd rather have James Barret. Did I tell you he used to give me little boxes of chocolate tied up with red bows whenever I'd stop in and see my dad at the factory after school?"

Romana grinned. "So that's how you developed your sticky fingers."

"Ha-ha." Fitz's expression softened. "What a hunk James was—is."

"The hunk's married to an heiress," Romana reminded her. "Think jailer with claws when you think of James Barret's wife, and confine your lust to more available men."

Fitz lapsed into silence before venturing a subdued "Warren Critch is out on parole."

Romana examined another bottle. "I know. A friend from the station called me three weeks ago and again on Monday when his parole was granted. I'm not surprised. By all accounts, Critch was a model prisoner."

"A lot of the people Belinda worked with in forensics are still there. Warren's a hot topic right now. I'm sorry, but so's Jacob Knight."

Romana gave in and let her mind slide back six years to a Cincinnati alley where one very out-of-control chemistry teacher had been holding a gun on one remarkably controlled homicide detective.

She'd been on patrol that afternoon with her veteran

partner. They'd been dispatched to a downtown alley after a witness had spotted a man with a gun. She and her partner had separated at the entranceway. She'd taken the rear approach.

To this day, Romana could still feel the adrenaline that had pumped through her system when she'd spotted Warren Critch. According to Critch, Jacob had pushed Belinda to have an affair. When she'd refused, Jacob had threatened to kill her.

Critch had been raving, oblivious to everything except the man in front of him. Anyone could have crept up from behind, it just happened to be Romana. With the barrel of her Glock pressed against his neck, Critch's mind had begun to function. He'd backed down and finally dropped his gun.

Two days later, his wife had been murdered.

Romana sighed as the memory dissolved. "I don't think I saved Jacob's life, Fitz, so much as I talked Critch into seeing reason."

"The consensus in the lab is that Warren Critch would have pulled the trigger, Jacob Knight would have died, and instead of being a free man today, Critch would be facing life without parole for killing a cop. Point being, I think Knight's dangerous, Ro. Gorgeous but dangerous."

A feeling of inevitability crept in. "Fitz, Jacob's…"

"Tall, dark and sexy as hell. Like a rock star. Or maybe a bad boy grown up."

"He's not James Dean."

"No, he's way better, and I'm betting a whole lot badder."

A picture flitted through Romana's head of an enigmatic face, slightly haunted, slightly hunted, narrow-featured and, yes, gorgeous. The collar of his leather jacket was turned up in her vision so his dark hair fell over it and skimmed his shoulders. Steely eyes stared at her, and his mouth—well, she didn't want to linger too long on that feature.

She felt Fitz tap her arm, noted her cousin's contrite expression and struggled with a laugh. "Let me guess, you're sorry. Again."

"Let's rewind to sitting on Santa's knee, and top it off with a trip upstairs for coffee and a Danish pastry. The Garden Room's been transformed into a Russian ice palace for the rest of December, and I gotta tell you, Ro, if ever anyone looked like a Russian ice princess, it'd be you."

"I'll try and take that as a compliment." Romana separated two bottles from the montage in front of her. "Tatiana perfume for my mother, the newly promoted radio station manager, and Opium for me."

"Former ice princess cop—really did mean it as a compliment—and current avant garde professor of criminology at the University of Cincinnati."

With a determined shove, the black cloud that had been hovering on the edge of Romana's mind dispersed.

Warren Critch was out of prison, that was a fact. The parole board felt he'd served sufficient time for his crime. True, he'd sent her a Christmas card every year of his incarceration, but the messages inside hadn't actually amounted to threats. She'd gone over them several times. So had a number of her police friends.

Critch was bitter—perfectly understandable. Didn't mean he'd jeopardize his newfound freedom by seeking revenge. He'd been blowing off steam in his prison cell. Romana taught the subject; she knew how the criminal mind worked. Or should.

"Wow." Fitz winced as the saleswoman held out a pretty blue bag and a short bill. "That's some hefty total. Guess coffee's on me."

Romana reached into her purse, felt the envelope that

hadn't been there an hour ago and, without looking, let her head fall back.

"Then again," she said to the reindeer suspended from the store's ceiling, "maybe no one really knows how the criminal mind works."

"Money, Ro." Fitz elbowed her. "Unless you're thinking of developing sticky fingers yourself."

Romana ignored the telltale red envelope as she hunted for her credit card. "Order me a cinnamon Danish, and a double-double coffee, okay? I need five minutes alone with my cell phone to call an old...friend."

"Is he as hunky as Patrick?"

A chill, possibly borne of fear, or more likely of some weird anticipation, feathered along Romana's spine. "Oh, he's hunky enough." She fingered the flap of the red envelope. "I'm just not sure how happy he'll be to hear from me."

DECEMBER DARKNESS FELL EARLY over Cincinnati. Snowflakes from an approaching weather system fluttered and danced and added to the already festive feeling in the air. Jacob Knight sat in his converted loft with his feet propped on the radiator and watched as pockets of red, gold and green lights winked to life around him.

He could see some portion of Fountain Square and the silver-blue glow that surrounded it. Thanksgiving had come and gone; it was all about Christmas now. About family and friends for most, more about bad memories for him.

When the phone rang, he debated briefly, then picked up.

"Knight."

"Well, what d'you know, he exists. I've talked to your voice mail so many times I was beginning to think you'd skipped the country without telling anyone."

Jacob swallowed a mouthful of coffee, kept his eyes on the expanding Christmas glow. "I'm still waking up, O'Keefe. Keep it short and simple."

His former partner released a breath. "Critch made parole two days ago."

"Yeah, I heard."

"He came across sweet as pie for the review board."

"I guess he figured surly wouldn't cut it."

O'Keefe grunted. "I'm worried about you, pal. Critch will want answers. If he decides to look for them, you know where that'll lead him."

Jacob finished his coffee, dropped his feet to the floor and pushed out of the chair. "Critch wrote his own answers six years ago when he found Belinda dead in their home. If he comes after me, I'll deal with him."

"Oh, he'll come," his former partner assured. "The question is how, when and where? Will he do it from the front where you can see him, or will he blindside you? I'm betting on a blindside."

"It's a good thing I'm trained then, huh?" Jacob glanced at his voice mail. Eleven messages, but the majority of them were probably from O'Keefe.

"You need a watchdog, my friend, or a mother. Better still, a wife. You also need to have some fun. Do you realize it's been two years since we've gone to a Reds game? Hell, it's been half as long since we even had a beer together."

"You're day shift, I'm night. The city's jumping, and the department's short-staffed."

"Yadda, yadda. Those are excuses. But pleasure aside, the fact remains, Critch is loose, and I don't think any shrink ever really got inside his head during those prison years."

"I'm a good cop, O'Keefe."

"I'm worried about Romana, too, okay? Lie and tell me you've forgotten that incredible face."

Jacob slid his gaze to the window. "No, I haven't forgotten her face." Or anything else about her. "He won't go after Romana, okay? I'll make sure of it."

"Ah, finally, we arrive at the crux of it. You'll make sure he doesn't go for Romana by getting him to come after you."

With his eyes still on the windows and his lips curved in a smile, Jacob asked, "Shouldn't you be heading home to your kid about now?"

"Nah, she's with her mom in Los Angeles. Indefinitely. It's one way to get custody, I suppose. Move to a place with sunshine, beaches and an excess of skater boys."

Jacob hunted for and located his keys and badge. "We'll have that beer before Christmas, Mick. And thanks for the heads-up on Critch."

"I'll keep an eye on Romana."

Jacob ignored the tightening in his belly as he shouldered his holster. "I'm late. Tell Captain Harris I'll be working on the Parker case tonight."

"Watch your back, Jacob."

His back, right. Except it hadn't been his back Warren Critch had been aiming at in that alley six years ago. And Jacob knew he hadn't done a damned thing to prevent the confrontation from taking place.

Shrugging into his lined leather jacket, he noted that the snow was falling more heavily now. He clipped his badge to the waistband of his jeans and headed for the stairs.

He didn't believe in signs or portents, but human tendencies and inherited traits were different matters. And while he might wish he could dismiss them, in six long years he'd never quite been able to get past what might actually be.

What he might have done.

He raised his eyes skyward, realized where he was looking and let wry amusement rise. His father was dead, but there was no chance he'd gone upward in the afterlife. If hell existed, his old man would burn there forever. Who knew, one day his only son might be joining him.

Because he didn't want to think about the night ahead—or anything or anyone else right then—Jacob concentrated on his neighbor's music as he started down the stairs.

Seventy-eight-year-old Denny Leech had been blasting Rat Pack Christmas songs on her ancient stereo for the past two days. She claimed Frank, Dean and Sammy ignited her creative fire. Painters needed inspiration. The problem was, Denny was painting her entire lower loft with one very small roller and a brush she'd found in the trash. In her case, creativity could take until Easter to play out.

She waved to him through her open door. "I'm doing a northern lights ceiling mural, Jacob. My granddaughter's coming over Sunday to see it. You remember Penelope, don't you?"

"Yeah, she's very pretty."

"You'd make a lovely couple. She's growing her hair. She's a blonde now…"

Humor kindled as he pushed on the rear door. Denny's voice followed him out. She'd talk for five more minutes before she realized he was gone.

He'd parked his black SUV in the alley early this morning. Had he alarmed it? A movement near the snow-covered hood suggested he'd forgotten.

"Punctual as always, Detective Knight. I love that quality in a man."

Romana Grey. He'd recognize that seductive purr anywhere. He also recognized the act she put on as she strolled around the fender.

She did it well, better than most people, but she had to be as uncertain of him now as she had been after Belinda Critch was found dead on her living room floor.

Jacob ran his gaze over her long white coat and black boots, then back up until he encountered her striking gray-blue eyes. "You love too easily, Romana. Why are you here?"

She leaned on the hood with her customary teasing grace. "You didn't answer your phone this afternoon, Detective."

He felt the tightening in his groin and shifted position. "I work the night shift. I sleep in the afternoon."

"And let me guess. You don't listen to your messages or check your mailbox when you wake up." She produced a red envelope from her pocket, held it between two gloved fingers. "Wanna guess who sent this?"

Something black and oily slid through his veins. He paused before reaching out. "Is it the same as the others?"

"Not quite." At last the nerves jittered through. "This one's darker, more malevolent."

The light in the alley was bad. Jacob squinted at the red-lettered message inside. "Looks like he wrote it with his left hand."

"It looks like he wrote it with his left foot, but the print's consistent with the other cards. I'll have that verified tomorrow," she promised at his quick glance. "I still have friends in the crime lab."

"I thought the crime lab was your ex's territory." Jacob jockeyed for a clearer view of the words. "How's Connor doing these days? Living fat on the Hanson family money?"

"I'm not going there with you." Romana let her hood fall back, slid her gaze down the alley and breathed out. Her expression softened as her mental focus shifted. "I believed him when he said he could make his own way in life without his family. I know he believed it."

"Instead, he took bribes, cut deals and lied to you."

Her smile was fast and false. "Thanks for the emotional lift, Knight. I needed it after that card." She watched him for a moment, before arching a shrewd eyebrow. "Do you want me to tell you what it says?"

"If you can, you've got Superman's vision."

"What I have is an excellent memory. 'I send you a Christmas greeting, Romana Grey,'" she quoted. "'A kiss for you, for the murderer you saved. It is the Kiss of Death.' Nice, huh?" She bumped his tire with the heel of her boot. "There's a sprig of mistletoe on the front. Can't imagine what he came up with for you. It's a mass-marketed card. I checked it out first thing. They're sold all over the country, same as the other five he sent, except this time I have a creepy feeling Critch delivered it himself."

"Delivered it where?"

"Into my purse. Don't say it," she warned at his sharp look. "You shop in crowded stores, you get jostled. You open your purse for credit cards, parking money, donation drums."

"Hands slip inside, remove wallets."

"We're talking about something that was added not subtracted."

"You were a cop, Romana."

"And now I teach criminology. Fine, I should have noticed, but, ah, well, I didn't. I'm human, Jacob. Move forward."

Not the faintest flicker of annoyance marred her pleasant expression, and her tone was equally unruffled.

She could act, all right. She was also stubborn. And bold as hell.

"I'll check my mailbox." He handed the card back. "Obviously you know Critch has been out on parole for the past two days."

"Mmm. Lovely thought, isn't it? Although I've also been told he mellowed substantially after the first few years inside, so much so that he wrote a novelette about his childhood in South America. His daddy mapped waterways along the Amazon. My guess is he did a lot more than that, but then I'm jaded from my brief stint on the force." She nodded forward. "Your mailbox is at the front door, right?"

His lips twitched into a smile. "Are you curious to see if my threat's nastier than yours?"

"Not especially. I'm thinking your lobby has to be warmer than this alley. Plus I love old theaters." She scanned the worn brick facade, relaxed a little more. "My father's a huge fan of 1920s architecture. He knows the woman who owns this place. Her husband made her promise not to sell the building or allow it to be demolished after he died. I think he planned to haunt it—don't know if that worked out for him or not—but she kept her word, which is why you and three other people get to live here. She left the stage, audience area and lobby intact and still found a way to make the place pay its own taxes. End of local history lesson." She moved past him to the rear door. "Why are you staring at me, Jacob? Teachers lecture out of habit. I could tell you all sorts of things about the house my parents bought in Boston."

His stare became a headshake. "Do you ever run down?"

"Depends on the company. My cousin Fitz says I don't talk enough."

"Would that be Irish-born Anna Fitzgerald with the curly red hair, who insists that unpaid-for shop items simply follow her home?"

Romana grinned. "Followed. Past tense, Detective. She's my second cousin on my mother's side, I've known her forever and, all bias aside, I think she's one of the brightest forensic techs in the city. The hospital board was right to give her another chance."

"You must have talked long and hard to that board, Romana. Second chances are hard to come by in that arena."

She waited while he opened the rear door, then, with a glance at his profile, preceded him inside. "It's going to start again, you know."

"I know."

"All the gossip and the rumors, the speculation, the accusations."

"I've been through it before, Romana. I know how it'll be."

"Unless Critch is grandstanding, which is possible given his psychiatric evaluation before the trial. He's a brooder, but he tends to back down in the face of fear."

"Which makes his latest Christmas message to you, what? A slap intended to unnerve? He's sent you six cards, one for each of the six years he spent in prison. And this last one was delivered less than forty-eight hours after his release."

"You're determined to be pessimistic, aren't you? Why don't you… Oh, my God, is that fresco original?" Captivated by the dark heavenly forces clashing overhead, she swung on her heel. Then she frowned, paused and sniffed. "Who's using alkyd paint?"

"Keep moving," he suggested. "Why don't I what?"

"Hmm? Oh, try and keep a positive thought." Still absorbed, she executed another admiring circle. "Words aren't weapons in this case, and I find it hard to believe that Critch will want to spend the rest of his life behind bars for killing us. It won't bring his wife back, and if he's smart, which I think he is, he'll have realized by now that our lives—and yours in particular—haven't been fairy-tale perfect since she died."

Jacob studied her through narrowed eyes. With her guard down and enchanted by her surroundings, he could visualize her quite easily in a storybook setting. Somewhere snowy and nostalgic. Not a princess in a tower—she was too savvy for that role—but in one of those places he'd dreamed of as a kid, before reality had stumbled in and revealed the harsh realities of life.

Speaking of which… "How do you know what my life's like? You left the force years ago."

She wrested her gaze from the ornate overhead carvings and directed it at him. "I know you switched to the night shift after Critch's trial. You prefer to work alone. Your record's outstanding, but you don't interact with your fellow officers any more than necessary. You keep to yourself on and off the clock, which includes hardly even talking to your best friend, O'Keefe. And word has it you're the only male cop in the city who hasn't flirted with the pretty new dispatcher."

"I talked to O'Keefe twenty minutes ago. I'd say he's still in major lust with you."

She shrugged, unperturbed. "Mick O'Keefe is a nice guy who happens to be divorced. He likes European cooking—my great grandmother's from Moscow—film noire and helping out with minor home renos for people who would otherwise be in over their heads. There's no lust involved, and even if there was—" she gave his chest a poke "—it wouldn't be any of your business. FYI, Knight, there's a woman wearing a pink ball cap and holding a paintbrush waving at you."

"Later, Denny." He reached past Romana to open the front door. "After you, Professor."

"Don't be snotty." But she went first and peered through

the metal slats of the box. "I see something red in there. Want me to pull it out?"

He handed her the key.

A moment later, she was turning the red envelope, a twin to the one she'd received, over in her hands. "No stamp," she remarked. "Probably water-sealed like the others, so I imagine DNA's out. Barely legible scrawl on the back, same mistletoe on the front and—oh, well, but a much more succinct message than mine inside."

Holding the Christmas card open with her gloved fingertips, she turned it so he could read the five words printed there in bold, bleeding red.

YOU DIE NEXT, JACOB KNIGHT!

Chapter Two

"Be grateful he didn't send you a kiss," Romana said thirty minutes later. She ran her gaze over the face of a building that was as close to a safety hazard as city bylaws permitted. Tilting her head, she read the sign. "Taft House. I hope it wasn't named for President Taft."

"Aaron Taft." Jacob angled his vehicle into a No Parking zone and cut the engine. "Aaron was a rich man with a wayward son. He believed the Y chromosome was responsible for all criminal tendencies." At Romana's skeptical sideways look, he reached over to tug up the zipper of her white coat. "Taft was born in 1871 and maintained the unshakeable belief that women were incapable of committing crimes. This house is strictly for men. Don't expect pretty."

"All I want to do is get in, see Critch and get out before this minor snowfall turns into a blizzard. You should flash your police lights," she added as he adjusted his shoulder holster. "It's procedure."

"What, are you afraid I'll get a ticket if I don't identify myself?"

"Well, yeah, or get vandalized."

"You academic types worry too much."

"You homicide types take too much for granted. It's your vehicle, Knight, but I'd flash."

On the street, snow gusted over them in wind-whipped sheets. Romana brushed her hair back and drew her hood up. The faux fur tickled her cheeks; hardening snow pellets stung them. She let Jacob propel her through the crooked front door.

There wasn't much to greet them: bare linoleum floors, gray-green walls and the tattered remains of a rush welcome mat. Someone, probably a well-meaning social worker, had draped a stingy string of garland over the entrance to the communal living area, and an already dry Christmas tree stood, poorly decorated, in the corner.

"Home sweet home." Romana lowered her hood and loosened her coat. "At least it's warm." She caught Jacob's stare and felt a swell of impatience. "If my mascara's smudged, Knight, tell me. I'd rather hear about it than walk around looking like a Charles Dickens ghost."

Still watching, he moved closer. His slow advance made the skin on her neck tingle and her stomach do a slow turn. "Are your eyes really that color, or do you wear contacts?"

"Ah." Amused at her overreaction, she allowed a smile to bloom. "They're mine. I'm a throwback to my great-grand-mother Rostov. Mahogany hair and winter-lake eyes, or so my great-grandfather described her in the poems he wrote. He was a terrible poet, but he painted a portrait that I swear could be me. It's a bit spooky, actually."

"Winter-lake, huh?"

"My driver's license says blue. Is anyone here?" she called out. She waited a beat, then added, "Police."

Returning to the threshold, Jacob glanced down the hall. "I could cite you for impersonating an officer, Romana."

"I was hoping to attract someone's attention. Oh…hello."

She spied a man whose whiskers reached halfway down his chest. He was huddled in a lopsided chair, studying her intently. "I'm Romana Grey. Do you live here?"

He completed his head-to-toe scrutiny. "You don't look like police."

"Well, I am. I was." She pointed to the door. "He is. Is there someone in charge we can speak to?"

"Bevin." The old man watched Jacob leave the door. "He's doing a bed check. Gotta be in by nine. I stay down here to catch the stragglers."

"And get a mickey of whiskey for your effort," Jacob said in an undertone. The old man didn't hear him. Romana did and jabbed his ribs.

"Do you know a man named Warren Critch?" she asked.

"Met him once. Don't expect to again. This'll be the second night his bed's been empty."

"Broken the terms of his parole already, huh?" Somehow, Romana wasn't surprised.

The old man shrugged. "He spent Wednesday night here. Had to. But when I saw him leaving with his gear yesterday morning, I said to myself, this one's gonna skip. Sure enough, he did. Bevin's mad as a hornet."

"Has he reported it?"

"Don't know. It's a blot on his record, so maybe not. You wanna talk to him, go upstairs, but that pretty face of yours'll only make him madder." The old man showed a set of chipped, brown teeth. "The pretty ones never paid Bevin much mind. Stuck in his craw—like losing Critch is gonna do."

Romana turned to Jacob. "I'm okay with avoiding him. How about you? You and O'Keefe can get us the answers we need."

"Horse's mouth is faster." Jacob gave the door frame a contemplative tap. "Five minutes upstairs, and we're out of here."

Romana debated but let him go without an argument. "Blue Christmas" drifted into the room. She perched on the arm of a second chair and removed her gloves finger by finger. "Who's the Elvis fan?"

A smile split the old man's whiskered face. "Pretty lady who's not a cop, have I got a story for you."

"ONE ELVIS IMPERSONATOR KNIFED another Elvis impersonator over a woman they were both dating. Didn't mean to kill him, but he was a little drunk, and he had a temper. Evidently, this stabbing took place outside the restaurant where both men worked as singing waiters." Romana had forgotten how weird the world could be from a street cop's perspective. "It happened right here in Cincinnati, Jacob. How could I have missed it?"

"The Doran case," was all he said.

She didn't have to think about that name. "The guy who went postal six years ago, shot five of his coworkers in the office lunchroom, then went upstairs and killed his boss."

"Before finally offing himself."

"His coworkers earned more money than he did. Boss was responsible. Bang, bang, everyone's dead, and we're back to an even beginning."

"Or ending."

She ran chilled fingers through her snow-dampened hair. "You have an awfully gloomy perspective, Jacob. Still, any way you look at it, media-wise, Doran's crime would take precedence over the death of a drunk Elvis impersonator."

In retrospect, she supposed it might also have taken precedence over the investigation into Belinda Critch's death, which had occurred a mere two weeks later.

Opinion within the department had been divided on the

Critch case. Some people believed that Warren Critch had murdered Belinda, others thought one of her lovers had done it. And, of course, an ungracious few had pointed the finger of guilt at Jacob.

Unfortunately, the forensic evidence had been negligible, and the crime scene investigators hadn't done much better.

Throughout the holiday season that year, seven major homicides had been committed. Doran's rampage had been the biggest bloodbath. Media attention had remained focused on him even in the wake of Belinda Critch's death. Naturally, the department had downplayed any suggestion of internal impropriety and, by Valentine's Day, interest in her case had dropped to zero.

Romana looked over, but Jacob kept his eyes on the increasingly slick street. He drove one-handed, and with his elbow resting on the door frame, ran the fingers of the other under his lower lip.

Silence stretched out between them. She raised a speculative eyebrow. "Are you awake, Detective Knight?"

He glanced at her. "Sorry. I'm used to riding alone."

She couldn't resist. "Why no partner?"

"I'm better alone."

It was an answer of sorts, though not an encouraging one. When he reached out to turn up the heater, Romana welcomed the warmth on her face and hands. "I'm not sitting here comparing you to Doran, you know."

"Because you're absolutely certain I didn't murder Belinda Critch."

"You said you didn't, and I believe you."

Now he smiled. "Bull."

Her temper stirred. "If I thought you were guilty, Knight, I wouldn't be here with you now."

"Where would you be?"

"I might be grading papers." But probably not because the first term was over and the second didn't start until January. "I might also be having dinner with Sean—or Brendan, or Anthony. With one of my brothers, anyway."

A crease formed between Jacob's eyes. "How many brothers do you have?"

"Six, all older than me. They've given me eleven nephews and one niece named Teresa. My oldest brother's an engineer. He and his wife lived in Chile for a while. When they came back, they brought two-year-old Teresa with them. She was an orphan, very sweet, and, because females are rare in our family, completely spoiled."

"Are you spoiled, too, Romana?"

"By my parents and my mother's very Irish parents, yes. By my father's mother, no. I'm Grandma Grey's namesake, and she's one tough cookie. She raises thoroughbreds in Kentucky. She's putting one in the Derby next year. I have a great deal to live up to, in her eyes."

"In what way?"

"Top of the list, I'm obliged to bear another namesake. My brother, Brendan, hoping to ease the pressure on me, named his first son Roman, but it didn't work. Grandma Grey wants a girl. She came from a completely male-dominated world, and she's hell-bent on flipping the status quo."

"Huh. How did Grandma Grey feel about you becoming a cop?"

"Oh, she was fine with that. Didn't agree with my college-age marriage, but she helped me get through the divorce and the repercussions of Connor's unlawful activities relatively unscathed."

"How did your ex come out of it?"

"The way a Hanson always does, with only a few surface scratches, and a huge family debt, which he'll pay for the rest of his life."

"You don't sound very sympathetic."

"I don't, do I? But I'm not as resentful as you might think." She played with the fingers of her white gloves. "It seemed like everything came to a head six years ago. Belinda Critch died and her husband tried to kill you. Connor's crimes were discovered, the hospital and the police department were simultaneously roasted in the press, I started to realize that being a cop wasn't what I wanted, and on and on and on. Before Critch even went to prison, I realized I couldn't shut off my emotions, and I couldn't push them down far enough on a daily basis to be a really effective officer. So I sat down and thought."

"About your marriage or your career?"

"Both. I shouldn't have married Connor, I knew that almost before the ceremony ended. But I was eighteen, and he was twenty-seven, and our mothers were college roommates, so I've known him for pretty much my whole life."

"And he was charming and handsome, and he swept you off your feet."

"This is my fairy tale, Knight. I'll draw the characters."

"But he was charming."

"To an eighteen-year-old, yes. He was also handsome and insecure and a lot angrier than I realized."

"Angry at his family?"

"Cigar's yours, Detective. Getting back on track, I thought about the decisions I'd made, both marital and career. I even made a pro/con list. Topping the pro list was the fact that I'd graduated from high school at sixteen, so I already had three years of college under my belt when I entered the Academy.

Long story short, after a visit to Grandma Grey's Kentucky ranch and a couple of really gruesome CSIs, I decided to go back to school. Now I *teach* kids rather than arrest them. So you see, it all turned out well in the end."

"You like teaching, huh?"

"Love it." She cocked her head, sent him a grin. "As it happens, I'm also good at it. When my parents moved to Boston two years ago, my father wanted me to come with them and work there. But I grew up in Cincinnati, five of my brothers are here, and I just plain enjoy the city. End of the Romana Grey story." She let a teasing light enter her eyes. "That was a lot to say, Knight, even for me. Now I know you're not a talker, but play fair, and tell me one small thing about your life. Anything will do, even your favorite color."

When he braked for a red light, Jacob regarded a twinkling Christmas logo on the delivery truck ahead. "Belinda and I were involved for three months twelve years ago. It ended before she married Critch. The goodbyes were mutual."

Surprised he'd taken that direction, Romana offered a casual, "Obviously you stayed friends."

"We were never friends."

"Then why did…?" She waved a glove. "Sorry, not my business."

"And that's going to stop you from asking?"

"I don't pry. Well, not much."

"Prying's what we do."

"Not on a personal level. I've always been fastidious about separating my career from my private life." She summoned a sweet smile. "What did Critch's parole officer have to say?"

His stare seemed to reach right into her head. When amusement tickled her throat, Romana went with it and gave her drying hair a final fluff.

"Weapons down, Knight. We're not fighting a duel. This is a third-party threat, directed at both of us. My guess is Critch plans to pull the trigger on the twenty-first."

"Don't count on that."

"Why not? It's logical. That's when his wife was killed."

"And what he'll expect us to think." Jacob glanced in the rearview mirror. "Snow's getting heavier. To answer your question, Critch's parole officer is pissed off as hell that he's lost one of his charges. He said he was going to report Critch in the morning. He did it tonight instead."

Romana laughed. "You have such a persuasive way about you, Detective. Does he have any idea where Critch might be?"

"None that I could persuade him to share."

"So we're down to Critch's family, his friends, maybe his teaching cronies."

"And his theater buddies."

"Critch was an actor?" She tried to form the image, but no matter how she sketched it, she couldn't picture the lanky chemistry teacher with his sandy-blond hair and semirugged features on a stage. "I thought he was into nature and weird experiments. I read that he had an extensive lab in his basement."

"Science lab in the basement, costume storage in the garage."

"Huh. What kind of theater?"

"Local amateur stuff. I imagine Belinda got him into it. She belonged to a community arts club."

"Really. That sounds so Rob and Laura Petrie, so suburban and, I don't know, happy, I suppose."

"Maybe they were happy."

"Then why did she…?" The question that had almost slipped out earlier came close to slipping out again. With a sigh for the quirk of his lips, she finished it. "Okay, I'll pry. Why did Belinda want to meet with you two days before she died? You weren't friends, she might have been happy with her husband. What did she want from you?"

Jacob checked the mirror again. "She said she was being stalked."

"I take it she didn't know by whom."

"She said she didn't. That could have been the truth. Belinda flirted with men." At her silent look, he added, "All men, Romana, not just your ex."

"Go in another direction, okay? Belinda was being stalked. Could it have been by her husband?"

"It could have been by any number of people, with names known only to Belinda. She wouldn't give me anything specific. She simply wanted to know how to obtain a restraining order."

"And after you told her, she… What is it, Jacob?" Romana demanded when his eyes strayed to the mirror for a third time. "Is someone tailing us?"

"For the past two miles."

"And you're only telling me about it now?" She zeroed in on the headlights behind them. "So that's why we're zigzagging all over the city core." She tried to gauge the distance, but it was difficult with the heavy snowfall. "I think he's closing in."

Jacob turned left, away from the busy downtown streets, toward Riverview Park. The vehicle behind them made the same turn.

They wove a path into an older part of the city. Tall, thin houses seemed to sprout straight out of the white-coated ground. Many of the windows were dark, a few were boarded up. Romana counted five Christmas trees in total, plus a trio of inflatable snowmen rocking in the wind.

In the middle of the street, a woman pulling a toboggan

piled high with bags walked against the wind. Jacob swerved to avoid both her and a parked car. At the last minute, so did the vehicle behind them.

"I'm not sure playing cat and mouse is the best idea here, Knight." Romana scanned the dash. "What's your dispatch number?"

"Ninety-one-Vector."

She would have called it in if he hadn't reached over and removed the radio from her hand. "No backup, okay? Let's keep this unofficial." When she started to argue, he added an even, "Like you are."

She blinked, drew her hand back. For a single, unguarded moment, she'd slapped on her old hat, the one she'd packed away after a few short years on the force, a painful personal evaluation and a brief struggle with guilt.

Still amazed by the easy switch, she refocused on their pursuer. "He's pulled to within thirty feet."

"He's also using his high beams." Jacob squinted into the mirror. "Can you make out the vehicle type?"

"I think it's a GM off-road. Dark color. No front plates. And either he's speeding up or you're slowing down, because he's ten feet off your back bumper."

As she spoke, the truck's engine revved. The vehicle leaped forward, rammed into Jacob's SUV, backed off and prepared to charge again.

"This is ridiculously predictable." Romana fought a ripple of fear with irritation.

After another solid hit, Jacob unsnapped his holster. "Can you shoot out a front tire?"

"Yes, but that'll make things pretty official."

He handed her his gun. "Just don't kill him."

Lowering the window, she braced her left knee on the seat

and waited for the truck to close again. "You'd think a guy who'd spent most of his youth in the Amazon jungle would be a bit more inventive, wouldn't you?"

Jacob checked the side mirrors. "Whatever works, Romana."

She started to lean out but was suddenly jerked sideways as Jacob swerved yet again. Unanchored, she toppled into his arm, and almost into his lap.

"Jacob, what are you…"

"Civilians."

She pulled herself upright. Shoving the hair from her eyes, she peered through the snow until she spotted a pair of men in baggy parkas. They were carrying lunch boxes and holding their hoods up with their free hands.

Behind her, the truck's engine roared again. Snow spat out from under all four tires.

With her rib cage pressed to the door, Romana stuck her head and hands through the window, took aim and fired.

The truck immediately skidded sideways, struck a mailbox and spun in a wild half circle.

The engine subsided for a moment, then gave a growl like an enraged bull. More streams of snow shot upward. The back end of the truck fishtailed before gaining traction. With the front bumper now pointed toward the city, it bounced across a corner lot and vanished into the darkness.

Jacob reversed.

"Wait." Romana caught his arm. "Critch knocked the mailbox onto one of those men."

Clearly frustrated, he watched the taillights fade.

She hopped out and ran to the sidewalk where the second man kneeled next to his friend. "Are you hurt?"

"Foot's caught." The pinned man's breath whooshed out. "Was that guy playing chicken with you?"

"In a way." Going to her knees, Romana examined his trapped foot. "There's a cushion of snow under your ankle. It might have prevented a break."

"We should call the police." The man's friend fumbled for his cell phone. "That guy was a nutcase."

"It's covered." Jacob revealed the badge on his waistband. Crouching, he snagged the top corner of the box. "On three," he said to Romana.

Within seconds, the trapped man was free. He flexed his foot. "Feels okay," he said in relief. He frowned at Jacob. "Don't chases involving the police usually work the other way round? You go after him?"

"Guy's a nutcase," his friend repeated. "He started shouting when his tire blew. I didn't catch all of it, but I heard the last part clear enough."

She didn't want to know, Romana told herself. Really didn't want to know. "Can you tell us what he said?" she asked.

"Yeah, he said this was the first threat. How many more you get depends on how he feels. But the real thing's coming, and when it does, it's gonna make you real dead. Then he spun his tires and yelled, 'Merry Christmas, murderers.'"

IT WAS DONE, ANOTHER THREAT had been delivered. Damn, but he felt good.

He knew when he wanted to do it; the gray area remained the manner of their execution.

He'd been working on his plan of revenge for years, since before those prison doors had clanged shut. He'd created and re-created Christmas cards for both of them, constructed and deconstructed a thousand bloody scenarios. He'd visualized them in death. He'd pictured himself placing mistletoe on their graves.

Whatever else he did, however it went down, mistletoe would be included in the killings, because mistletoe leaves had been scattered around Belinda's cold body.

Could you strangle a person with it? He didn't think so. Stab a rough sprig through a frantically beating heart? Probably not.

He pictured Romana Grey. She had a dazzling face, and, he suspected, an equally amazing body. Another time and place…

No, he wouldn't think like that. Couldn't. He was going to kill her. Knight would watch, then he would die. Revenge complete, all wrapped up like the perfect Christmas present.

It would be perfect, too, because no matter how long and hard the authorities searched afterward, they wouldn't find their man. Warren Critch knew the Amazon basin as well as anyone alive. He wasn't about to be captured.

A dark Christmas song dribbled out of the radio. Sadly, he couldn't run Romana and Jacob over with a reindeer—he'd have enjoyed that—but he could shoot them. And with something other than bullets.

Ah, yes, now there was a tantalizing prospect. He wouldn't implement it too soon, of course. They needed to suffer first as Belinda had, but in time, in time…

Smiling, he picked up a handful of darts and began launching them at the wall. The first one struck Jacob Knight in the throat, the second got Romana Grey below her lovely left breast.

His smile widened. Killing them was going to be worth the six-year wait.

Chapter Three

With the exception of several colorful additions during the holiday season, nothing ever really changed at the station house. Reports were typed in cubbies by officers who'd rather be anywhere than behind a computer. Suspects, cuffed and uncuffed, shuffled in and out, phones rang, conversations ebbed and flowed. Once in a while, an overstressed lieutenant barked out an order.

By early December, tinsel had been stapled around desk fronts, and most of the tall plants were draped with twinkling lights. An animated Santa ho-ho-hoed boisterously in the corner. Menorahs stood next to fiber-optic pine trees, snowflakes hung from the ceiling, and there were snowmen and penguins plastered to every glass partition. As a rule, no less than three platters of cakes and cookies sat on the front desk, the largest being in full view of the captain's office.

Jacob entered through the alleyway door. He snagged a raisin square, made a detour to Records, then headed upstairs to the homicide division. Night would give way to day in less than an hour, but O'Keefe, being an early riser, invariably arrived long before his shift began.

"Morning, Detective Knight." A pretty female dispatcher

offered the cheerful greeting. "Captain Harris wants to see you."

"On my way."

As he passed, she picked up a shortbread cookie and let it dangle from her fingertips. "Are you coming to the Christmas party?"

Jacob couldn't remember her name. Her badge said Officer Dyson. "I'm not big on Christmas."

"It's Clare," she stage-whispered across the desk. "And you don't have to celebrate Christmas. Use it as an excuse to eat, drink and be merry."

He glanced at the captain's office. "I'll think about it," he said, and moved on before she could push for more.

"You're such a social animal, Knight." O'Keefe gave him a hearty slap between the shoulder blades. "Did you even notice that she was coming on to you?"

"I noticed." But he was absorbed again in the report he'd copped downstairs and by one name in particular. "Do you know James Barret?"

"I swear you'd be better off dead." O'Keefe gave his head a sorrowful shake. "Yes, I know him. You've heard of the Barret Brown Furniture Concept, right? Well, J.B. is half of that rapidly expanding business."

"It says here that his partner, Ben Brown, died under questionable circumstances six years ago."

"Really?" O'Keefe peered over his shoulder. "What file are you—ah, I should have known. Belinda Critch. They weren't my cases, Knight, and they sure as hell weren't yours." He caught the back of Jacob's jacket. "Hold on. I need caffeine, and the coffee inside's complete crap."

Jacob skimmed the file. His instinct told him it should be

fatter. "Dylan Hoag," he read while his ex-partner dropped quarters into a vending machine.

"Belinda Critch's brother." O'Keefe fished in his pockets. He deposited quarters until a cup plopped down. "I think he works for a security company. Maybe he owns it. You still take yours black?"

"Yeah." A steaming cup appeared in Jacob's hand. "Patrick North's name is here. I don't know much about him."

"Doctor Death." O'Keefe set a palm over the printout. "Why are you doing this?"

Jacob raised his head, absorbed the thrust of his ex-partner's stare. "Because Critch is after us."

"Damn, I knew it. What happened?"

"He missed his bed check twice. Romana and I went to the transition house last night. When we left, Critch followed us in a truck. No visible license plates. He knocked a mailbox onto a civilian, apparently yelled a threat out the window and took off."

"Well, hell." O'Keefe ran a hand through his unruly brown curls. "That's not good."

"According to the witness who heard what Romana and I didn't, Critch plans to string us along with threats before he kills us."

"Where's Romana now?"

"I dropped her off at her place around midnight. The building's secure," he added before O'Keefe could object. "I checked it out myself. Even if Critch could get past the front entrance, he'd need a code to access her floor, and her door's state-of-the-art. Her father made sure of it."

"Be glad he did."

He was, but the mild derision couldn't be helped. Or if it could, he wasn't interested in making the effort. For a moment, he saw his own father's face, twisted into an unrecognizable mask. Blocking the image, Jacob drank his coffee. "Why does the captain want me?"

"Probably to tell you Critch has disappeared." Another round of quarters clinked into the machine. "You gonna fill him in on the details of your shift?"

"Only as far as the Parker case is concerned."

"Figured as much. Jacob." O'Keefe stopped him when he would have walked away. "Do us all a favor, and let someone else handle this."

Jacob smiled past his shoulder. "While I do what?"

"Take a well-deserved vacation. Go to Tahiti, or Fiji or Hawaii. Swim. Drink. Get laid. Hell, connect with your mother's family."

"Yeah, right. I'll rehash my mother's life in New Zealand and follow it up with her death here in Cincinnati. Thanks, but I'd rather stay and do battle with Critch."

"He's obsessed, Jacob."

"I'm not a rookie, Mick." He countered O'Keefe's frustrated stare with a steady one of his own. "I won't let him hurt her."

"Or you."

A faint smile crept in. "Or me."

O'Keefe rumpled his hair again. He reminded most people of a tall, well-built teddy bear, with his perpetually kind face, his soulful eyes and a mop of brown curls that were only now, in his mid-forties, beginning to creep back from his forehead. But Jacob knew the man behind the facade. He'd worked with him for eight years—and had seen firsthand just how deceptive teddy bears could be.

The eyes before him grew troubled. "You know she's not your type, don't you?"

He'd been waiting for this, Jacob reflected, and made himself look away. "I never thought she was."

"But you're interested."

"No." Jacob met his eyes. "I'm not."

"Hmm, you lie so well, I can't tell the difference anymore. You don't want her, she doesn't want you—or probably me, either, for that matter, but I'm a hopeful schmuck who needs to be rebuffed to his face before he'll give up. My kid likes her."

Jacob glanced down at the file. "Why don't you send Romana to Hawaii for the holidays?"

O'Keefe opened his mouth, but it was a more velvety voice that replied, "Won't work, Knight. Romana's not a run-and-hide kind of person."

She strode up to them from the side, smiled at O'Keefe, then went toe-to-toe with Jacob. If she'd been a hothead like Mick's ex-wife, she'd probably have punched him. Come to think of it, that might not be a bad idea. If nothing else, a punch would ease the gridlock of tension and mounting desire in his stomach.

"What are you doing here, Romana?" Jacob kept his tone calm and his expression neutral.

A sideways glance drew O'Keefe into her answer. "I got a phone call forty minutes ago. The guy claimed to be an elf, said he wanted to go over my Christmas wish list with me. Since I'd just stepped out of the shower, I told him my only wish was for him to hang up. To which he replied, 'Wrong answer, cop saver. What you should wish is to be a cat. But even nine lives won't help you now. Santa Critch is going to hunt you down and poison your holidays. Sad to say, Romana Grey. You've seen your last merry Christmas Day.'"

SOMETIMES, ROMANA REFLECTED with a shudder, a photographic memory was just plain creepy. The verse at the end of Critch's early morning phone call sang in her head all day.

In the same elfin voice he'd used—which only made the effect that much freakier.

Naturally, the call was untraceable. Critch had stolen a cell phone from a Cincinnati resident who'd been standing, half-asleep, at a bus stop. He'd used the device for his own purposes, then ditched the phone. Mission accomplished, from his perspective.

From Romana's, life carried on. She wasn't prepared to let Critch affect it, even on the smallest level.

After leaving the police station, she spent Saturday morning and most of the afternoon Christmas shopping with two of her sisters-in-law and six nephews under the age of five. As a rule, she enjoyed taking them to toy stores, loved watching them bounce on Santa's knee; however, by five o'clock, even her abundant energy was sapped. In fact, she was so wiped out that the path lab at the hospital was starting to look good.

Or not, she amended as she pushed through the side door and began her solitary descent.

Organ music wafted out of invisible speakers. Critch's rhyming threat jangled in her brain. "Sad to say, Romana Grey, you've seen your last merry Christmas Day."

"Jerk," she muttered, and, twitching a shoulder, pushed through another door.

An attendant she didn't recognize passed her in the antiseptic green corridor. The woman wore headphones and a blank expression as she hummed along to a hip-hop song. But even her off-key humming was better than the churchlike version of "Sleigh Ride" currently playing on the path lab's sound system.

Although weekends tended to be quiet on the lower levels, Romana knew Fitz was here somewhere. The trick would be

to locate her cousin before she bumped into someone who remembered her as Connor Hanson's wife.

"Romana?"

Too late. The man's voice came from her right. Steeling
herself, Romana turned—and exhaled with relief when she
saw who it was.

"Dylan, hi." She rubbed her left temple where a headache
had been brewing since lunchtime. "What brings you to
Death Central?"

Belinda Critch's brother, Dylan Hoag, closed the electrical box he'd been examining. "I'm checking out the security
system. They had a wiring problem down here yesterday."

"Heard about it. Fitz," she explained at his elevated
eyebrow. "Have you seen her?"

"We had a chat, but Patrick whisked her away, said he
needed help. Must be hard to trim a corpse's fingernails all
by your lonesome."

Romana strolled closer, ran a teasing finger over his
shoulder. "I sense a chip here, Mr. Hoag. Toward Patrick, I
wonder, or the forensics team in general?"

"The team could be better. Standards have slipped since
Doctor Gorman retired."

Now she patted his shoulder. "Hate to tell you this, Dylan,
but they were slipping while Gorman was here. He was well
past his prime when the hospital board decided to force the
retirement issue."

"Then there were Connor's indiscretions." Dylan's tone
soured. "And Belinda's death."

A tick in his jaw accompanied the bitter statement. Romana
wanted to respond, but couldn't think of anything comforting
to say. She settled for another pat and left him to finish his inspection of the breaker box.

Dylan hadn't changed much in the eight-plus years she'd known him. His hair was light brown, short and spiky. He kept his tall frame trim and his somewhat angular features a deliberate blank. It was his idea of a cop look. Sadly, although they'd entered the Academy at the same time, Dylan had washed out halfway through the program.

Romana didn't know why the memory should strike her right then, but she recalled Dylan's reaction quite clearly as he'd been given the news. Resentment had flared for about five seconds before he'd doused it. He'd aimed a long, steely glare at the sergeant, then turned on his heel and stalked away.

Six months later, he'd formed his own company—with a handful of employees and the endorsement of one extremely influential businessman.

James Barret…Romana rolled the name over, caught Dylan staring and set it aside.

"You look frazzled," he noted in his more usual low-key fashion.

She regarded the ends of her hair and tried not to picture what his idea of frazzled entailed. When his gaze slid to her face, she caught just enough of his expression for comprehension to click in. "You thought it was because of Warren Critch, didn't you?"

He jiggled a wire. "He's never been happy about what you did in that alley."

"I don't believe this." With a fatalistic laugh, Romana circled away, then returned. "I'm surrounded by enigmatic men. Give me something, Dylan. You hate me, you don't. You want Critch to hurt Jacob and me, you want him to fail. You've seen him, you haven't—what is it? Talk to me. React. Emote."

He straightened, and his eyes—not as penetrating as Jacob's—captured hers. "Warren and I talked on the phone the day he was released. One conversation, two minutes long. I thought he wanted money. He said he didn't. He just wanted me to know he still thinks about Belinda every day, and he lives in that downtown alley every night."

Romana's hackles rose. "Jacob didn't kill her, Dylan."

"Someone did."

"Yes." Her mind slipped sideways. "Someone did." Then with conviction, "But it wasn't Jacob."

Dylan's chuckle had a raw edge. "You know, I can almost believe you. You sound so sure of yourself." He stepped closer. "But I don't think you're as certain as you pretend to be."

No way would she be intimidated by him. Romana held her ground and her nerve. She lifted a finger to his chin and tapped it in a manner intended to provoke. "You know, Dylan, it seems to me that someone must have redirected all those cards Critch wrote to Jacob and me while he was in prison. The postmarks said they were mailed from northern Kentucky. And you are, or were, his brother-in-law."

Dylan's eyebrows came together. "Warren wrote to you?"

"Subtly threatened is the way I see it now. He made sure that Jacob and I received Christmas cards every year, to let us know, I imagine, that he wasn't going to forget about us, or the part he felt we played in Belinda's death."

Wilted organ music hovered in the air between them. Dylan's features remained cold. "If Warren's been threatening you, then he must still believe Knight murdered Belinda. I sorted through her stuff after she died, Romana. There was nothing that incriminated anyone else."

"Anyone else?" Romana challenged softly. "Or anyone at all?"

If human features could take on the characteristics of a granite carving, Dylan's did at that moment. She could almost hear the war that raged inside his head. He so wanted Jacob to be guilty. He needed to hate a specific person, not a faceless, nameless entity.

Before he could respond, they heard a rustle of fabric in the hallway. Romana didn't have to look to know who was there.

Jacob's hands were jammed in the pockets of his leather jacket. His expression was far less promising than Dylan's. "You want to take a swing at someone, pal, take it at me." He started toward them, slowly, deliberately. "Romana did her job in that alley. I'm the one who saw Belinda before she died."

Dylan's gaze flicked from Jacob to Romana and back again. When he finally spoke, it was in a controlled undertone. "Belinda said that Warren used to go down to the basement and brood when he got angry. Sometimes, he'd stay down there for hours, once for a whole day. Eventually, he'd come up, and when he did, he'd always find a way to get back at the person who'd angered him. Warren's had six long years to brood about you two. Now that he's out, my guess is he'll let his vindictive side take over—until the source or sources of that feeling are eliminated."

"I AM SO, SO TIRED OF BEING threatened." Romana stalked back and forth in the hospital parking lot. Her white coat flapped open around her ankles, and a playful wind blew her long hair around her face. "Critch is convinced that you murdered his wife. Dylan's ninety percent sure of it. Even Fitz, my own cousin, thinks you're dangerous. Me, I still choose to believe you didn't do it, because I think you're a good person, and I know you're a good cop. No, better than good, you're an excellent cop." She paused, slanted him a contemplative look. "The kind of cop female rookies fresh out of the Academy probably still fantasize about."

Jacob had been leaning against the front fender of his SUV while she vented her frustration. Now his green eyes shifted from the distant line of freeway traffic to her face.

"Did you have fantasies about me, Romana?"

She resumed her pacing, but at a slower tempo. "I might have." Amusement kindled at his expression. "Come on, Jacob, I was young, not happily married and not liking that fact one bit. You were an unattainable male. You didn't notice me." Amusement blossomed into a laugh. "Don't be polite and pretend you did. Rookies are a pain, necessary to the force, but a pain just the same. I remember one time…" A sudden thought struck. "Oh, no!" She started to look at her watch, remembered she'd loaned it to her sister-in-law and grabbed Jacob's arm. "What time is it?" A frustrated sound escaped. "It can't be seven o'clock? I'm supposed to be in the park, watching Teresa figure-skate."

"Are you serious?" He trapped her wrist before she could search for her keys.

"It's for a Christmas play, Jacob. *Pageant in the Park.* The deputy mayor's wife put it together. Tonight's only a dress rehearsal, but I promised I'd be there, and I never break a promise, especially not to a seven-year-old child."

He held fast even when she gave her wrist a tug. Romana knew she could have made a more determined effort to release herself, but her skin felt oddly warm under his fingers, and there were fiery little arrows currently racing up her arm to her throat.

"Huh." She paused for a moment to marvel. "Didn't expect that."

Jacob's expression altered slowly, went from exasperated to intrigued. He loosened his grip, but didn't release her. Instead, he drew her closer and looked down into her eyes.

The pulse at the base of her throat beat like an erratic drum. Logically speaking, she should feel uneasy about this. After all, wanting to believe wasn't the same thing as actually believing. Jacob had no alibi for the night Belinda Critch had died. But he did have the most riveting features, especially his eyes, sea-green with the barest hint of gray. And then there was his mouth…

"I'm…uh…hmm—lost the thought." And possibly her mind with it. But right then she didn't care. She was too busy wanting to pull that incredibly sexy mouth of his down and kiss him until she couldn't think about anything else.

She'd wanted to kiss him almost from the first time she'd met him. Being married, she'd felt guilty about that, so she'd made a point of not looking any more than necessary—until Connor had cheated on her.

"Probably a good thing," she murmured.

Jacob's eyes fixed on hers. "Good things have the potential to turn bad, Romana. His lips twisted slightly. "Voice of experience."

She tipped her head to regard him. Surely one kiss couldn't hurt. She was no longer married—thank God and Grandma Grey—and dress rehearsals, even when run by political figures, seldom came off on schedule.

As was her habit, Romana deferred to her feelings, or in Jacob's case, her hunger. Maybe it hadn't been appropriate at the time, but she couldn't deny that she'd fantasized about the gorgeous, dark-haired cop who'd made detective even before she'd entered the Academy. She'd glimpsed him from time to time at the station, had actually worked with him once on a murder investigation. But she'd been young back then, painfully inexperienced and probably fortunate that her male partner had watched over her like a scowling papa bear.

Romana eased forward, smiling as his eyes heated up. Danger spiked through anticipation. Her skin was already hot, and he'd barely touched her yet.

She rolled her hips, just a bit. "Are you going to let me seduce you, Detective?"

His eyes strayed to her mouth. "Thinking about it."

Large flakes of snow drifted from a starless sky. The traffic noise became a distant buzz in her ears. As she raised her head, he ran his thumb and fingers upward along the curve of her throat until they formed a V beneath her chin.

Excitement glimmered. The desire she felt for Jacob had been in hibernation for a long time, and it wasn't taking much to wake it up. This probably wasn't a good idea, or a smart one. But it was just forbidden enough to be irresistible.

A blanket of snow covered the ground. The city glowed silver and gold. The night air had a bite, but it was nothing compared to the jolt that ricocheted through Romana's system when Jacob took that last step and lowered his mouth to hers.

Her head spun in delicious circles. He tasted like sex and cool water, a tantalizing contrast. His tongue made a thorough exploration of her mouth, and she felt a sigh rise up in her throat.

Now this, she thought hazily, this was a kiss. A wicked, soul-stirring, heart-hammering kiss. And it was exactly what she'd wanted, what she'd needed from him tonight.

But even off balance, there were limits. Giving his lower lip a nip, she pulled away. It was either that or move the whole thing into his SUV.

"Guess I still have a few lingering fantasies." She disentangled her hair from his hand. "You're a great kisser, Detective Knight—for a man who prefers his own company."

He ran a thumb over her jaw. "Are you trying to get a rise out of me, Romana?"

She shimmied her hips against his. "I don't need to try. I already have." She gave him another quick nip.

His eyes tempted her to do it all again—until she spied the gleam deep inside them.

She took a wise step back. "I need air, Jacob. You're making me dizzy."

"Sounds promising."

In spite of herself, Romana couldn't resist hooking two fingers in the top of his waistband. Smart was one thing, but there was no need to end the moment in a blind rush.

"You're such a conundrum," she murmured as he ran his hands up and down her arms. "I have a feeling I'm going to…" The thought died when she spotted the object several feet in front of her. Rectangular shape, bloodred color and all too familiar to her these days. "Oh, damn," she breathed.

"What?" Jacob swung his head, followed her gaze to the windshield of his SUV.

"That's one of Critch's envelopes." She made a quick sweep of the lot. "And I swear it wasn't here a moment ago."

Jacob yanked it free and handed it to her even as he stuffed his gun into the top of his jeans. His eyes never stopped moving.

Romana regarded the flap, visualized briefly, then opened it. Her hands wanted to tremble, but she sucked it up and steadied her nerves. This was a scare tactic, an effective one, but she'd be damned if she'd play Critch's game, no matter how rattled she felt.

Still scanning, Jacob drew her into the shelter of his large vehicle. He gave her a few seconds to read the message before he murmured, "Out loud, Romana."

She frowned at the poorly printed words. "'If you're keeping score,'" she read, "'this is your second threat.'" She turned the paper over, searched for more. "What threat?"

As if cued, a pair of projectiles whizzed past her ear. She heard two soft *thwacks,* then found herself on her knees in the snow. Jacob held her firmly in place while he combed the shadowy fir trees on the perimeter of the lot.

"Why did I ask?" She pushed at his hands. "I'm not going to jump up, Jacob. Do you see him?"

"No."

Crawling forward, Romana stole a look around the bumper. "There aren't any vehicles over here," she said. Then she raised her sights, and her heart gave a single, hard beat. "Ah—well."

"What?"

"I found our second threat."

Still on her knees, she indicated Jacob's windshield—and the pair of neat, round bullet holes Critch had fired through it.

Chapter Four

Jacob woke with a hiss and an image in his head that had him reaching for his gun before his eyes were fully open.

It was the same dream, always the same—his father shouting, his mother closing doors to keep the worst of it in.

Monsters under the bed had nothing on Jacob's father in a rage. As a boy, he'd been willing to join the hidden demons so he wouldn't have to hear what he knew would come next.

He remembered the way his heart had thudded. That helped block the sound. Beside him, Kermit sang in his silly frog voice. He thought it was good to be green. Jacob thought it was better to pretend.

The dream rolled forward. Morning came. Everything seemed fine, back to normal—except his mother wore a long-sleeved, high-necked shirt in mid-July, his father snarled into his coffee cup, and no one spoke, not even Jacob's chatty Muppet frog.

Then the scene shifted. Cold crept in. Snow blanketed the ground. Jacob's father dragged a Christmas tree inside through the garage. His mother watered it. She laughed because she had pine needles stuck in her hair when she emerged from under the low branches.

Jacob remembered her laugh most of all. It echoed in his head even as the atmosphere altered and his father entered the house.

He'd had a bad day, they saw it in his face. A police officer had died. The shooter had escaped. His father's fists were clenched. So was his jaw.

Everything had turned red after that. Red smears on his mother's face, long red streaks on his father's hands, drops of red clinging to a Christmas candle beside the freshly watered tree.

It was the same red they'd found on Belinda's body....

Swearing, Jacob fell back on the mattress and stared at the shadowy ceiling.

New shapes formed in the corners, indistinct people shuffling around in unknown places. Jacob felt his heart slamming, both then and now. Too late, he spied the silhouette behind him. He felt a slash of pain in his skull, remembered O'Keefe yelling, then—nothing.

Still staring upward, he worked the tense muscles in his jaw. He pictured Belinda Critch, a tall rangy blonde, not delicate in feature or demeanor, yet sensual in a way that drew men toward her and drove women away. No matter how he tried, though, Jacob couldn't hold the shot. His mind kept changing it, refining the features, darkening the hair, softening the expression—and ultimately turning up the sex appeal by a good eighty-five percent.

Frustrated by his thoughts, he rolled from the bed. It was after 5:00 p.m., snowy, cold and, unfortunately, Sunday. He had no official work to do tonight, but he did have a file on his kitchen counter, copies of three recently delivered Christmas cards stuck to his fridge and a memory in his head from yesterday that had started with a kiss and ended with an aborted pageant rehearsal in the park.

The power had failed at the outdoor pond that served as a rink, so Romana hadn't been able to watch her niece skate, although how a child of seven could be expected to do anything on ice when she was dressed up like a pink-and-white spotted elephant was beyond Jacob. He'd barely been able to stand on skates and hold a hockey stick at that age.

They'd try again tomorrow night, the deputy mayor's wife had promised a small crowd of onlookers.

While coffee brewed and the radiator made ominous clunking sounds, Jacob paged through Belinda's file. But, like his mental picture of her, the reports blurred; names and faces ran together. Romana's winter-lake eyes stared up at him. Her mouth tempted him to taste. The scent of her hair and skin shot straight to his groin.

Losing it, he reflected and seesawed his head to loosen the muscles in his neck.

Someone had murdered Belinda. Did he want to find out who'd done it, or slap the file closed, take O'Keefe's advice and head out to the airport?

A knock on his door prevented an answer, but if he was honest, he'd admit that New Zealand paled next to the prospect of spending time with Romana Grey. So really, he should be thinking airline ticket all the way, and leave O'Keefe to do what he could surely do better than his former partner to keep Romana safe.

Another knock. "Jacob?" Denny Leech's raspy voice reached him. "You up yet?"

Jacob let his head drop back. She'd have her granddaughter in tow, he just knew it.

"Yeah, I'm up."

He used the peephole out of habit, glimpsed a pink ball cap and a movement beside it. This should be uncomfortable.

It was the prolonged squelch of rubber on tile that alerted him. It sounded wrong. The thud that followed it was even more out of place.

The skin on Jacob's neck prickled. "Denny?"

When she didn't respond, he reached for his gun in its holster by the jamb. Twisting the latch, he sidestepped. With the barrel pointed upward, he kicked the door open—and stumbled as he swung onto the threshold.

A door clanged shut below. Jacob looked down, cursed, jammed his gun into the back of his waistband.

The leg that blocked his path belonged to his neighbor. His neighbor who was lying face up in a seeping pool of blood.

NINETY MINUTES LATER, ROMANA rushed into the crowded emergency room. She spotted Jacob through a sea of bodies and made her way over.

"How's Denny?" she asked. From his expression, she suspected not good.

He stared past her at the treatment room. "Possible skull fracture and a concussion." His expression was calm, but that was practiced, like his tone when he added, "Critch clubbed her from behind with a broken brick."

Romana's stomach pitched. Apparently prison hadn't mellowed the man one bit. "How old is she?"

"Almost eighty."

"Does she have a strong constitution?"

"I'd say so."

A man in a wrist cast jostled Romana's arm. With a sideways glance, she drew Jacob toward the water fountain. She wanted to remind him that this wasn't his fault, but any solace she offered would go unheard. He'd blame himself for what had happened because he hadn't gotten to Critch first.

"I assume the brick Critch used has been found."

"In the alley, next to my front bumper."

"Fingerprints would be nice," she mused. "Or a strand of hair. But if it's like the cards he sent, there won't be anything to connect him to the crime. I don't suppose you saw him."

"No, only Denny."

Romana wanted to touch his cheek, but Jacob simply didn't invite that kind of contact. She settled for brushing the hair from his forehead. "You know, my grandmother's in her late seventies, and she handled a concussion last year as if it were a scraped knee. She was up and riding her horses within a week. Totally against her doctor's orders, but she insisted she knew her body's limits better than a man she sees only once a year. Where's Denny now?"

"They're taking her upstairs." He slid his gaze from the treatment room to her face. "You weren't supposed to come here, Romana. I called so you'd make sure your door was bolted and alarmed, not go flying out into the night and possibly into Critch's waiting hands."

Romana studied his face. The strain of the past few hours showed most clearly in his eyes, but there was subtle evidence of it around his mouth and in the side of his jaw, where she saw a muscle tick.

Because she needed what he appeared not to, Romana flattened her palms on his chest. "You've done all you can here. Someone can call you if there's any change in Denny's condition." She curled her fingers around his T-shirt and pulled. "Right now, you need to come to the park with me."

He gave a disbelieving laugh, scanned the bustling corridor. "Are you on some kind of street drug, Romana?"

"No, I'm on some kind of mission to locate and capture Critch before he hurts another innocent bystander. Or better still—" tightening her grip, she forced him to look back at her "—to locate and apprehend the person who murdered his wife."

"And you think we're going to do one or both of those things in a public park?"

"No idea, Knight." She stepped closer, partly to distract him and partly because a woman in a wheelchair was rolling past. "What I do know is that Belinda Critch was—I'll be polite and say *acquainted*—with one James Barret. And my well-informed cousin Fitz told me this afternoon that, since his godchildren are part of it, Mr. Barret will likely be attending tonight's pageant rehearsal."

"If Critch'll attack an old woman—an uninvolved old woman—he'll attack anyone." Jacob threaded his way through traffic on the busy streets of Mount Adams. "Anyone, Romana, any age."

"Thank you, I realize that." And it brought a chill to her skin thinking about it. "Fortunately, my niece had to pull out of the pageant. She tripped over a toy truck and sprained her ankle." Romana stared through the window at the decorated houses they passed. "The city looks so festive right now, doesn't it? Pretty lights, Christmas music. I swear I can even smell chestnuts roasting in the park. And yet your neighbor's in a hospital bed, I'm glad my niece hurt her ankle, and I'm trying to think up an excuse not to go anywhere near Fitz tonight."

Jacob located a parking spot on the edge of the makeshift lot. Directly across from them, on the far side of the pond, a high school band played "Holly Jolly Christmas." He watched them as he spoke. "I can talk to Barret on police time if it makes you more comfortable."

"It doesn't." She pulled on a pair of black leather gloves,

a striking contrast to her long red coat. "I'm not going to let Critch win, I just don't want anyone I know to get hurt. Having said that, I still think our best plan to stop him is to figure out who murdered his wife."

"While we do or don't search for him?"

Resolved, she slid from her seat and slammed the door. "Eggs in more than one basket, Knight. We search for both of them."

He set his arms on the hood. "I hate to remind you, Romana, but you're not a cop these days. You shouldn't be searching for anyone."

"Critch shouldn't be taking potshots at us. What's your point, Detective?"

"You'd be better off in Boston with your parents."

Ah, they were back to the safety issue. She tucked her hair behind her ears, tugged on a black hat. "Only in your eyes. In mine, I'd be exposing them to danger."

"He wants me more than he wants you."

"Again, your opinion. I figure if I so much as try to leave the city, he'll turn on my brothers, or worse, their kids."

"Romana…"

"Not running, Detective. Accept it." Her lips curved. "On a more salient note, in case you haven't noticed, you're standing next to a cobalt-blue Porsche. That car is the same color as James Barret's eyes, which is undoubtedly why he bought it."

"And you know that because…"

Her smile deepened to a tease. "I guess that means I either know him well enough to be aware of his vanity, or Fitz told me."

At his vaguely suspicious look, she sighed out a laugh. "Fitz had a crush on him as a kid. Her father's an upholsterer for Barret Brown Furniture. A younger James Barret used to give her candy, and bat his baby blues at her. If she says he and Belinda were involved, they probably were. One thing Fitz can do better than anyone I know is ferret out information that she feels is relevant to her life. Don't say it." She deflected the obvious question. "Fantasies are as relevant to a lot of people as reality is." She should know, Romana reflected with a shiver. She was standing three feet from hers.

Beyond a faint twitch of his lips, Jacob didn't react. He simply held out a hand for her to precede him.

She told herself to focus, not be sucked into an emotional whirlpool. It would be so easy to fall for Jacob Knight, to let herself want him in a way that, sadly, she'd never wanted her ex-husband. Big girl, big desires, she reflected with a twinge of regret. But Santa couldn't make everyone's Christmas wishes come true, and even if he could, Jacob was still a dark horse with the department and a largely unknown, albeit incredibly sexy, commodity to her.

"Ro!" Any hope she had of avoiding Fitz died as her cousin swooped in, out of breath and pink-cheeked. "You have to help me. James wants to talk. Don't know why, but I can't say no. The thing is, I managed to drag Patrick here tonight, and I don't want him to disappear while I'm gone. So I need you to—oh." The fingers she'd wrapped around Romana's arm loosened, then did a speculative tap dance. "Hello, Detective Knight. I didn't see you." But now that she had, she took a long, assessing look. "Talk about coincidence. I ran into your old partner last night at Franconi's. He was alone and lonely. We had beer and pasta together."

"He's missing his daughter." Jacob surveyed the park scene. A crease formed between his eyes when his gaze reached the pond.

Romana followed his gaze. "What? Is it Critch?"

"No, it's a guy from Vice dressed like a jack-in-the-box."

"Charlie," she corrected. At his uncomprehending look, she grinned. "He's a Charlie-in-the-box. Island of Misfit Toys, Knight."

"You need kids," Fitz said, then snapped her mouth closed. "Or not. Uh, Ro, could you… She'll be right back, Detective." She nudged Romana toward a cluster of benches, wiggled her fingers at a man seated on the farthest one and didn't release the breath she'd evidently been holding until Jacob moved away to set his forearms on the makeshift guardrail. "Can't believe I said that," she muttered. "Dumb, dumber, dumbest."

Romana didn't correct her. Tonight wasn't about fixing misconceptions, it was about exposing a murderer—and keeping Warren Critch away from the people she loved.

"Talk to James," she told her cousin. "I'll distract Patrick."

Fitz started off, but backpedaled to drill a warning finger into Romana's arm. "Only distract, okay? No making him think things he shouldn't." She fluffed her curls. "You could talk me up a bit, though, if the opportunity arises. I mean, honest to God, Ro, if the guy was a horse, I'd figure he was gelded."

"Nice image," Romana murmured. "Thanks, Fitz."

As she picked her way through the snow, Romana noticed that Jacob was already surrounded by a flock of girls. All wore bright-green jackets, which would make them members of the performing high school band.

"What is it about cops and hormonal teenagers?" Patrick wondered aloud when she came within earshot. He lounged on the bench with his head resting on the back and a cup of something hot in his hand. "It's like they have radar. Cop in the vicinity. Line forms to the left, girlfriends."

"Cynic." Romana dusted snow off the seat beside him. "They probably think he's a hot guitar player."

"I spotted the badge on his belt loop from here, Romana. He's the big *D* to them. Dangerous, and older to boot."

The night air had a bite, like Patrick's tone. Romana turned up the collar of her coat and wished she'd worn heavier clothes.

With a crooked smile, Patrick produced a thermos from the snow beside him. "A red-headed elf told me to come prepared. Hot chocolate?"

She blew on her gloved hands. "Smart elf. I'd love some."

"Myself, I'm a warm-weather man."

"How warm?"

"I was born in Houston. This white stuff's acceptable on Christmas Day, but otherwise I'd pass."

"Not into winter sports, huh?"

"I'm not into any sports, unless you include channel and web surfing."

He sounded completely bored. Romana's female pride would have been stung if she hadn't known he used the same dull tone with everyone. It might not be kind, but she had to wonder what Fitz saw in him.

Oh, he was handsome enough in a scruffy, mismatched sort of way. He also had height, a good inch over six feet, which was about the same as Jacob, actually. His features were strong and his eyes dark brown, a match for the perpetual tangle of his hair. Romana suspected the stubble he wore was intended to be sexy, but all she wanted to do was find him a razor.

Funny she never felt that way about Jacob…

"Houston Control to Professor Grey." Patrick waved a steaming cup under her nose. He lowered his hand in disgust. "Oh, God, you're staring at the cop, aren't you?"

"Well, I did come with him."

"You need to watch your step," he said. "Knight's not what he appears to be."

Romana took a cautious sip of her drink. As she'd antici-pated, it was heavily laced with rum. "Neither's your hot cocoa, Patrick. Why the red flag?"

"It's the same flag Belinda held up a couple of days before she died." At her questioning glance, he shrugged. "We worked together. We talked."

"Only talked?"

Patrick's laugh had an edge. "Okay, right, here we go. I knew when Critch was released the whole question-and-answer thing would erupt again. We were friends, coworkers. She was married. I respected that. She respected my respect… And you can eighty-six the look, Romana. Don't you have any male friends? By that, I mean the kind of friends whose sole purpose in life isn't to jump your bones?"

"We were talking about Belinda's bones, Patrick, not mine."

"We were talking about Jacob Knight initially. The guy's trouble in caps. You want it straight, that's exactly what Belinda said."

Romana blew on her cocoa, squashed the uneasy prickles in her stomach. "It sounds like you and Belinda had some pretty involved conversations."

"You do that when the alternative is to let it sink in that you're slicing up dead organs while extracting bodily fluids."

"You didn't have to choose forensic pathology, Patrick."

"My father was a mortician. My mother was a morgue atten-dant. What else was I going to do? I'm John Patrick North, only son of Mr. and Mrs. Coffin and Slab." He laughed without humor, raised his cup in her direction and drained the contents. Sadness replaced the laughter. "We were friends, Belinda and me, and whether you want to hear it or not, I believe Knight killed her."

Summoning an easy smile, Romana passed him her drink. "Spoken with great conviction. But you haven't specified why you're so sure Jacob did it."

"He argued with Belinda in a restaurant before she died."

"That's a matter of record. Did he threaten her?"

"She didn't say exactly, but I could see by her body language that she was upset. And afraid."

"Of Jacob?"

"No, of Santa Claus." He polished off her cocoa, hesitated, then moved a reluctant shoulder. "But come to think of it, Dylan's name came up a few times."

"She was frightened of her brother?"

"Step."

It took Romana a moment to understand. "Step—" she stared in amazement "—brother?"

"You didn't know?"

"Why would I know?"

"You were a cop. I thought you people knew everything."

"It wasn't my case to investigate."

He eyeballed a glittering pine tree across from them. "No, Stubbs and Canter got that gig. Short, fat guy with salt and pepper hair and no chin—that was Stubbs. Canter was a foot taller, with arms like Popeye and a butt to match."

"Odd detail to notice," Romana commented.

"I'm a details kind of guy."

If his lopsided grin was intended to charm, the attempt fell flat, as he likely would when he tried to stand. Romana didn't envy Fitz the remainder of her date.

Abandoning pretense, Patrick ditched his cup and drank from the thermos.

Romana waited until he lowered it to remark, "You wanted her to come on to you, didn't you?"

Patrick stared at the pond where two dozen kids ranging from five to fifteen years of age struggled to glide, twirl and hop in full costume. "What I wanted wasn't something I shared with Belinda. I told myself I'd wait. I never believed she'd last with Critch. He was possessive and gruff and, from what I'd seen, potentially violent. He had a tendency to freak whenever he caught her talking to another man. I figured when the marriage ended, she'd need a friend, and there I'd be."

"A friend who'd segue into a lover."

"We all have our pipe dreams, Romana. Mine died with Belinda six Christmases ago. If Knight didn't kill her, maybe Warren did. But like I said, I lean toward Knight."

"Because they argued."

He hitched an irritable shoulder. "Well, it's really more because of what she said afterward."

A light shiver chased itself across Romana's skin. "Which was…"

He swung the now-empty thermos by its silver neck. "This wasn't part of our personal conversation. I heard her on the phone in the staff lounge. She sounded halfway to hysterical. She said she'd just had lunch with Jacob Knight."

"That's not news, Patrick. Jacob admitted in court…"

He halted her with a raised finger. "Not done yet, former Officer Grey. Belinda stated very clearly that she was frightened for her life. She said she wouldn't have thought it possible, but Jacob Knight really did want her dead."

"You pretend to ride the ostrich, Broderick, you don't drag it around like a bag of trash. Play the game, young man, or there'll be no trip to Disney World this spring."

While Jacob observed the exchange from the guardrail, James Barret straightened from his crouch, snicked his elegant coat cuffs back in place and gave the back of an eight-year-old boy's head a light tap.

"Go. Cooperate. Act like a godson I can be proud of." When the boy slumped off, he gave his head a rueful shake. "That one has delinquent written all over him." Without turning, he raised his voice. "What do you think, Detective Knight? Will you be arresting him in ten years' time?"

Interesting that Barret would recognize him. Unfazed, Jacob went with the question. "I doubt it."

"You can't deny he has an attitude."

"But no venom. He's dragging his feet, not using them to kick anyone."

Barret flashed neon-white teeth and twitched his cuffs again. "I'll have to trust you there. He's the son of my wife's best friend. My wife wanted to be a godparent, and what Shera wants, Shera usually manages to get."

Had Shera wanted Belinda Critch dead? Jacob set the question aside as Barret extended a well-manicured hand.

"You were questioned during the investigation into Belinda Critch's death," he noted. "How did you know her?"

Fitz appeared at Barret's side and slid her arm through his. "James makes a point of knowing everyone and everything that matters. I thought you two might need an introduction, so I came back. Guess I needn't have bothered."

"You needn't have," Barret agreed, "but I'm glad you did. Fitz can liven up even the most awkward conversation, Detective."

Jacob regarded him without emotion. "Are we having an awkward conversation?"

"If you came here tonight to ask me about Belinda Critch, then, yes, we are."

"You knew her personally?"

"I did."

Fitz glanced from one to the other. "Uh, listen, guys, this probably isn't the best place to…"

"How well?"

"That's a very broad question, Detective."

Barret's practiced smile had a snap far more vicious than the wind that slapped at their cheeks. Because he relished a challenge, Jacob let his anticipation rise and his own eyes gleam.

"I'll rephrase. Did you have an affair with her?"

"Whoa—hi—now that's a loaded question, Jacob." He felt his own arm being snagged and squeezed as Romana added through her teeth, "Mayor's a good friend of his, Knight." She offered a smile that would have bewitched a corpse. "Hello, Mr. Barret. I'm Fitz's cousin, Romana Grey. We met a few years ago at a university alumni dinner."

"Met and danced. I remember the event very well." He took her free hand, didn't raise it to his lips as Jacob had expected, but held on and transferred his full attention to her. "You're even more beautiful than I remembered."

Fitz craned her neck to peer across the pond. "Where's Patrick, Ro? You promised to, uh—keep him company for a while."

"He drank too much hot cocoa and fell asleep. I buttoned his coat and stuck a pair of earmuffs on his head. But you should probably check on him. The wind's a bit nasty tonight."

Among other things, Jacob reflected.

Fitz fluttered at Barret. "Guess I'll go, then." She gave Romana's hip a swat in passing. "Call me," she said in an undertone.

"If I survive." Romana squared up, refocused. "You know, you two, this really isn't the place…"

But Barret brushed aside her objection. "It's as good a place as any. I have no idea why my godson's riding a wooden ostrich in this pageant and no particular desire to watch him do it."

She sighed. "Doesn't anyone but me know about the Island of Misfit Toys?"

Because Barret still hadn't answered his question and likely wouldn't head-on, Jacob opted for a roundabout approach. "How did you meet Belinda?"

Barret's eyes, already cool, iced over. "I could tell you it's none of your business. Unfortunately, in my experience that response seldom works with the police. It's a matter of record that we met at a New Year's Eve party nine years ago."

Before Jacob could counter, Romana reaffixed her dazzling smile. "I love New Year's Eve. It's such an uninhibited night. Was Belinda's husband at the party?"

Surprisingly, some of the ice in Barret's eyes melted. "No, he wasn't. I can't tell you why. What I can say is that she never mentioned a husband while she was coming on to me. Sorry to sound crass, but that's what she did for the first part of the night."

"Where was the party?" Jacob asked.

"Also a matter of record, Detective Knight. It unfolded at Gilhoolie's Pub, and before you make a snide remark about the earthy nature of the venue, I'll remind you that I'm a self-made man whose father traveled from Galway to America at the age of fifteen and worked in a Portland, Maine, fish processing plant for much of his life. As a teenager, I worked hard alongside him."

Romana gave Jacob's ankle a kick before venturing a pleasant, "How on earth did you go from processing fish in Maine to making furniture in Ohio?"

Barret's eyes glinted. "My father, bless his whiskey-soaked soul, met a man very similar to him in a bar. His name was Ben Brown. Ben had an idea, and my dad had every dollar he'd saved since arriving on these shores. I was nineteen at the time and more than ready to leave the smell of fish behind. We formed a three-way partnership. My father passed on three years into the deal, leaving Ben and me to build on the framework of our infant business venture. We built well. Our partnership held fast until Ben died six years ago."

"The same year Belinda Critch died. And under somewhat questionable circumstances." Jacob's prod was deliberate. It earned him another kick from Romana and a cool arch of Barret's left eyebrow.

"Did I mention, Detective, that I wasn't the only man Belinda came on to that cold New Year's Eve?"

"You haven't mentioned much at all—about that night or any other." Jacob ignored Romana's hissed, "Mayor's your boss, Knight," and countered Barret's visual dagger with a level one of his own. "I've read the police report on Belinda's death. Details are sketchy in several areas. Yours is one of them."

"Possibly because I was never a viable suspect. I cooperated with your department in as much as I was required to. However—" Barret revved up the false smile again and gave his right cuff another vicious snick "—if it's details you want, I can give you one I neglected to pass on to any of the officers I encountered."

"Not going to be good," Romana predicted from Jacob's side.

"Is this detail connected to Belinda's death?"

"Your call, Knight. I'm sure you know that off-duty police officers frequently stop by Gilhoolie's for an after-shift drink. The pub's divided into two sections—public front, private back. On that particular New Year's Eve, about seventy of us were partying it up in a back room that was as tight for space as the sardine cans my father and I used to stuff. It was approaching midnight, and I needed air to counteract Gilhoolie's special blend of whiskey. I stepped into the front of the pub and immediately spotted a group of off-duty officers. I also spotted Belinda. She was wrapped around a guy with curly brown hair who had cop written all over him. Now the guy might have been wearing a wedding ring, but I'll tell you this for nothing. From my vantage point, he wasn't using it to fend her off."

Although Jacob maintained his neutral expression, he sensed where this was heading. Still, he shrugged. "Spit it out, Barret. I don't shock as easily as you might think."

"Cop's name was Michael O'Keefe," Barret obliged. "Married for ten years, I discovered later. One kid. Impeccable record on the force. Apparently, not quite so impeccable on his own time." His eyes glittered, steely-blue. "I saw your partner slip the publican a C-note, Knight, then watched him fumble his way toward the upstairs rooms in the company of one very drunk, very married Belinda Critch."

Chapter Five

"He's lying." Romana tried to sound adamant but knew she fell short. "Even if he was having problems at home, O'Keefe wouldn't have had sex with a married woman." She slanted Jacob a mistrustful look. "Unless you introduced him to Belinda Critch before that New Year's Eve party, so she wasn't a complete stranger to him."

"Which would make it okay for him to have had sex with her?"

"No." She breathed out. "No, it would just make them not strangers." Frustrated, she pressed on her temples. "I'm trying really hard to untangle this mess of knots we've tied, Knight."

And coming to a lively restaurant—his idea, not hers—in even livelier Mount Adams probably wasn't the best place to do that. The chili at Bitte might be the best in the city, and the owners, a pair of second-generation German brothers, might be famous for bursting into song, but Romana had had two bombshells dropped on her that night—one involving Jacob, the other his former partner—and neither one was sitting well.

As she struggled with her thoughts, she moved her gaze around the room.

Holiday oompah music underscored laughing patrons

at more than three dozen tables. Being German, the brother/owners had Christmas trees stuffed into every nook and cranny. The one precariously angled over their booth tended to grab Romana's hair every time she moved.

She swirled the lager she hadn't really wanted and, beginning with the less complicated prospect, backtracked through the newest knots.

"What was the state of O'Keefe's marriage nine years ago?"

Jacob gave a small laugh. "Come on, Romana, guys don't talk personal on the clock."

"In my experience, they don't talk personal off the clock, either. But even a guy can get a sense of another guy's life. Was he snappish, moody, tense, depressed? Or the opposite—upbeat, relaxed, eager to leave when his shift ended?"

"He was O'Keefe, steady and dependable. A solid cop. We talked baseball, football, politics and punks." Jacob took a long drink of beer. "If you're interested, Barret's friend, the mayor, is a dick."

She tugged on strands of her hair that were currently snagged in the tips of the Christmas pine. "Really? I'll have to mention that to my colleague at the university. The mayor's her stepfather."

"Steps can be dicks, too."

Although the word *step* triggered a third line of thought, Romana wanted to deal with O'Keefe and Belinda first. "Straight answer, Knight. Did O'Keefe know Belinda Critch before he allegedly went upstairs at Gilhoolie's and had sex with her?"

"Alleged sex."

"Don't nitpick. It wasn't an official question."

"Then the unofficial answer is, no, I don't think he knew her, but yes, he'd met her."

"Through you?"

"Through the department. We deal with people in forensics every day. It's part of our job. And Belinda was very people oriented."

Mostly male people, as Romana recalled, but she let it go and ran a contemplative finger around the rim of her glass. "It could have been a one-time thing between them. New Year's Eve festivities gone awry."

"Could be. Why aren't you looking at me?"

She'd been expecting this. Raising her head, she forced a steady stare. "Better?"

He leaned over his drink, and it took all of Romana's willpower not to grab his T-shirt and haul him closer. Or shove him away and escape.

Jacob watched her but didn't speak until the young restaurant owner, who'd launched into a boisterous rendition of Handel's "Hallelujah" chorus, finished to a round of applause. Jacob's green eyes moved over her face with a slow, almost dangerous kind of seduction. Her skin warmed, and her heart made a dizzy revolution in her chest.

"Who did you run into in the park?"

She could lie and call herself a coward, or go with the truth and brace for impact.

She took a deep breath—then sighed it out. "One of Belinda's phone conversations was overheard during that weird and eventful forty-eight-hour period prior to her death. Your name came up."

"Not in a good way, I assume."

"She told whoever was on the other end that you wanted her dead."

"Did this eavesdropper happen to know who Belinda was talking to?"

"I'd guess no." Now that it was out, Romana gave in to temptation, slid closer and ran a fingertip from his cheek to his jaw. "Deny it, Jacob. I'd rather believe you than someone who listens in on private conversations."

His eyes fixed on hers. "Why would I want Belinda dead when I didn't want her in the first place?"

"That's not a denial, Detective."

Catching her fingers, he brought them to his lips. "I didn't want her dead, okay? I didn't want anything from her."

She reminded herself to breathe. "Did you argue about the restraining order she requested?"

"We might have. I know she wanted me to obtain it no questions asked."

"Surely she knew that was impossible…" A cloud of doubt scudded in. "What do you mean, you might have? Don't you know why you argued?"

Turning her hand over, he ran his thumb lightly across her palm. The shiver that skated along her spine had as much to do with apprehension as desire. "What aren't you telling me, Jacob?"

He held her gaze, but his lashes fell to shield his expression. "I remember meeting her for lunch, and I know we talked about a restraining order. It's leaving the restaurant when things start to get…blurry."

Romana's latent cop sense kicked in. She curled her fingers around his. "Define *blurry*."

He stroked the skin on the back of her hand. "Hazy, as in unclear, like a slow spin through a black hole."

Concern had her capturing his chin. "You have blackouts?"

"Had them six years ago, for a three- maybe four-week period."

"Did you tell Stubbs or Canter?"

"Canter and I have several post-Academy issues, and the code book is Stubbs's bible."

"Doesn't mean he'd have crucified you. Why a month's worth of blackouts?"

The lines around his mouth deepened. "Long story short, six years ago, O'Keefe and I pursued three homicide suspects on foot to the waterfront. It was early December and icy. O'Keefe went down. I kept going. I lost sight of one suspect, but the other two were visible and, by the time I reached them, penned in by a high warehouse fence. The one closest dropped his weapon when I approached. The other didn't. I heard O'Keefe shout, but didn't turn fast enough. The third guy blindsided me. When I regained consciousness, two of the suspects were gone and the one I'd managed to graze was on the ground, howling that he was bleeding to death."

"Let me guess. When the paramedics arrived on scene, you sent the runner to the hospital but never considered going there yourself."

"Something like that."

She shook her head. "Men." Then on a note of exasperated amusement. "Cops." The humor faded. "Untreated concussions have been known to cause blackouts, Jacob. You must have realized you needed attention after your first one. Or was the restaurant the first time?"

"Fifth." A crease formed between his eyes. "I think."

Okay, this wasn't good. But it didn't necessarily damn him, either. It was simply another knot.

A limb caught her hair, causing several decorations to jingle. The approaching server apologized and helped her untangle. Transitioning smoothly, he recommended the house chili with wild rice and a bean and herb salad.

By the time he left with two full orders on his pad, Romana had her hair smoothed and her doubts firmly locked away.

"You should have said something—" she stabbed Jacob's chest to emphasize her point "—long before you reached number five. Did O'Keefe notice anything?"

"Yeah, he told me I looked like crap and suggested I get a vitamin shot." He nudged aside his empty glass. "O'Keefe was going through a messy divorce, Romana. He'd lost the custody battle. His father had been killed in a motorcycle accident a few months earlier."

"His father was a biker?" she interrupted. "I mean…" She frowned. "I thought when O'Keefe said his dad rode bikes he meant ten speed or mountain. Hell." She visualized O'Keefe's face on the dark wood tabletop. "I'm not much of a friend, am I?"

Jacob almost hid his smile. "You said yourself, you don't pry. O'Keefe doesn't really talk about his private life. He's even less forthcoming about his father's death."

Which wasn't quite the point. Any way Romana looked at it, she should have known.

She took an absent swipe at the air—and realized her thumb was covered with tree sap.

"Having a bad karma day." She rubbed at the sap with her napkin. "I need soap and water." As she slid from the booth, she patted his cheek. "Think explanation for five unreported blackouts, Knight, and I'll be right back."

There were only two people in the women's washroom, a mother and daughter who appeared to be having a *Freaky Friday* episode.

Romana tuned them out and set her mind on Jacob. He didn't remember leaving a restaurant with a woman who'd wound up dead two days later. He thought he remembered why they'd argued but wasn't sure.

Like the conversation Patrick had overheard, those facts couldn't have come out at the hearing. There'd have been headlines if they had. So did that make Jacob a liar, or did it mean that the overall picture was intact and only the details were fuzzy?

Her head buzzed with possibilities, far too many to sort through in a washroom where a teenage girl's voice was growing louder by the second.

"Let it go, Lacy," her crimson-faced mother finally ordered. "You're embarrassing both of us."

Romana could have told her that very little embarrassed a police officer, past or present, but she stopped herself and used the air machine to dry her hands. She was re-shouldering her purse when the door shot open and a man in full Santa costume rushed in.

He didn't hesitate, merely flicked a glance at the women in the corner then lunged at Romana, his nearest target. He had her arm wrenched painfully behind her back before she could dip a hand into her bag.

"Mom?" The girl sidled behind her mother.

"It's okay," Romana gasped as her arm was yanked higher. "He wants me, not you."

"Smart lady," the fake Santa growled in her ear. "Pretty, too. Bad-luck, good-luck scenario for me. You!" He jerked his whiskered chin at the frightened pair. "Lock yourselves in a stall, and stay there. You—" he returned his mouth to Romana's ear "—come with me."

She was trained, Romana reminded herself. One unguarded moment, and she could take him down.

"Where are we going?" she asked and was rewarded with

a crack in the region of her elbow. But he had hold of her other arm as well, she realized through the pain, so if he was carrying a weapon, he wouldn't be able to access it easily.

"Rear entrance," he snarled, then more softly, "Quiet, now, gorgeous. We're gonna leave here like mice, you and me. Open the door and take a peek outside."

Adrenaline pulsed through her. She reined it in and exhaled. "I need my hand."

He squeezed her hard. "Screw with me," he warned, "and I'll snap your elbow like a twig."

Then he shifted his grip.

The instant her wrist was free, Romana used her boot on his instep, spun out of the arm lock, brought her knee up between his legs and mashed his nose with the heel of her hand.

Blood spurted. Santa howled and stumbled headfirst into the door. When it crashed open, the impact sent him staggering backward into the sink.

"Let it bleed," Jacob advised from behind the barrel of his police special. He held out a hand in her direction. "Romana?"

"Sore arm." She gave it an experimental shake, then curious, bent to inspect the seething Santa. "Critch?"

When he didn't respond, Jacob lowered his gun to a point below the man's Santa buckle. "Lose the whiskers, pal, unless you'd rather lose a vital body part."

Bloody fingers gave the beard a yank.

Not Critch, Romana realized. Close—he had the rangy build and rugged features—but this man was younger, and not as tough as he'd wanted her to believe.

She tried a question while he gulped air through his mouth. "Do you know Warren Critch?"

He started to swear, but swallowed the worst of it when he saw Jacob's face. "No."

One-handed, Jacob hefted the man to his feet. "Romana?"

"Dialing." She used her cell phone and at the same time knocked on the closed stall door. "It's okay. You can come out."

The daughter was slumped like a rag doll against the metal wall. Only her mother emerged.

She touched Romana's arm. "Why did you think he was after you?"

"Very long story," Romana replied. "But take my advice. If your daughter ever decides to become a cop, tell her to make sure it's what she wants." She regarded the bleeding Santa, let her mind rewind to the telephone threat she'd received only yesterday and her eyes stray to Jacob. "Because no matter how hard you try, if you decide to leave the force, the break will never be totally clean."

WELL, WELL, NOW WASN'T THIS AN intriguing twist? Someone else, someone completely unrelated to his purpose, had done the terrorizing tonight. He hadn't needed to lift a finger. True, the guy hadn't rattled them too deeply; but there must have been a moment when they'd been unsure, when Romana in particular had feared for her life.

He warmed to the idea. Prolonged fear. They should never be sure where Warren Critch might pop up or what he'd do when he did. Yes, he liked that scenario very much.

He'd use uncertainty to his advantage, throw them off-balance then swoop in for the kill.

He smiled the smile of a smug, nasty Grinch. Who said revenge had to be dull?

"ANSWER'S NO, FITZ. I'm not going. End of conversation."

"Come on, Ro, I need you there for support. Anyway, functions like this are fun. When you were on the force, you told me police parties had the potential to get wild."

In the kitchen of her Clifton apartment, Romana removed a final tray of Christmas gingerbread from the oven and glanced at Fitz's half-empty glass of eggnog.

They'd been baking the parts for a gingerbread house all afternoon. Romana was comfortably barefoot in her favorite black sweats, a stretchy white tank and three pairs of jingling Christmas earrings. It might have been thirty degrees outside, but a gas fire burned warm and inviting in her living room, the air smelled of ginger and other spices, and Loreena McKennitt sang haunting Christmas melodies on her MP3 player.

She listened to her cousin's dramatic pleas and told herself not to laugh. No matter what her initial mood, Fitz always had the ability to amuse her. But go to a police/forensics party after she'd left the force? Not in this lifetime, not even for Anna Fitzgerald's sake.

"You're slurring your words, Fitz." She rearranged the trays in an attempt to figure out which pieces went where. "No more brandy until I can understand at least half of what you're saying." Still arranging, she shoved at her cousin's hand. "And don't eat the walls until they're up."

"Say no all you like, you're coming to the party." Despite her thick tongue, Fitz's expression grew sly. "Bet Jacob Knight'll be there."

Romana slid Fitz's glass out of reach. "Jacob does parties like I do boring faculty dinners—which is to say, he only goes when threatened by a higher power. Don't eat the roof, either."

"I'll cut you a deal, Ro. I'll stop nibbling if you'll tell me about the mean Santa who nabbed you in the bathroom. You rushed through it too fast the first time."

Although she didn't want to repeat the story again, the

alternative—to be badgered for the next hour by her tipsy cousin—was even less palatable.

"The guy was a thief, Fitz. He dressed up as Santa Claus, marched into a liquor store, waited for a lull, broke a bottle and used it on the cashier. Manager was in the back. He found a knife and charged. Santa took off. He didn't have time to lose the costume, so he left it on and ran into Bitte, where Jacob and I were having dinner. The women's washroom door was right there. He saw it as a refuge and ducked in."

"Where was Jacob?"

"Heading for the men's room. The liquor store manager spotted his badge and told him he'd followed a would-be thief into the restaurant. Jacob reasoned it out. Result? Mean Santa's going to be spending Christmas in jail with a few badly bruised body parts and a broken nose."

Fitz fingered her own nose. "Remind me never to sneak up on you from behind. So time passes, and you and Jacob have been doing what?"

With the gingerbread set out in semiformation, Romana began capping the spices. "We've been questioning people who knew Belinda Critch, and a few who knew her husband. One of Warren's amateur theater cronies manages a toy store. We're seeing him tonight."

"Yeah? Downtown store or shopping mall?"

"Mall."

Fitz made a face. "I like street shops better. Crowded malls suck."

Romana grinned. "Too many security guards lurking in the shop shadows, huh?"

"You're never going to let me live that down, are you?" Her cousin's elbows hit the granite counter with a thud. "Man, you swipe a few small things..."

"Like a Rolex and a handheld PC, two pairs of Jimmy Choo shoes…"

"I get it, Ro. Sticky fingers—bad. Straight and narrow—good. Don't forget I have serious childhood issues. My father's an alcoholic." Fitz's elbows slid away and her forehead landed on the counter. "James says he's on the bottle again."

Romana swung around. "Oh, Fitz, I'm sorry." She leaned over the island. "Is he sure?"

"Ninety percent. He told me about it in the park. I kind of passed it by Dad, but you know how he is. Deny to the death, or the unemployment line if he isn't careful." She eased her head up to peek out from under her bangs. "I don't suppose you could, you know…"

"Talk to him?"

"He likes you."

"Doesn't mean he'll listen." But at Fitz's stricken expression, Romana relented. "Yes, all right, I'll talk. Tell him I'll drop by for tea on Saturday."

"Sunday. Saturday's the police party, and setting aside the fact that I want you there, you should want you there. Think about it, Ro. A lot of cops worked on Belinda Critch's case. You can talk to them. Or Jacob can. And don't tell me he won't show, because you can con anyone into anything when you put your mind to it." A lopsided smile appeared. Using her fingernails, she inched her eggnog forward. "So, does the cutie pie detective have as great a body as I think he does under those jeans and that super cool leather jacket?"

Amusement tickled Romana's throat. "No idea, Fitz." Which was a lie since she had plenty of ideas, not to mention last night's deliciously graphic dream still shooting around in her head. To tell Fitz anything, however, was to risk announcing it to the world. "We kissed, okay? Nothing more erotic than that."

"Was it great?"

Eyes sparkling, Romana drew the eggnog back out of range. "Get invited to the police officer's New Year's Eve party, and you might find out."

"Yeah, right, like Knight's going to do New Year's Eve."

Sliding her gaze to the wide condo window, Romana watched tiny snowflakes drift down from a dove-gray sky. "Trust me, Fitz, if Jacob and I make it through Christmas to New Year's Eve alive, we'll be in the mood to celebrate." She jingled the bell on one of her earrings. "At least his neighbor's better. Sort of. She's awake and aware."

"That sounds good. Why don't you sound happy?"

"Oh, I'm happy, just—I don't know—puzzled, maybe. She says Critch was wearing a ski mask when he grabbed her."

Fitz searched for the point. "And that puzzles you because…?"

"Why would he bother?"

"Uh, so she couldn't identify him?"

"Yes, but we know it was him, so I repeat, why bother?"

"Maybe he's shy."

"Mmm." Romana considered it from Critch's point of view. "I suppose he could have been thinking that as long as he was disguised, even if we believed he was Critch, there'd be no actual proof."

"Isn't that what I said?"

"I mean if Denny had died, Jacob could have said he thought it was Critch who hit her, but he couldn't be absolutely certain. And any potential witnesses, say another neighbor, wouldn't have been able to provide a description, either. Becomes conjecture in the eyes of the court—ergo, no murder charge."

"Until he gets around to you and Jacob."

"That's different, or it will be in Critch's eyes. He'll have an escape plan in place, an immediate one. In Denny's case, he knew he'd have to hang around, and he couldn't risk an increased police presence."

Fitz propped her chin in one hand. "Being a cop sounds complicated, Ro. So many procedures and loopholes and bad dudes flipping them the bird, then walking. No wonder some go bad." Her finger crept across the counter. "Are you sticking to your belief that Jacob didn't kill Belinda?"

The doubts that rose up scuttled into the corners when Romana pictured Jacob holding his gun on the Santa who'd grabbed her at Bitte. "There's no reason not to stick."

"So if you're right, that means someone else, probably someone who knew Belinda in the back bedroom kind of way, did the killing."

Romana slanted her a mildly suspicious look. "Why the tone, cousin?"

Eyes rolling, Fitz hopped from the barstool. "You're a cop to the bone, Ro. No tone, no problem. Come on. Let's haul out the big stepladder and hang twinkling lights around your gi-normous city-view window."

Romana bit her lip, glanced at the phone. She should call Jacob. Or—well, maybe not. No, she really should.

Frustration escaped on a sigh. Yes, no, maybe—what she really wanted to do was scream. Then call him.

Her fingers tapped the countertop. Of course, he could have called her. How did he know she knew about his neighbor? She also had no idea when he wanted to leave for the mall. Or why her blatantly sexual dreams about him were beginning to disrupt her thought processes.

Actually, that was one question she probably could answer, if she allowed her thoughts to veer in that direction. The problem was, she wasn't sure she'd like the answer, or the other, more disturbing questions that would accompany it.

"Damn you, Knight. What secrets are you hiding in that gorgeous head of yours?"

While Fitz hunted noisily for the ladder, Romana set her elbows on the counter, plunked her chin in her hands and debated. She was glaring at the handset when her cousin gasped.

"What?" Reacting automatically, she grabbed a spatula and darted into the living room.

She'd been expecting a spider since Fitz was terrified of anything with more than four legs. Instead, she found her cousin staring at the computer screen.

"You had an envelope. I opened it."

Romana stared with her—and felt an icy finger of fear glide along her backbone.

A color image glowed on the monitor. The subject of the picture was positioned exactly as Belinda Critch had been in death. Unlike Belinda, however, she was lying naked in the alley where Critch had tried to shoot Jacob. Mistletoe leaves were scattered around her. Some of them floated in the blood that had seeped from the wound in her chest. Half-lidded gray-blue eyes stared at them, cloudy and dull, like the eyes of a very old doll.

Her eyes, Romana realized through a layer of shock. Winter-lake blue, and just as dead as Belinda's had been.

Directly beneath the photo, a single word wafted across the screen.

Soon…

Chapter Six

Jacob needed to punch something. Not because he was angry but out of sheer frustration. In three nights he'd had three dreams about Romana, and she'd been naked in all of them.

There'd been other dreams as well, long-accepted nightmares that left him tense and wanting a drink, but never ones that absorbed him so completely that nothing he thought or did could shake their hold on him.

At 7:00 p.m., pumped on caffeine and with a gym bag over his shoulder, he walked through the door of the Riverside Gym. So many officers frequented the place that over the years it had become their off-duty training center.

Thankfully, Christmas wasn't the busiest time of year. Jacob spied a handful of his cohorts, sweating, grunting and adjusting weight machines, but he wasn't going for weights tonight. He wanted his workout fast, painful and exhausting as hell. It was the only hope he had of dousing his desire for Romana. He aimed a narrowed look at the ceiling. God help him, this wasn't a thing he needed right now.

Circling the floor mats, he headed toward the change room. A man who'd been beating up on a large bag stopped when he spied him. The leather took a last vicious punch as he called out to Jacob.

"You looking for a self-defense partner, Knight?"

The room's echo gave his tone an extra whip of anger. Jacob's lips curved, but he didn't alter his stride.

"I've got ten years on you, Hoag."

Dylan rounded the bag, began untying his gloves. "The year count between us is only six, as I recall."

"Street years count differently." But Jacob halted, unzipped his jacket. Considered. "You want to fight out your mad?"

"My mad, my hostility, my contempt for a judicial system that favors cops above all others."

Anticipation kindled in Jacob's belly. "We're on our own time," he reminded. "I won't hold back."

"Wouldn't want you to." Despite the acid in his voice, Dylan's face remained a blank canvas. "I might have washed out at the Academy, but I haven't been sitting around mourning the loss. In fact," he dropped his boxing gloves on the floor, "I don't see it as a loss at all these days."

Yes, he did, Jacob thought, because as a cop he'd have had easy access to his sister's file. He'd also have had the means to investigate any and all claims made at the hearing.

With a shrug he replied, "Up to you, Hoag. Street rules."

Dylan's fists balled. "What does that entail?"

The light of anticipation flared as Jacob paused in the doorway to look back. "Means no rules at all."

"HE'S NOT HERE, ROMANA." O'Keefe pressed weary fingers to his eyelids. "If he's not answering his cell phone, I don't know what to tell you."

"He's not answering any phone." She perched on the edge of O'Keefe's desk and tried not to notice the bags developing under his eyes. "But there is something you can tell me."

"Shoot."

"How did you spend your New Year's Eve nine years ago?"

O'Keefe raked the hair from his temples. "Nine years. I don't… Ah, wait, maybe I do. Gilhoolie's Pub?"

"That's the one." Romana wasn't sure why she felt guilty when he was the one who'd been spotted going upstairs with Belinda Critch, but it probably had to do with a friend's loyalty and the sense that she'd let herself believe a stranger's story just a little too readily.

With no way back, however, she waded in deeper. "James Barret saw you with Belinda Critch, Mick. Handing money to the proprietor, going upstairs."

O'Keefe's hands fell and with them, Romana's hopes. She'd wanted him to deny it, to be disappointed at her lack of faith. She absolutely did not want him to look at her with those big dog eyes of his and offer a sheepish grin.

"Weak as water, Romana, that's me. Or was nine years ago." His chair creaked as he leaned back. "My wife and I were— well, let's be civilized and say we were having problems. I was drunk, and Belinda was there, coming on to me."

She'd come on to James Barret, as well, yet Barret had managed to stay downstairs. "Belinda and Critch had only been married for eighteen months, Mick. He was still buying her presents, sending flowers to the lab."

"Nothing happened."

"I—" Romana blinked in surprise. "Nothing? As in no sex?"

"I couldn't—you know, get it up. God, it was embarrassing. Still is." He kneaded his eyebrows. "Anyway, she got annoyed and started flouncing around the room. She said she'd wasted her New Year's Eve. There were other parties she could have gone to and far better men she could have seduced. Then she marched downstairs and disappeared into the back room."

"Where the private party continued."

"At full volume."

"Was Barret still there?"

"His car was in the lot when I left—which was about twenty minutes after Belinda blew me off. It took me that long to screw up enough courage to go back down and face what I thought would be a round of jeers from my buddies. But I guess Belinda didn't say anything, and they didn't see her come down, because all I got were winks and thumbs-ups."

Romana visualized the scene, told herself there was nothing funny about it. Still… "Honest to God, Mick, you men and your trophies." She slid from the desk. "Okay, relax. Interrogation's over. What time does Jacob's shift start?"

"Nine." He waited a beat, then said, "You've got that thing happening for him again, don't you? No lies, Romana. We've been friends too long for that."

"No lies." She brought her head around. "No comment, either. Direct me, Mick. He's not here, he's not at the hospital, he's not on duty, and he's not answering. I need a location."

"Try the gym," he suggested. "When Knight has a problem crawling around in his gut, he likes to sweat it out."

She wouldn't ask, Romana promised herself. Didn't want to know. She made it as far as the office door before glancing back.

O'Keefe's smile was resigned, but all he said was, "I wish to hell I had an answer for you. I know there's something that didn't come out at the hearing, something that's been eating away at him ever since." His eyes held hers. "Whatever it is, and with Critch on the loose, hell bent on having his revenge, my gut feeling is that you're going to wind up in the middle of it—with no way back, and, more than likely, no way out."

ONE OF DYLAN'S FISTS nicked his jaw. Jacob licked blood from the corner of his mouth and felt the fire inside swell.

Dylan danced back and forth on his toes, expending energy, breathing in controlled bursts. Jacob preferred a mental dance and slow, assessing circles that, for the most part, took him out of range whenever his opponent bounced in.

"Kick it back up, Knight," an impatient Dylan growled. "We're not cats in an alley."

They weren't kangaroos in the outback, either. "I'll kick it up," Jacob replied. And offered a dangerous smile. "When it feels right."

Dylan blew out more loud breaths. His lungs appeared to be tiring, which actually surprised Jacob a little. From the look of his muscles, Hoag should have been in better shape.

He let Dylan come to him, offset the left hook and faked a right. Dylan was so busy protecting his face that he missed the body blow completely. It caught him in the solar plexus and elicited a rush of air that left him doubled over and gasping.

But only for a moment. Then the dancing stopped, and he charged.

It was exactly what Jacob wanted.

Dylan's fingers missed his throat by inches. When Jacob snaked an arm around his neck, he felt an elbow plunge into his stomach. It hurt, but not enough to throw him off. Snugging his grip, he gave Dylan's ribs a hard jab. In response, Dylan butted him on the side of the neck.

Jacob felt sweat slither down his spine. The desire for more was a hunger inside him. The pain felt good, and every punch, every kick, every lash knocked another cobweb loose.

His mind felt clearer than it had in days. Didn't diminish his desire for Romana, but the clutter around it was disappearing. He could meet his feelings for her head-on and, hopefully, put them in their place. Wherever the hell that was.

Reading Dylan's body language, he anticipated the next blow and dipped his left shoulder just enough that Hoag's knuckles bounced off bone. With adrenaline zinging through his veins, Jacob spun, kicked Dylan's legs out from under him and planted him face-down on the mat.

Dylan's curses emerged in a rough growl. He jerked under Jacob's body weight but couldn't free himself.

Jacob leaned over. "Had enough?"

Dylan snapped up his head and swore. "You're bigger than me, Knight. You have a longer reach."

"You weigh more than I do." Jacob held him down for another moment before relaxing his hold. "No rules, Hoag."

"Yeah, you said that before."

As he spoke, Dylan worked himself onto his back. His lips peeled away from his teeth. Without warning, he doubled his fists and raised them like a hammer.

But Jacob wasn't foolish enough to have trusted a spiteful adversary. Despite Dylan's weight advantage, he blocked the worst of the blow.

The spark reignited. He'd have let it erupt if he hadn't caught a movement in the doorway.

Glancing up, he saw Romana leaning on the wide jamb. She had one hand hooked over the opposite elbow as she observed the fight.

The mistake was his. If he hadn't looked, he'd have seen Dylan draw back his foot. What he saw instead was the expression of shock that bolted across Romana's face.

Only a kick aimed straight at his crotch could elicit an expression like that. A split second before Dylan's foot contacted, Jacob rolled sideways. He plunged his heel into Hoag's side, directly into his kidneys.

While Dylan crumpled and wheezed, Jacob did a slower roll into a crouch. With one hand dangling between his knees, and the fingers of his other checking out the cut on his mouth, he regarded Romana from the ground.

"How'd you track me down?"

"I talked to O'Keefe." Wincing in sympathy, she pushed off to approach them. "Is he all right?"

"Will be." Jacob located his towel and stood. "We said nine for the mall, didn't we?"

She sent Dylan a last commiserating look, then refocused. "We didn't specify." Accusation gleamed in her eyes. "And you didn't call."

"Was I supposed to?"

"No, but I'm feeling irritable, and here you are, fresh from a head-clearing workout that I wish I'd thought of for myself."

A faint grin appeared. He held his hands out to the side. "You wanna go, Officer Grey? Tank's not empty yet."

At his offer, her approach, in fact her entire demeanor, altered. Instead of simply walking, she began to sashay, in a way that could only be called bombshell seductive. "Are you challenging me, Detective Knight? Because I'm always up for that."

Still nursing his injured side, Dylan gained his feet. "Watch for silent bullets, Romana. It's the only way Knight knows how to deal with a woman."

She kept moving, her eyes locked on Jacob's. "Oh, I think he knows one or two other ways. Your left cheek's bleeding, Dylan."

He touched the bone, swore and limped away.

"I think you riled him, Knight."

He heard a soft snap in his head, wondered where all the light had gone. "I might have."

"He's wrong, you know."

"So you said." Off-kilter and edgy because of it, Jacob watched her closely. Dylan Hoag he could handle. Romana in this mood was a more difficult proposition. To say nothing of more dangerous.

She halted less than a foot in front of him, made two fists and jammed them against his stomach muscles. "You look good without a shirt."

"Clothes are restrictive." His eyebrows went up. "You gonna take your shot now, or wait until you've destroyed my guard completely?"

"No rules, Knight." Her eyes danced. "Besides, I prefer to bide my time in hand-to-hand combat."

He wondered if a person could drown in eyes like hers. It seemed possible since simply breathing had become a major undertaking. If he'd been hot before, it was nothing compared to the way he felt now.

And wasn't that just what he needed after everything he'd done to close down his feelings for her tonight?

She pressed her fists in deeper. "So what's the deal? Are we going to do it or not?"

He had to realign his thoughts. "You want to fight?"

"It's an option." The dance became a tease. "But I like my idea better."

With a quickness Dylan Hoag could only dream of, she snatched up two handfuls of Jacob's damp hair and yanked his mouth onto hers.

HE TASTED OF HEAT AND SEX, like fire in a snowstorm. Two seconds in, and Romana's blood went from a sizzle to a roar. She'd plunged into the kiss unthinking. She wanted him to respond the same way.

To her surprise, he did, and with a swiftness that both excited and intrigued her. His mouth devoured hers. His lips explored and his tongue probed in such a wonderfully thorough way that she wished it could go on forever. She wished more that the soft warnings deep inside her mind would disappear.

Shoving them back, she released Jacob's hair, let her hands streak across the smooth lines of his shoulders. The workout with Dylan had heated his skin and now, she thought with a hazy smile, it was heating hers. Couldn't get much better than that, even in a dream.

Jacob's grip on her waist shifted lower. He snugged her hips against his. She felt his arousal, and with a satisfied purr, bumped herself against him. Drawing his full lower lip into her mouth, she regarded him through her lashes.

"You should punch out your rivals more often, Detective. I like the aftereffects."

"You're only feeling the ones that don't involve bruises." His lips trailed upward over her cheekbone, but while his breath on her temple brought a shiver, she really wanted that mouth back on hers.

He did truly amazing things with his tongue. However, pretty much anything he did right now would only fuel her desire to tear off his sweats and have sex with him on the gym floor.

Her roving hands snagged his waistband. For a second, she considered tugging on the drawstring. But even as his mouth returned to feed on hers, she knew she wouldn't do it. Wasn't quite that uninhibited. She feathered her fingers over his back instead, then upward again until they were tangled once again in his hair.

Now if only the nagging voice in her head would go away. But it kept sneaking out, reminding her that no matter how much she wanted him, the ice she stood on was far too thin to be trusted. What would she do if it cracked, if everything she believed, needed to believe, turned out to be a lie?

The question haunted, almost as much as he did. Jacob Knight rocked her senses in a way that no one else ever had. He threw her off-balance, tripped her up when he kissed her, then, piece by piece, stripped away every last scrap of her common sense.

Ah, but if she was honest, wasn't that what she wanted him to do? After all, she'd been the one to initiate the kiss.

Romana supposed it was fortunate that a sergeant from Internal Affairs, a woman who knew them both and who'd been on the force for more than thirty years, should breeze into the room with a sarcastic, "Oh, knock it off you two. If I can't smoke in here, neither can you. Heads-up, Grey. You might want to think twice before letting this one get you on your back. Beautiful he might be, but I can tell you firsthand, pretty much every female under sixty at HQ is lined up and itching to take their best shot at him. And not with bullets."

Romana didn't look at the woman, nor did she step away. She did, however, let her eyes sparkle up into Jacob's.

"Does that lineup include you, Sergeant Davenport?"

"Would if my hubby wasn't still the love of my life."

She kept walking. Like Romana, she didn't glance over or pause as she passed. "I was just at HQ if you're interested. Word's out that Critch has jumped parole, and he's on a vengeful tear. No surprise, Knight, your captain decided to have a chat with Critch's prison shrink this afternoon. I won't go into detail, but suffice to say the shrink figures his patient's either cured and functional, or he's completely off the map and incurably, nonfunctionally, carry-his-grudge-to-the-death insane."

Chapter Seven

"You know," Romana mused, "just once it would be nice to talk to someone who had something positive to say about this situation."

Jacob surveyed the bustling main aisles of the north-side shopping mall. "Like what?"

She thought for a moment. "Well, the Cincinnati police force does have an excellent reputation for apprehending lunatics before they strike."

"Do we?" Still scanning, Jacob grinned. "That's news to me."

"It would be, seeing as you cops in Homicide always look at life from the dark side. I teach criminology, Jacob. I see the stats. When it comes to apprehending crazies, this city's police officers are among the finest in the country."

"Either that or the majority of the nutcases gravitate to warmer climates."

"So what—you're saying most of the nut balls live in Florida, or California, or Texas, or Louisiana, or…" She knocked his arm with her own. "You know I could go on for quite a while here, don't you?"

"Yeah, I've discovered that about you. I'd rather you went on about that e-picture again."

She shuddered off the sensation of floating, ghostlike, on the ceiling and staring down at herself in death. "Surrounded by mistletoe leaves," she murmured. And halted the thought there. "I wonder why he used them?"

"Who? Critch or the killer?"

"Either. Both. Okay, Critch was re-creating his wife's death with the picture he sent today, but what do you suppose was going on inside the murderer's head when he placed mistletoe around Belinda's body?"

"Maybe we should ask Critch's shrink."

"If that shrink's name is Raymond Haines, don't bother. The man's at least two hundred years old. God, Jacob, he was ancient when Doctor Gorman retired, and Gorman was in his late seventies by the time he left Forensics—which he only did because the hospital board put an enormous amount of pressure on him."

"Should I know what you're talking about?"

Exasperation swept in. "You're in Homicide, Knight. You must have met Gorman at some point."

"Tall, shriveled guy who looks like a cross between an undertaker and a cadaver? Yeah, I met him. Belinda said he made several passes at her."

Romana twitched a shoulder. "I have absolutely nothing to say to that." But she did and he knew it, damn him, because he merely waited her out. As they stepped onto the escalator, she kicked the metal step with her toe. "Was there a man in this city that Belinda Critch didn't sleep with?"

"I never said she slept with Gorman."

"Come on to, then."

"I didn't say that, either."

"I know Doctor Gorman, Jacob. For the last five years of his tenure, staying awake and reasonably aware occupied the

expert." Jacob set a hand on her back to keep her moving
"You're a woman of many talents, Romana."

"My brother…"

"Runs a chain of office supply stores, I know. I've hear
stories," he said at her questioning look.

She wanted to respond to his mocking tone, but she glimpse
holiday Barbie and couldn't resist making a beeline for it.

"This is a retro doll, Jacob, you know, from the earl
xties. Teresa would love her."

He set his cheek on the side of her hair. "How many sever
ar-olds do you figure are into retro toys?"

"Lots, but okay, maybe I'd love her more." She searche
the price, but he started pushing. "Jacob, I only want to.
my God!" Her eyes lit up. "Is that Fozzie Bear?"

he felt the change instantly, and the zap of tension th
mpanied it. He whipped his head around. It took her
ent to realize he wasn't staring at the Muppet bear she
ioned, but at the frog beside it.

ou like Kermit?" She watched his face in profile. Som
here, she realized. And the memory attached to
ht such a dark expression to his face that a shiv
ly rippled along her spine.

cob?" She touched his arm. "Uh, Critch's actor frie
ding by the plastic tricycles."

ah, okay."

ave the frog one last look, then motioned her forwar
ough part of her longed to ask the obvious questio
swallowed it and, taking his hand, led him to the e
isle. "Looks like the guy could use a few of She
tranqs." She forced a pleasant smile. "Hello, M
I'm Romana Grey. This is Detective Knight. V
you yesterday."

bulk of his time, to say nothing of his thoughts. The only way
he'd have noticed Belinda Critch or any other woman is if
she'd plunked herself down in his lap naked and made a
blatant attempt to seduce him."

"Maybe she did."

"But you just said…"

"I said she said he made several passes at her. Doesn't
mean she didn't invite them."

"Uh-huh." Romana took a quick look around the upper
level. "I think you're contradicting yourself. That says to me
you're preoccupied, which in turn suggests you think Critch
is tailing us."

"There's a good chance he is, and the idea doesn't sit well
with me in a crowded shopping mall."

"At least it isn't peak time." But she cast her eyes along the
rows of glittering storefronts and wondered how far a carry-
his-grudge-to-the-death insane person might go to achieve his
goal. "Maybe we should meet this toy store actor away from
his work."

"In a theater, for instance?"

"Is he doing a Christmas play?"

"He's in an amateur version of *Charlie and the Chocolate
Factory*. He's the techno-geek kid's father."

Romana slowed her footsteps as they neared The Toy Box.
The crowd around them seemed much larger all of a sudden.
"Local theaters are smaller than malls," she reflected. "But his
home would really be the logical…" She stopped speaking as
her eyes landed on a woman across the mall.

"What?" Jacob followed her line.

"Over there. Tall woman in the cream coat. That's Shera
Barret." Amusement stirred. "She looks harassed."

He studied the rail-thin woman with her sleek blond

hair, Prada boots and shiny shopping bag. "She looks like she's on speed."

"It's her natural state when she's not on tranqs." Romana grinned. "I've heard stories," she added at Jacob's sideways glance. "That little Gucci bag she's carrying is probably worth 10k or more. I hope she didn't park underground." At his even more dubious stare, she laughed. "I'm being serious, not catty. Think street patrol, Detective. Thieves love underground lots. Ah, here we are, The Toy Box. Kiddy heaven. I wonder if Mr. Geek has the latest PS in stock. My nephew's so into that right now."

"If you have money to buy Christmas presents like that, Romana, you're grossly overpaid." Although he spoke to her, his attention lingered on Shera Barret.

Curious, Romana cocked her head. "What's on your mind?"

"Ben Brown died of respiratory failure."

"According to Fitz, he also suffered from asthma."

"He was at home in front of his television, drinking a glass of brandy when he died. No exertion. Not pets or outside pollution to trigger an attack, and his house was conspicuously dust free."

Romana moved aside so a pair of adolescent girls in Santa hats could enter the shop. "You think Barret's partner was murdered?"

"I think it's strange that he'd have a fatal attack of asthma under those circumstances."

Hooking his arm, she drew him with her to the display window, where a group of animated elves played board games, listened to music and baked elf cookies in a miniature oven. "What did the medical examiner think?"

"The autopsy report claimed there were no foreign substances in his system."

"So either the report was true and his death was natural, or someone involved in the autopsy process faked his or her results." She dredged up a sweet smile. "Just how honest was Belinda Critch?"

"How honest was your ex?"

She removed her black gloves. "Fair enough. Bottom lin_ Belinda went after Barret nine years ago. Maybe she didr_ a_ score the first time around, but who knows what might ha_ happened at a later date? The question is, did Barret want_ s_ partner gone, and if so why?" She arched a speculative eyeb_ "Think you could get a look at Barret Brown's books?"   ye_

"He'd have cooked those long ago."

"Then why are we having this conversation?" She str_ for_ ened both herself and the front of his jacket. "Let it go f_ Oh_ okay? We came here to talk to Critch's theater frien_ s_ things first. Or at least one thing at time."   acc_

Not that she expected Jacob to set his thoughts a_ mor_ she needed time to assimilate all the things that see_ men_ happening so quickly around her. She was ratt_ "_ picture Critch had sent her, and still reeling from J_ thing_ back at the gym. A chat was about all she had_ broug_ tonight. Then she'd either jump Jacob and have v_ actua_ him, or topple into bed and shut the world out u_ "Ja_ is stan_

She had to squeeze past a group of ten-year_ were salivating over a rack of skateboards. No_ "Ye_ dozen senior-aged women chattered in th_ He g_ section. The jackets they wore identified them_ Alth_ Grannies. Scores of other customers, mostl_ Roman_ parents, wandered aimlessly up and down t_ of the a_ Barret's_

"These shelves are piled too high." R_ Mitchell_ head way back. "And the boxes are too cl_ spoke to_

"Police officer, university professor_

The man, balding and obviously uneasy, stabbed at his glasses with a ragged fingernail. "I'm a little busy right now."

"Five minutes," Jacob said.

Mitchell regarded his badge, nodded and drew them past the plastic toys through a swinging stockroom door.

It was a tight squeeze between the mountains of cardboard boxes, the dollies and a long red lunch table straight out of the 1950s.

"I don't know what I can tell you." His reindeer name tag read Manager Mitch. He smelled of peppermint, perspiration and unclean clothes. His Adam's apple bobbed vigorously as his gaze swung between them. "Warren and I weren't doing a play when his wife, er, died."

"What did you think of the man overall?" Jacob asked.

"He was nice enough, you know, a regular sort of guy."

Romana unbuttoned her long black coat in the stuffy room. "Was he a good actor?"

The man laughed, revealing crooked teeth. "Good Lord, no. His movements were rusty, and he was as wooden as Pinocchio with his delivery. He did the plays for Bel—for his wife. She was very good," he added. His neck flushed red. "At acting."

Jacob studied him, half-lidded. "Did Critch seem agitated before his wife was killed?"

"Not especially, no. He was a tad possessive of her, but if you'd asked me back then, I'd have said he seemed more relaxed than he'd been since before they were married."

"When was the last time you saw him?"

"Two weeks before Belinda died. Oh, no, wait, I passed him in the liquor store once after that."

Romana picked up a napkin and waved it in front of her face. If there was air in the room it wasn't moving, and judging from the smell of smoke wafting past, someone on staff liked cigarettes.

"He wasn't quite so relaxed that night," Mitchell elaborated after a prod from Jacob. "He said something about his wife being in trouble. Or was it threats? Yes, he said she was being threatened by someone. I think he was mostly upset because she wouldn't tell him who was doing the threatening."

Jacob rested a hip on the red table. "Did he say anything specific?"

"Not that I can…" The man sniffed the air. "Do you smell something?"

Besides dirty clothes and stale cigarettes? Romana shook her head. If she'd had a weaker stomach, she would have gagged. She set her makeshift fan aside instead. "You should tell your employees to take their cigarette breaks outside, Mr. Mitchell."

He blinked at her. "Only two people on my staff smoke, and they're not working tonight."

"Then you should empty your trash cans more often."

Jacob set a hand on her nape, glanced at the stockroom door. "That's not cigarette smoke, Romana."

She spied it as he did, filmy, gray tendrils clouding the window of the door.

A moment later, that door slammed open and three salespeople ran in. "The toddler's toy section," one of them revealed as an alarm began to shriek. "And the games counter." The panicked associate pointed in no less than six directions at once. "Coming up and over the shelves. The store's burning, Mr. Mitchell. The fire's between us and the front door."

FITZ SAT IN THE ATTIC SUITE she rented in her father's house and stared at the roofs of the neighborhood where she had lived since the two of them had moved here from Belfast twenty-plus years ago. She wanted more out of life than to live in a shabby-chic suburb in a Midwestern city that too many people still tended to associate with a 1970s sitcom. Or if she had to stay, she wanted to do it in style.

She wished she'd been born beautiful like Romana. Unfortunately, the most flattering description she'd ever received was the time James Barret had called her "a sprightly lass." Still, she'd learned how to turn a man's head. She paid attention to what each one liked and used that knowledge to stroke their egos.

Belinda Critch had taught her that single valuable lesson years ago, in the days when Romana had been a cop and she, Fitz, had been a mere gofer in Forensics.

The hospital underworld had revolved around Belinda back then. All the men had wanted her, except old Doctor Gorman, who'd been so feeble that snickering techs had occasionally stuck mirrors under his nose during his several-times-daily catnaps.

Men had adored Belinda; women had hated her. So why did everyone think a man had killed her…?

Giving her head a shake, Fitz sat cross-legged on the window seat and dumped the contents of her treasure box on the cushion. This was her secret stash, mementoes mostly, nothing of value, just trinkets that had stuck to her fingers when she'd been feeling low. She separated out a pair of Patrick's sunglasses, one of Belinda's watches, a pair of James's cufflinks—actually, those would be worth something—a woman's antique pin, another of Belinda's watches and a ten-karat gold ring that Dylan, the so-called security whiz, hadn't missed even though she'd slipped it off his finger in the middle of a Fourth of July picnic.

He'd been glowering at someone, she recalled. James? Patrick? His brother-in-law? His sister?

Fitz couldn't remember. Not about that day. But she remembered other events, like the Christmas party where Belinda should have been dancing with her then-fiancé Warren Critch, but had instead been wrapped around twenty other men.

Had she ever unwrapped herself from any of them? Fitz picked through her treasures and tried to line it all up in her head. The men, the marriage, the men.

Maybe it didn't matter.

Then again, maybe it did.

She turned to stare at the soft blue lights her father had woven through the limbs of a chestnut tree. Romana was important to her, like an older sister in many ways, except she was two years younger. *Ah, but hey, serious childhood issues,* Fitz reminded herself.

She forced her mind back to Belinda and the upshot of the woman's death. Critch claimed someone had threatened his wife's life. Now he was threatening Romana's. Because she'd saved a cop.

But what if Romana was right, and the cop was innocent? What if someone else had killed Belinda?

Fitz rubbed her forehead, had to think. What had Belinda said to her in those last days they'd worked together? If she hadn't been so busy trying to liberate Belinda's silver bracelet watch from her wrist, she might have paid more attention.

Picking up the coveted silver watch, Fitz ran her thumb over the tarnished inner band. Letters and numbers emerged through the black, enough of them to pique her interest.

Ten minutes later, her hands trembled, her cheeks had lost much of their color…and her fear for Romana's life had shot off the scale.

man, even one as stoical as Ben, you're bound to feel something when he moves on." She flicked at the broken fingernails on her right hand. "Such an annoying night. I had more shopping to do. The early whisper is that the fire might have been a prank. For the alleged prankster's sake, I hope that's not the case. I have excellent lawyers and a great deal of animosity for people who inconvenience me."

An influential daddy didn't hurt either, as Romana well knew. With Jacob starting toward them and her lips going numb, she got to the point. "Do you like mistletoe, Shera?"

Something glinted in the woman's brown eyes, but vanished a moment later.

"I hang it in the house during the holidays. A kiss at odd moments never hurts, don't you agree?"

"That would depend on who you're kissing."

"I have to think Detective Knight would be quite proficient that area. If I weren't married…" She set a hand on her roat and gave it a considering pat. "Never mind, James is re than enough for me, and he's wonderfully faithful."

Like a cocker spaniel. Romana smiled. "You're a fortunate an, Shera. More fortunate, I think, than Warren Critch."

es." Shera's expression faltered, but she brushed the aside. "I've always had luck on my side. Have a nice g, Romana. Tell the detective who's closing in that I e's hot enough to burn."

ptic remark from an unfulfilled and likely unhappy Romana watched her click away on those impossible eels, amazed that she didn't so much as wobble on vement.

ced up. A ring of clouds circled the moon. Romana untless nights like this when, as a child, she'd de with Rudolph across the face of that moon

Chapter Eight

Romana couldn't recall ever spending a more chaotic three hours in a mall, and that included the time one of her brothers had released seven gerbils in a busy department store. It had been Christmas then, too, and there'd been shrieks and squeals and a great deal of running by sales associates and customers alike.

But those had been small, terrified animals. This was a fire, or rather several fires, lit in trash cans throughout the complex. It was also, she discovered sometime during the first hectic hour, no less than seven smoke bombs, set off with crude timers near the outflow air vents.

Shoppers didn't squeal so much as scream and stampede. In rushing for the exits, the more hysterical ones knocked down and injured a number of those who were somewhat more bewildered.

Mall security did its collective best. So did Jacob, Romana and three off-duty officers who'd been endeavoring to chip away at their Christmas lists.

Two of the doctors they found refused to help due to possible malpractice suits. Two others sighed and rolled up their sleeves.

Firefighters arrived and evacuated the mall, but of course

that took time with a number of the exits shrouded in smoke and only a brave few willing to dart past the blazing cans to access them.

It took until midnight for the smoke, flames and screams to subside. The wounded, thankfully none seriously, had been transported to the hospital, disgruntled storeowners congregated in the parking lot, and Jacob was talking to the fire chief near one of the main entrances.

As the last of the ambulances pulled away, Romana spotted Shera Barret clicking across the parking lot with no regard for the ice under her designer boots.

"You." She stabbed a gloved finger. "I know you, don't I?"

"My father knows your father." Romana took shelter from the wind behind one of the fire trucks. "TriBel Productions makes global travel documentaries. My father produces them. Yours is part of the media conglomerate that airs them." She held out her hand. "I'm Romana Grey."

Three tiny shopping bags hung from Shera Barret's thin wrists. She had two broken fingernails, her hair was rumpled, and a streak of black marred her cream cashmere coat.

She worked the hair from her face. "I feel like I've been hit by a very long train. What happened in there?" She waved Romana off. "Not a question really." Her eyes sharpened. "It isn't through your father that I remember you. You're that police officer who stopped Warren Critch from shooting a man. Detective Knight. Handsome, sexy and stupid to have been involved with a woman like Belinda."

Romana's interest kindled. "You knew Belinda?"

"Of her. We spoke twice. Once, I picked up the telephone and she asked for James. The second time, she was sitting in a car across the street from our house. As you might expect, I had a few choice things to say."

Romana envisioned the fireworks, but remained silent and let Shera vent.

"She told me she had business with James." Shera scoffed and slashed a finger across her chest. "Of course I bought that whopper with her wearing a dress cut down to here. Stupid woman. Did she think I'd just fallen off the turnip truck?"

Her insecurities were showing, Romana reflected. Off tranqs and on a verbal tear, who knew how informative she might become?

"Did you talk to your husband about the incident?"

"Apparently it's a rather crowded turnip truck." Unable to claw her hair back into place, Shera settled for sweeping it out of her face. "Yes, I talked to him. He said Belinda Critch had been coming on to him since he met her. A case of wanting the one thing she couldn't have, I imagine."

Romana turned up her collar against the rising w "When did this confrontation take place, Ms. Barret?"

"Shera's fine. Shortly before she died, in mid-Dec

"Before Belinda died, but after Ben Brown pass

"A month after Ben's death, yes."

"And you'd been married to your husband for that point?"

"Eight months, three weeks, five days." Sh the bulge under her glove that was undoub ment ring. "My family is very wealthy an nected. I knew I'd land a big fish from th I have to say I didn't expect to fall in lo unsettling." Her eyes ran the leng "You're very pretty, Officer Grey. A

"Not anymore. Were you surpris

Shera shrugged. "Surprised bothered James, but I suppose whe

Now she longed for a different sort of adventure, with a man she barely knew, in a world she hadn't expected to visit again.

Funny how life never worked out as planned. Unless you were Shera Barret and had the ability to rewrite whatever scripts didn't suit you.

As she continued to stare at the sky, Romana sensed Jacob's approach. His features, mesmerizing and mysterious, drifted through her mind. She felt his mouth on hers, remembered the way his hands had explored her body, drawing her closer until she almost couldn't breathe. Certainly couldn't think.

Not about Warren Critch, or dark alleys or Muppet frogs. And only for a moment about the image of herself in death, with mistletoe leaves floating in the pool of blood that surrounded her.

"IT WAS A PUNK PRANK," Dylan Hoag maintained early Thursday morning. "Happens all the time, and there's not a thing your people can do about it. Apparently."

Jacob saw O'Keefe's lip curl. They were gathered in his former partner's cubby, volleying theories and getting their facts straight.

Dylan had dogged Jacob through the front door earlier, with the claim that since he had clients whose security systems had been damaged in the chaos, he had a right to be part of the investigation. He didn't, but Jacob had let him tag along anyway.

"The smoke bombs were rudimentary," he noted now as he flicked through the preliminary report. "A kid of fifteen could have constructed them, with or without help from the Internet. The trash-can fires were even less complex. Smoldering cigarettes in four of them, smoldering rags in the rest. But the starting sequence of the bombs was timed and charted. It ran a circle around The Toy Box, where Romana and I just happened to be having a chat with a man who knew Warren Critch."

"What are you saying?" O'Keefe poured himself a glass of water. "That Critch knew you'd be at the store and set everything up prior to your arrival?"

Jacob continued to scan the report. "More likely he followed us in, saw where we were headed and set it up then. I walked the route, Mick. Five minutes is all it would have taken to plant the smoke bombs and ignite the cans."

"To what end?" Dylan challenged.

"The one he achieved, I imagine. A bunch of injured shoppers intended to engender guilt. A message sent to Romana and me that he's watching, and he can take us out any time he chooses."

Dylan sipped his latte. "Why doesn't he, then? Why not off the pair of you and beat it out of the country?"

O'Keefe arched an eyebrow at Jacob. "Torment?"

"That'd be my guess."

"So all the damage to my clients' businesses is your fault?"

"And you get nothing out of it, right?" Jacob countered Dylan's charge without looking up. "No clients suddenly deciding they should upgrade their security systems to allay shopper panic?"

"There are systems that do that?" Momentarily impressed, O'Keefe downed his water. "You know, one day we'll all be replaced by robots, just like that life-size Santa standing next to Lieutenant Markham's desk."

"It was a figurative question, and Santa has an electrical short." Setting the report aside, Jacob glanced at the murky dregs in his friend's coffeepot. "Word is, Dylan, that you and Belinda were steps."

O'Keefe swung around. "Seriously? Man, how'd I miss that?"

"You didn't. Stubbs and Canter did. What's the story, Hoag?"

"No story." But both his jaw and his shoulders tightened visibly. "My dad married Belinda's mother when I was ten and she was seven. Like punk pranks, it happens all the time. Our parents died within a few months of each other, and we were all we had left."

Starved for caffeine, Jacob gave in and poured a cup of the thick coffee. "How old were you when your last parent died?"

"This is irrelevant, Knight. And invasive."

"You wanted to join the party."

Dylan hissed out a breath. "I was twenty-three." At Jacob's steady stare, he growled, "Okay, I was eighteen, just. Old enough to work and take care of my sister. We had money. We were fine. She went to college and came out the other end a damn fine lab technician."

"While you washed out at the Police Academy."

"I was older than most of the other prospects. I had my own ideas. I didn't fit in."

"That's what we in the biz call a major attitude problem," O'Keefe remarked.

"Sell it to Rudolph." Dylan's eyes went cold and flat. "This isn't about me. It's about smoke and fire and pissed-off clients, and…"

"It's about Warren Critch." Jacob speared him into silence with a look. "It's about revenge for a crime I didn't commit and Romana had no part in. You want to chase punks, go ahead, but what happened last night was executed by someone with a plan."

"Well, that someone's flying solo, Knight. Tap my phones if you want to. Except for that two-minute conversation I told you about, I haven't spoken to Warren. I don't know where he is or how he's getting by. I do know he loved Bel, and so did I. Am I sorry he's taken it upon himself to go after you? Not especially. Do I think it's right? No. Do I think he'll succeed? I'd say the odds are in his favor."

"Such faith in us cops," O'Keefe scoffed. "It's no wonder they cut you loose from the Academy."

Dylan tossed his empty cup into the wastebasket. "No one cut Romana loose, and yet she's gone, too, isn't she? Makes you wonder about misplaced faith and expectations placed just a little too high on humans who, like the rest of us, are often a little too low for the positions of power we seek."

"Now he's a philosopher," O'Keefe muttered.

"What I am is observant." With a derisive swagger, Dylan started for the door. "You're overthinking that fire and giving Warren too much credit for cleverness. He used to shoot fish in the Amazon. Hardly ever missed, I'm told." Outside the door, he turned. "My question is, why would he bother to be clever when all he wants is to kill the pair of you? Bang, bang, two shots, you're gone forever. And once he's safely tucked away in the South American rain forest, so is Warren Critch."

JACOB FELL INTO BED AT 1:00 P.M. He felt like a zombie and hoped his mind would let him sleep like one. But the dream came as it often did. It played out to the point where the blood appeared, then suddenly veered off course.

In the blink of an eye, he traded his parents' living room for a grungy downtown alley that smelled strongly of human waste. Shaking hands pointed a gun at his head. Red-rimmed eyes bulged at him.

"You want her to die," Critch accused. He cocked the gun.

"Finally—finally, it's all good, it's all right, and you want to take her from me. To kill her because you can't have her."

Jacob had made the usual attempt to placate him. Why would he want Belinda dead? Someone might have threatened her life, but it hadn't been him.

The quiet click had surprised him as much as it had startled Warren Critch. He hadn't seen Romana slip into the alley. She'd moved with the shadows, used them, caught them both off guard.

"Put the gun down," she'd ordered Critch from behind. "Toss it toward the trash cans."

"He wants to kill my wife," Critch had insisted, stiff-lipped. "I won't let him do that."

"Drop the gun," Romana had repeated. Not once had her eyes flicked to Jacob's face. "Do it, Critch. Now."

Critch's arms had trembled. He'd made a low, agonized sound. His entire body had seemed to vibrate. Then the sound had ended, and his weapon had clattered to the pavement.

"Kick it away," Romana had instructed.

"Belinda told me she's been threatened. I know they had lunch. They argued. Knight was angry with her. He wants to kill her."

"It's up to the police to investigate that allegation," Romana had replied. "It's not your job or your right to execute vigilante justice…"

The scene changed with an abrupt sideways slash.

Belinda Critch was dead, and Jacob was talking to his captain. The captain wanted answers he didn't have. O'Keefe knew the truth about the blackouts, but for his partner's sake he had kept silent.

They stood like the points of a triangle around the captain's desk while Kermit sang a silly Christmas song in the background.

A hand touched Jacob's arm. He whipped his head around. Romana stood behind him. She wore a white coat with a long red scarf.

"Look in the mirror," she said.

He didn't want to do it, but his eyes were drawn to the glass, magnet to metal. He saw his father's face staring at him and felt hollow inside, like the void his mind had suddenly become.

Dropping his head back, he stared at the white ceiling tiles. He wasn't his father, please, God, never his father, and yet his father was in him. Some of his father's traits lived on through him. Romana needed to know that, to understand.

It was past time he told her the truth.

When he turned to her, she set her hands on his chest. Before he could speak, her eyes widened in alarm. He caught her arms, tried to keep her from falling. But it was too late. He could do nothing but watch in horrified disbelief as the tails of her red scarf turned to twin ribbons of blood.

And the light that was life drained out of her stunning winter-lake eyes.

JACOB SHOT UPRIGHT IN BED, again, pried his clenched teeth apart, again. It took several seconds for the worst of the nightmare to fade. Once it had, he reminded himself that these images came from him. From his very deep feelings of guilt.

An ambulance raced past on the street below. Horns blared as the rush hour began.

A shower helped, hot at first to relax his tight muscles, then cold to counter the effect Romana continued to have on him. She hadn't been naked in his latest dream, but it made little difference. When he thought about her, his body reacted. He could only imagine what actually seeing her naked might do.

The phone rang while he brewed coffee. With his hair dripping and his mind distracted, he picked up.

"Knight."

The response was immediate, whispered words that blew across his soul like an evil north wind.

"You're a dead man, Detective Knight, at my whim. You and the exquisite Romana Grey. She won't be so exquisite when I'm finished with her. In fact, she might not be exquisite already. I'm holding a sprig of mistletoe, Jacob. But do you think the leaves are on the sprig where they belong, or on the ground beside her?"

Chapter Nine

Romana leaned on the intercom button, counted to five and leaned on it again. As a rule, she found the theater where Jacob lived delightfully atmospheric, but tonight it felt plain old spooky. Even the little cherubs floating high on the ceiling seemed to be leering at her.

She checked her watch. He went on duty at nine. His truck was in the alley. The hood was hot, so he'd been out, but he was here now, and she was going to see him.

Finally, he responded. "Mick?"

Romana stepped in front of the camera. "No, it's me. I can't find Fitz. We were supposed to go shopping after she finished work, but she didn't show. She always shows, Jacob, or calls to say why she can't. It's one of her best qualities. She never leaves me hanging."

He said nothing, and she was just cranky enough to consider smashing the monitor.

"I've had a bad day, Knight," she warned. "Please don't choose tonight to go all moody and withdrawn on me."

Five seconds passed, then ten. Romana zeroed in on the stairwell door. She was yanking on the handle when the elevator opened and Jacob emerged.

He strode right over to her, took her by the arms, jerked her up on her toes and kissed her. At least it resembled a kiss. In some ways, it felt more like an assault on her senses, but there was heat behind it and under that a measure of desperation that confused and unnerved her.

"What?" She dragged her mouth free. "Did something else happen?"

"Phone call." Trapping her chin between his fingers and thumb, he examined her face.

"Uh, Jacob." Closing her fingers around his wrist, Romana gave a subtle tug. "I wasn't outside long enough to get frostbite if that's what's worrying you."

Then she remembered what he'd said, and her heart jittered. "Did you hear from Fitz?"

"I heard from Critch." Setting his forehead against hers, he closed his eyes. "He wanted me to think you might be dead, that he might have killed you. O'Keefe and I have half the Cincinnati force out searching for you. I checked the alley where you nailed Critch myself."

Half the force? It was difficult to think past that, more difficult still to keep from wrapping herself around him. "You could have tried my cell phone. It's always on."

"Is it always charged?"

"Your point." Then, recalling her reasons for being there, she snagged the sides of his jacket. "Jacob, I can't find Fitz." She shook him so hard his hair brushed her cheek. "I have to find her."

"We'll find her." Jacob ran reassuring hands along her arms. "If Critch has her, we'll get her back."

Romana's heart beat so fast it made her feel lightheaded. "He'll hurt her, I know he will. If he hurt your neighbor, he'll hurt Fitz."

"Unless he doesn't have her. Romana, she might have gone out with someone, spent the night with him."

Romana had already considered the possibility. "I couldn't get hold of Patrick," she allowed. "And Fitz does have a thing for him."

"What about Barret?"

"Ah, well." She dropped her hands, fingers spread. "Different story there. Shera insists that James flew to Cleveland this morning. My sources at the airlines claim he's not on any of their flight lists, so either he was traveling incognito or…"

"He didn't go to Cleveland."

She forced herself to relax, had to or she'd lose her ability to think. "The scuttlebutt at Barret Brown is that he has a mistress."

"Is this scuttlebutt reliable or the usual half-baked bull?"

She seesawed her hand. "It came from my Uncle Dan—Fitz's dad. He wasn't overly clear, and I couldn't push without frightening him, which I don't want to do at this point."

Jacob regarded her for a long moment, then shocked her with a kiss that sizzled her blood and zapped almost every thought from her head.

"Let's go." Turning her by the shoulders, he propelled her toward the door.

She fingered her still-tingling lips, had to give her mind a shake. "Where?"

"Where I'm assuming your cousin should have been today but wasn't."

"Jacob, stop pushing. I went by the hospital earlier. She didn't come in for work this morning." Panic clawed at her insides. She refused to let it win, but swung around. "If Critch has her, what can we do? We can't even find him."

With his hands still on her shoulders, he stared into her eyes. "We'll do what we have to do, and we will get her back."

"And you know that because…"

"If Critch took your cousin, Romana, he did it for a reason. I think he'd be more than willing to return her in exchange for the person he really wants. Me."

No matter how hard she fought, Fitz couldn't stop her teeth from chattering.

What would happen to her? She wanted to ask, but really didn't want to know.

What an idiot she'd been. She had no experience in these matters and no business launching her own half-baked investigation. True, she'd stumbled in unknowing, but she should have taken her suspicions straight to her cousin. She'd be home right now, safe, warm and wrapping Christmas presents rather than scared, frostbitten and shaking in a damp cellar.

She shrank against the wall as footsteps approached. When the door creaked open, she avoided the beam of light that illuminated the person outside.

"Not the brightest bulb in the package, are you, Anna Fitzgerald?" She registered annoyance and amusement in equal proportions. "You've given me a problem, and I thought, I'd hoped, I was done with those long ago."

"You killed Belinda." The statement fell from her mouth unbidden. It made her jailor laugh and her insides coil into greasy knots.

"Well, now, that is a brilliant deduction. Maybe you should have been the cop instead of Romana. Except she isn't a cop anymore, is she? And her attention these days, when not fixated on Jacob Knight, is pretty much centered on finding Warren Critch. But what about the person who murdered his wife? Why isn't she focused on that task as well? Makes you wonder, doesn't it, if your cousin might not be a little unsure about her not-so-white Detective Knight. Oh, dear, no, mustn't think like that. Locate Critch, apprehend him, then worry about that other niggle. Or let it go. Stick Critch back in prison, and we all return to square one. We've been there for six years with no more harm done. Maybe that's where we should stay."

"I never thought it was you…" Fitz began, but her voice died away when a finger reached out to tap her chin.

"I realize that now. But when I saw you attempting to play detective, I thought you had it all worked out. What could I do but react as if you had? End result? Here we are, you and me, in a place where I'm very much afraid no one will ever think to look for you."

Tears burned Fitz's eyes. Her wrists and feet were bound. She couldn't even try to escape.

"Please don't…" she began.

The eyes in front of her rolled. "Oh, God, spare me the spiel. 'Don't hurt me. I won't talk. Secret to the grave.' The lines are old and tired. And you're forgetting one vital detail." The face she didn't want to see at close range dipped to her level and smiled. "I'm a murderer. Did it once, won't have a problem doing it again. But just so you know, I don't make a habit of this. Now Critch, he's hungry for the kill. Whereas I only killed because I had to. Sort of." The eyes in that face clouded slightly. "Had to. Wanted to… So long ago in some ways, yesterday in others."

To Fitz's horror, the mouth began to twist. She didn't need Romana to tell her that was bad.

"I don't blame you for wanting her gone," she managed to whisper. "I mean, she deserved to die, right?"

"In spades, Anna Fitzgerald. You don't treat people the way

she did and simply walk away. Have I told you the Belinda Critch story as it relates to me?"

What would Romana do? a frantic Fitz wondered. She swallowed her tears, shot for a tremulous smile. "You haven't, no," she replied. "But I'd like to know."

The eyes watching her narrowed. "Maybe I wouldn't mind telling someone about it at that. It's not like you'll be going anywhere with the news. Do you like chili?"

Another nod.

Her jailor's head cocked. "Can you cook it?"

"Any way you want it."

"Chili and a story." The thought appeared to sit well. "I could handle that. But you do realize you're going to die."

"I know." Fear flopped like a fish in Fitz's stomach, but this was the way, the only way. Her only chance. "One last meal," she said. "I mean, if it has to be the last, it should be good, right?"

"Oh, it'll be good." The finger that had been on her chin snaked out to stab the ribs above her heart. "Then it'll be over." A hideous smile formed. "Isn't life a bitch?"

FITZ'S ATTIC APARTMENT was compact, colorful and bursting with character—just like her.

Romana ducked under a trio of red hanging balls and peered into the tiny bathroom.

"Her hair dryer's not on the counter," she called back to Jacob. "Neither's her favorite coffee mug. She wasn't here this morning."

"Wouldn't her father have noticed that?"

"I don't imagine he noticed anyone or anything until at least noon." Romana recalled her uncle's red whiskey eyes and the breath he'd attempted to disguise with cinnamon mouthwash. "Anyway, Fitz leaves for work two hours before he does on Thursdays."

She returned to the living area, pivoted on her heel and wished just once that a clue would jump out at her.

"No tree yet," she noted while Jacob poked through the kitchenette. "She wants a live one, but there's not much room up here."

"Did you check her messages?"

Romana tossed her coat on the sofa. "Her supervisor called twice. I'm numbers three, four and five, and my brother Noah wants to know if she thinks I'd like a gift card or a Hermes handbag for Christmas."

Jacob smiled as he opened a cupboard. "I'd go with the handbag."

"Cigar's yours, Detective." On her third scan of the room, Romana spied a jar of silver polish and a blackened cloth. "What's that?"

He opened another cupboard. "Let me guess. You don't polish your Christmas silverware?"

"I don't have Christmas silverware. Neither does Fitz." But her cousin did have a black metal box with a combination lock sitting on the shelf above the desk. Interesting.

She glanced at Jacob. "You any good at cracking safes, Detective?"

"I've done a B and E or two in my time."

He was a man of mystery on both sides of the law.

"Job's yours." Because she wanted to rock him as he'd rocked her earlier, Romana strode into the kitchen and gave him a hard, smacking kiss. "You open Pandora's box. I'll try James and Patrick again."

She'd called James Barret's home twice already, but Fitz swore third times were lucky. Not in this case, however. According to a slightly winded and decidedly out of sorts Shera, her husband wouldn't be returning from Cleveland until Friday. Which told Romana nothing. Except that her cocker spaniel hubby likely wasn't as faithful as Shera wanted to believe.

An unpleasant thought wound its way through her head. Fitz had always liked James, lusted after him in fact. If Barret had flown to Cleveland, he hadn't done so under his own name. And Fitz, who adored him, was missing.

"Okay, that's just plain unworthy," she decided and punched Patrick's number with more vigor than necessary.

He answered with a yawning, "I was asleep, Romana. I hope this is important."

Call display still threw her sometimes. Romana pushed the hair from her cheek, held it back. "Patrick, I can't find Fitz. Did you see her at all today?"

"What? Uh—no, I didn't. I worked the graveyard shift last night. Left at six this morning. Went Christmas shopping."

Romana would have smiled at his gloomy tone if her thoughts hadn't been bouncing around like a pinball. "Her supervisor said she didn't clock in."

"Well, he'd know." The gloominess gave way to guarded concern. "Can't the police put out an APB on her?"

Romana circled the small room. "Fitz is a grown woman, Patrick. No matter what I think or feel, it's too early for APBs."

"Everything by the book, huh?"

She slid her gaze to Jacob. "Most things, anyway." She stopped pacing when he tipped up the lid of the box. "Gotta go, Patrick. Let me know if you hear from her." She hung up. "What is it?" she demanded when Jacob didn't speak. "Don't give me that inscrutable look, Knight, just show me what's… Oh… Damn." Even in dim light, the contents of the box winked and glittered and told her far more than she wanted to know. "Wonderful." She dropped to her knees. "I should have guessed."

Jacob maintained his easy crouch. "Lucky for Fitz I'm in Homicide."

"Luckier still that she's not here so I can kick her butt." Romana dipped a hand inside, let cuff links, rings and pendants slide through her fingers. "I really have to stop believing in fairy-tale endings." Nudging aside a cameo, she picked up a silver watch. "This is interesting. No sign of tarnish."

Jacob took it from her, flipped the band over. "It's engraved."

Instantly protective, Romana took it back. "It could have been a gift."

"Uh-huh, just not to Fitz."

"Maybe she bought it at a garage sale."

"And maybe I'm Father Christmas in disguise, but it's not a good bet."

"You're being a cop, Jacob."

"You're happily-ever-aftering again. Is there a name?"

There was something. Romana switched on a table lamp. Purple light spilled onto the watchband and the ornate script lettering that covered it.

"Still not psychic, Romana," Jacob prompted gently. "You'll have to read it out loud."

She really didn't want to, but the words had already scored themselves into her memory.

She breathed out the worst of her fear and read,

Belinda.
May our secrets live on. Forever.
Love, James.

IT MEANT NOTHING, ROMANA told herself. So James Barret had given Belinda a watch. So Fitz had cleaned it up and locked it in a box. And yes, both Fitz and James were unaccounted for. That didn't mean James Barret had taken her. Critch was still the most viable suspect—in everyone's opinion except hers.

"I'm staying with Critch on this one," O'Keefe said when Jacob updated him by phone. "Think about it. How would Belinda's murderer even know Fitz had the watch?"

It was a valid question, Romana admitted. And still the pesky little whispers continued.

At Jacob's suggestion, they drove to the police station— via James Barret's riverfront warehouse. The streets were slick, the Christmas music on Jacob's radio Kentucky bluegrass. Not a far stretch in Romana's mind from Irish folk. Which sent the whispers into overdrive.

"You want to tell me what's wrong?" Jacob sent her a glance. "Or am I supposed to guess all the way to headquarters?"

Because it was foolish to live in denial, Romana relented. "It's part of an old Irish verse."

"What is?"

"The inscription on the watch." She played with the hem of her long coat. "'Though life cannot be so, and our bones do turn to dust, may our secrets live on. Forever.' Fitz is Irish. She knows the verse. Barret's also Irish. And Belinda's dead. Okay, maybe Barret murdered Belinda—no idea what their secret might have been, though logic says affair. Or maybe he paid her to doctor his partner's autopsy report. Very big secret there. Worth killing for? Possibly. But how could he have known that Fitz had Belinda's watch?" She pressed her fingers to her temples. "I want to go with O'Keefe and believe Critch has her. So why can't I?"

With a glance in the side mirror, Jacob geared down. "Believe it's Critch, Romana. And put your seat belt on."

She lifted her head. "Are we being followed again?"

"Seat belt," he said and reached a hand toward it.

As she buckled up, Romana finally noticed what she'd missed during her emotional outburst. No matter how often Jacob used the brake pedal, nothing happened. He was relying on his vehicle's gears to slow them down.

Her training kicked in, and she braced her hands on the seat. "Where does this street end?" She regarded the ice slick in front of them. "Please say before the river."

"Yeah, it ends before the river." The transmission screamed as he rammed the gearshift down another notch. "It dead-ends at Gloster Road, at the old brick building that used to be the Merriman Meat Factory."

She saw the building then, in silhouette, an immovable mountain of wood and concrete set behind an even more imposing wall of bricks.

"Oh, hell," she managed to whisper.

The tires slipped. The SUV spun. And all Romana could do was stare in horror as the wall grew closer and closer.

Chapter Ten

Jacob disliked hospitals at the best of times and even more so when he was being threatened with admission. The E.R. doctor wanted to observe him for at least twenty-four hours. Jacob just wanted to get the hell out of there. When the doctor left, he picked up his jacket, reclipped his badge and went in search of Romana.

A man dressed as Frosty the Snowman slumped past with his costume head tucked under one arm and a bandage over his right eye. "Who gives exploding peanut jars as Secret Santa gifts?"

Someone with a grudge or a sick sense of humor, Jacob supposed. But better exploding peanuts than a Chevy Blazer with a slashed brake line.

"I don't have whiplash, Dr. McGee, and you're holding up three fingers." He heard Romana's patient voice inside one of the treatment rooms. "I'm not phobic, I don't feel dizzy, and you're still holding up three fingers."

A smile tugged at Jacob's lips. Apparently, neither of them intended to spend the night here.

"Jacob, are you..." O'Keefe rushed toward him in a baggy coat, a striped pajama top and jeans. He grabbed his former partner's arms and inspected him from head to toe. "All in one piece." Relief spread across his face. Then fled. "Where's Romana?"

Jacob nodded at the treatment room. "Giving McGee a hard time. She's fine. He'll badger her for another forty minutes, but she'll convince him."

"Give me the rundown."

"Someone—Critch—cut my brake line, probably while we were at Fitz's place. We were heading along March toward the river. I wanted to check out Barret's furniture warehouse before checking in at the station. Brakes failed."

O'Keefe shook his head. "I think you're wrong about Barret. If anyone has Fitz, it's Critch." He tucked the pajama top into his jeans, squinted past Jacob's shoulder. "Is there any coffee?"

Jacob motioned to his left. "Critch might have her, Mick, but the watch says something, and I want to know what it is."

O'Keefe waved his badge at a harried-looking nurse and stuck his head around the corner. "Smells like coffee and diapers. Makes you want to move right in." He picked up a tall pot, sniffed the contents and blew into two mugs. "Barret's coming to the Christmas party Saturday night as the mayor's special guest. His wife RSVP'd, so I'm thinking he'll show. You can feel him out then."

A young nurse walked past, paused and backtracked with a twirl. "Guess I deserve a pick-me-up, too."

While she poured and chatted, Jacob relived the scene in his Blazer.

Every cop knew how to stop a runaway vehicle. Jacob had done it twice in his first rookie week, and countless times as a homicide detective. Unfortunately, he hadn't done it on a street with a grade as steep as the one on March, a layer of ice under the tires and a brick wall looming in front of him.

Thankfully, Romana hadn't panicked. She'd simply buckled up, shut up and braced.

Lounging against the wall, O'Keefe cleared his throat. Jacob returned to earth and swallowed a mouthful of the tepid coffee. "What?"

"She's gone. You can zone back in."

"I didn't…"

"Yes, you did. Your mind goes into space, Jacob, whenever you're not interested in a thing. My question to you is, how can you not be interested in a woman who looks like Madonna in her prime, isn't married and is so obviously coming on to you? Did you see the cleavage she displayed for you?"

"Yeah, I saw it."

O'Keefe dropped his gaze to the front of Jacob's jeans. "So what, are you made of stone or just so damn besotted with Romana that your brain doesn't register other females?"

"I'm not besotted."

"In lust with, then. We had every available officer out searching for her tonight. Not because I requested it but because you told the captain to just do it and you'd explain why later."

"What's your point?"

A muscle twitched in O'Keefe's jaw. "You're in love with her, probably have been since before Belinda Critch died."

Jacob's smile had a fatalistic edge. "I didn't even know her back then."

"You knew her well enough. You observed from a safe distance, thought you were immune, then got the shock of your life when you realized you were gooney over her." Grieved acceptance marked O'Keefe's features. "The irony of it is, I think she feels the same way about you. Cool cop Jacob Knight, homicide detective with a stack of commendations as thick as my wrist. You got it all, Knight. The looks, the brains, the guts, the glory and now the girl. You must have been born under one frigging lucky star."

"Are you done?" Jacob asked when his friend lapsed into silence.

O'Keefe expelled a weary breath. "Is there more left to say? Yes, I'm done, and while I stand by all of it, I shouldn't have unloaded on you like that. I know you've had a lot of valleys with those peaks. Deep ones. The suspicion surrounding Belinda Critch's death, the memory thing, the threats." A frown appeared. "The brake line… Damn. You were filling me in on the details before I went off half-cocked."

Jacob knew he could walk away now, and O'Keefe would understand why. But they'd been partners for years, friends longer. And if he was honest, not much of what O'Keefe had said was untrue.

By way of a peace offering, Jacob topped their mugs. "Come into the waiting room, and I'll tell you about a patch of ice the size of Lake Michigan, a rusted-out fence and just how much damage a brick wall can inflict on the back end of a truck."

TIME TICKED ON. DARKNESS gave way to light. Romana felt as if she had a metronome embedded in her brain. No Fitz, no Critch, no way to contact James Barret.

Her parents arrived in Cincinnati unannounced early Friday morning. Her father insisted that his grandchildren should miss school and go tobogganing. Later, he'd treat them to dinner and the Festival of Lights at the Cincinnati Zoo.

He roped in Romana and her brother Noah to help. He would have added Fitz to the list if Romana hadn't told him that the path lab was overrun, and Fitz couldn't possibly get away from work.

Feeling every one of the bruises she'd incurred the evening before, she bumped down snowy hills, ate pizza and chicken wings and wandered through the spectacular Christmas light display with her family. By 8:00 p.m., rosy-cheeked and tired, the kids were back at their homes, and Romana's parents were en route to Grandma Grey's Kentucky ranch house.

"And that's a thumbnail sketch of my entire day," Romana said to Jacob, who'd knocked on her door fifteen short minutes after she'd collapsed on the sofa. "How did your daylight hours pan out, Detective?"

"I've had worse." He looked around at her high ceiling, tall windows and wide-open floor plan. "You have urban written all over you."

"My home's urban, but I'm going to inherit a Kentucky horse ranch, and believe me when I tell you, I've mucked out more than a few stables in my life."

He grinned. "I wouldn't mind watching that scene unfold."

She wagged a finger. "No, no, you don't watch at my grandmother's ranch, you participate. Means you get dirty. She has six dogs, a million cats and the most beautiful thoroughbreds you can imagine. And if you think the Christmas light show at the zoo is a wow, you should see her ranch on Christmas Eve. Think North Pole with a twist. She dresses up as Mrs. Claus and invites the entire town of Evanwood to walk around and gape. All donations of food and money gratefully accepted and passed on to local charities. I'm playing the part of Snow Miser this year, and while I'm sure you have no idea who he is, visualize icicles and snow control, and you're pretty much there."

Standing at the living room window, Jacob scanned the city. "There's still no word on Fitz."

"I know." She ran a hand along her arm, joined him at the

glass. "I hate that I don't know who has her. Critch makes sense, but I keep thinking about Belinda's watch and seeing James Barret's face." Guilt crept in as she glanced at Jacob's profile. "When I'm not seeing yours."

He gave a brief laugh. "Not the best time for that, is it?"

"No, but then I'm not big on timing. Fitz says it's one of my more promising flaws." Unable to shut down her feelings, she went with the moment and walked her fingers up his arm. "I'm liking the shoulder holster, Detective Knight. It screams power and sex appeal."

"You think guns are sexy?"

"When the right person wears them, yes."

"I'm not a saint."

She flicked at the ends of his long hair. "Good, because sainthood's totally overrated. Even Santa Claus shunned Rudolph for having a red nose."

"Then offered him the job of top reindeer."

"Because he needed Rudolph's nose to guide him through a winter storm."

A gleam appeared in Jacob's eyes. He slid a knuckle along her jawline. "Is this story going somewhere?"

"It made you smile." She took a rumba step closer, hooked two fingers into his waistband. "Any story that can do that is worth the telling."

"You have a warped mind, lady."

"When you grow up with six brothers, you warp or go nuts."

The gleam intensified as he ran his thumb over her cheekbone. "I see your eyes when I'm asleep. Sometimes they're all I see. Other times," he wrapped his long fingers around her nape, "I see a lot more of you."

Tugging on the bottom of his T-shirt, she slid her hands over his skin. "That's pressure on me. It's not easy living up to people's expectations. I should probably warn you, I'm not a good emotional risk."

"Why not?"

Head tipped to the side, she regarded him at a deliberately seductive angle. "Too changeable. I have trouble sticking. On the flipside," she eased in to bite his lower lip, "I don't seem to have any trouble at all…"

The rest died in her throat as his mouth crushed onto hers and began to devour. Nothing else registered. It was as if a giant wave of lust crashed over her, drenching her with wet heat.

And color. Pure white fire with splashes of jeweled light. Or was that the city skyline? Whatever it was, wherever it came from, sensation after sensation tore through her.

God, did Jacob Knight know how to kiss. The taste of him drove Romana's excitement level up until she was clutching his hair to keep him as close as possible. She pressed her body against his and simply let herself revel.

Should she be doing this here and now, though, with her cousin missing and her brain so crammed with thoughts that it might take her until next Christmas to sort them out?

When he raised his head, the room tilted slightly. Big yes, she decided, and swore she could see Fitz sending her a delighted thumbs-up. She marveled that her mouth felt numb and gave her upper lip an experimental touch with her tongue. "So that's what a nuclear explosion feels like, huh?"

"Or a tidal wave." He framed her face with his hands, looked into her eyes. "We shouldn't be doing this, Romana."

"Probably not." Her movement against his lower body drew a hiss of reaction. "But I sense a conflict in you, Jacob." Her smile teased while her fingers roamed. "A big one."

He pressed his lips to her forehead. "Very clever, Professor Grey. I meant there are things I haven't told you."

The smile gave way to understanding as she brushed at his dark hair. "You don't remember the night she died, do you?"

"Only a part of it."

"Jacob, you didn't kill her. Aside from the fact that you're a cop and sworn to uphold the law, why would you have wanted her dead? It doesn't make sense, and it doesn't mesh with your character."

"Not the character you know."

Romana sighed. "Did you love her?"

His eyes slid past her to the window. "I don't think I had any feelings for her. She wanted help with a problem. I'm a cop. She came to me."

"So you see? We agree. You didn't do it—as I've said from the start." She nipped his lower lip, smiled just a little and set her hands on his shoulders.

Taut muscles, lean body, awake and aware. Troubled he might be, but he wanted her, and God knew she wanted him.

Still, timing mattered, and this wasn't their moment. Tonight they needed something different, something active and purposeful.

"I have an idea."

"Should I be worried?"

"I'm worried enough for the both of us, Jacob." Her eyes narrowed. "Captain Harris has people looking for Fitz, right?"

"As many as he can spare."

"Good, because we need a break."

"Okay, now I'm worried."

"That's the idea." Jumping up, she wrapped her legs around him. One final, long kiss, deep and dangerous, then she nuzzled his ear and whispered, "Grandma Grey swears a change is as good as rest for sharpening the mind."

"And that means?"

"It means, Detective Knight, that you and I are going to climb into your new vehicle, point it north—and go shopping for Christmas trees."

SURVEILLANCE WAS A DULL SPORT, but what had to be done had to be done. He'd been following Romana all day with little opportunity to strike. He had no particular desire to involve children in his revenge. Besides, Knight was with her now, and twofers were always more exhilarating.

Take the incident last night. Watching them career down that hill, skid, spin and finally crash through a rusty fence into the meat factory wall had gotten him hard. Wonder what a shrink would say about that?

A sprig of mistletoe on the dash taunted him. Knight had used it as a prop in Belinda's death. It seemed only fitting that Warren Critch should make his counterstatement in much the same way. One clear, life-ending statement. Then, *hasta la vista,* he'd be gone.

Inside his truck, he pulled the hat he wore down low on his forehead, tucked his hands under his arms and slumped deeper into his seat. He had an arsenal of weapons locked in the utility box behind him. When they left tonight, alone or together, he'd be right behind them, their very own ghost of Christmas past.

Feliz Navidad, Jacob and Romana.

Chapter Eleven

They drove to a Christmas tree farm ten minutes north of the city. Live trees, cut trees, small, medium and large trees, this place had it all.

Romana knew what she wanted—a six-foot blue spruce that could be planted in her brother's backyard after Christmas.

"It's eco-friendly," she told Jacob as they wandered through the labyrinth of green. "It's also a happy ending for the tree."

"Now you're into the psychology of trees?"

"Every living thing has a spirit. People, trees, even cockroaches. Maybe." At the tug of amusement on his lips, she grinned. "Hey, I teach criminology, not metaphysics. What kind do you want?"

He examined the burlap root bag of a traditional Christmas pine. The memory of a similar pine brought a stab of pain and a clutching sensation in his belly. He saw his mother's face and had to work to block it out.

"No kind, Romana. But thanks."

She left the blue spruce she'd been admiring and circled to where he stood. "You need a tree, Jacob, even if it's the Charlie Brown twig variety."

"Oh, look, Oscar," an elderly woman remarked. "There's a lovely spruce."

Romana gave Jacob's shin a light kick. "Your bad attitude just cost me my first choice, Knight. Pick a tree before they're all gone."

Humor stirred as Jacob made a sweep of the immediate area. At least three dozen people had braved the slippery roads to come here tonight. There were others wandering around in the barn, in search of wreaths and pine boughs. The smells of Christmas enveloped him. Funny, though, when combined with Romana's exotic scent, the memories felt distant and very nearly manageable.

Romana rubbed her arms to warm them. "I know there are unhappy thoughts running around in your head, but you won't exorcise them by letting them control you. You have to stare them down, put them in their place."

He kept his eyes on the line of frozen root bags and his hands in his jacket pockets. "Is that the Romana Grey philosophy for beating your demons?"

"Think of it as a game of cops and robbers. Cops good, robbers bad."

"In theory, anyway," Jacob remarked. "Some robber-demons can take a lifetime to capture and control. I'm thirty-eight. That's not even half a lifetime by twenty-first-century standards."

He gave her credit for patience. Squeezing his arm, she replied simply, "Not going to pry, Knight."

His gaze climbed the skinny tree in front of him. "Because you're afraid of what you'll hear, or because you have other weightier matters on your mind?"

"You really are obtuse, aren't you? Fine, more the second than the first. I want to find Fitz, and I don't know how to do it. You don't know either, and the department can't help. Officially."

"The patrols know the story. I talked to several officers last night. They'll watch for her."

Unhooking her arm, she skirted a puny fir that stood between two much more majestic ones. It tilted to the right at the top, and a number of the branches were uneven, but it looked as healthy as a live tree possibly could under full-blown winter conditions.

"This is Fitz," Romana said and detached an icicle from the trunk. "I'm going to buy it for her and decorate it in purple and red, her favorite colors. That's all I can do to combat my demons right now."

The skin on Jacob's neck prickled. Turning up his collar, he looked back but saw nothing except trees, darkness and an old man wearing a money apron.

There were more people here than he'd anticipated. Why, he couldn't imagine. What sane person left the city at nine o'clock on a Friday night to go shopping for Christmas trees?

He noticed Romana glancing into the shadows and knew exactly what she was looking for.

"Problem?" He kept his tone casual and his eyes on the snow-covered pots that dotted the path.

"Hmm? No. I was thinking."

"About Christmas trees?"

"And Fitz and Critch and mistletoe." She dusted loose snow from another spruce. "I know you know why I wanted to come here tonight. The purchasing of Christmas trees is a bonus. I figured, beyond the city limits, in bad road conditions and nasty weather, who'd want to wander around outside? Guess I underestimated the hardiness of the average Cincinnatian." She blew out a cloud of breath, swept an arm around the yard. "You see now why I left the force. I couldn't get a fix on the human mind, let alone the criminal one."

"Insanity's its own unique mindset, Romana. No one can get an accurate fix on that."

"Except the criminal in question." She shook the hair from

her face. "Let's just pick three trees, load up and hope that if he is here, he'll follow us back to the city before opening fire. I spent most of today jumping at shadows, terrified that he'd take aim at me and hit someone in my family."

Although he appeared to be examining the trees, Jacob watched for movement in his peripheral vision. "I'll take that one." He nodded at a spindly pine with too many limbs and not enough needles to cover them. "I was kind of into Charlie Brown as a kid."

Romana's sighing laugh eased the tension and immediately took his mind in a very different direction. Just for a moment, he pictured the two of them on the floor, under that spindly Christmas tree, making love and not worrying about any of this. A smile touched his lips. It would be one hell of a Christmas present.

The man in the money apron dragged a large sled behind him. He helped Jacob load the trees and offered his son's help strapping them onto the roof. At the rate the father moved, Jacob figured they'd be lucky to get out of there by midnight.

Ten minutes later, Romana joined them. "Okay, we're all paid up for trees, topiaries, wreaths and boughs."

Jacob secured Fitz's tree on the sled. "What are topiaries?"

"Balls of manicured greenery in a pot. Nothing you'd want, but my niece loves them."

Jacob's skin prickled a second time as a woman drew Romana aside to ask for advice. Instinct had him sliding a hand into his jacket. He fingered his gun and scoured the winter darkness, but he still saw nothing and no one.

A breath of wind whispered across his cheek. It played with the ends of his hair and blew the top layer of snow around in circles. He didn't realize he still had his hand in his jacket until the old farmer waved him off with a cheerful, "Money part's

done. I heard your wife saying she paid inside. Topiaries." He snugged the rope around Romana's spruce. "The missus has been making the silly things for sixteen years now, and every year we sell right out of them. Shows you what I know."

"Ditto." Jacob caught a movement in one of the larger shadows, but it was only a man with an ax emerging from the U-cut area.

"Which one's yours, then?" a new and deeper voice asked. Preoccupied, Jacob knocked the trunk of the spindly tree with his knee. "This one."

"Which vehicle?" the voice grunted.

"It's the black Pathfinder," Romana returned to say. She nudged Jacob's arm. "What is it?"

"Other than Paul Bunyon coming out of the forest, nothing."

"He's the owner's youngest son. Look, let's get out of here before the shadows really do come alive."

He nodded, took one last, long look, then swung around— and found himself staring at a chest twice as broad as his own.

"You must be the owner's oldest son," Romana said. "Your mother showed me pictures when I was in the barn."

The man flushed. "I hate it when she does that." A projectile whizzing past his head drew a scowl. "Damn kids and their snowballs."

No way could Jacob wrestle Paul Bunyon's big brother to the ground, so he merely drew his gun and shouldered past. "That wasn't a snowball. Get down."

"What was it?" Romana demanded.

"It looked like a dart."

Another object flew past. It missed Romana's arm by less than six inches.

Jacob didn't waste his breath. "Under my jacket, waist-band, right side," he said. "Cover me."

She pulled out his backup gun, searched for movement as he did. "So many people," he heard her murmur.

"There." He spied the weapon as it was raised. "Get down," he ordered a group of six in front of him. "Romana…"

He took off to his right, made a point of staying in the light. It would give Critch a target and Romana a chance to whisk the bystanders out of harm's way.

"Come on, Critch," he invited softly. "I'm the one you want, not them."

But he wanted Romana, too, and knowing that made Jacob hesitate, glance back when he should have been focused on his quarry.

Critch's dart came out of the blackness too fast for him to dodge it. The tip ripped through his leather jacket and scraped painfully across his upper arm.

He felt it instantly, the numbness that spread upward into his left shoulder and shot straight down to his elbow.

He slowed, but didn't stop. Away from the farm's flood-lights, he could make out shapes between the trees.

He spied a movement and took shelter behind a Scotch pine. But it wasn't Critch who tottered around a stack of cut trees; it was the old man in the money apron, oblivious to what was happening as he zipped his fly.

Jacob spotted another movement and swung out around the pine. "Get down!" he shouted.

The man gaped at his gun. The best Jacob could do was shove him sideways as another dart flew past.

This one embedded itself in the trunk of the pine.

Jacob crouched. "Stay on the ground," he warned the man.

He scanned the snow for footprints. There were dozens. Motionless, he listened for any sound, but like him, Critch had gone dead-still. Which made it a waiting game.

"Move, you bastard."

The old man bellied forward.

"Not you," Jacob said over his shoulder.

But the old man kept coming. He pointed with a woolly finger. "Boots," he rasped. "The toes are sticking out from behind that knotty pine."

Jacob touched the man's shoulder in passing. He kept low. His left arm was virtually useless, and his breathing felt tight.

He spied the boots and circled. But the old man behind him slipped as he struggled to his knees, and both Critch and the boots disappeared.

Another dart blew past. Snow gusted up. Jacob glimpsed an arm, fired, and heard a yelp—of pain, he sincerely hoped.

His head felt heavy, and he wanted to stumble. He cursed both Critch and the drugged dart, and kept going.

Feet thudded on the snow. Branches shook. Ice pellets scattered.

Jacob trailed Critch by sound, realized he was heading toward the U-cut grove and took a zigzag course through the leaning stacks.

He saw a group of teenagers, heard another dart discharge. Before he could locate the source, a gun fired behind him. The bullet zinged off a thick trunk and into the night.

The teenagers took a collective step back, then began to run. Jacob bent slightly to catch his breath. A half second later, someone crashed into his back.

"Ouch!" Romana grabbed his arms for balance. "Why did you stop?"

He motioned at the kids. "Bystanders. Two o'clock."

He dropped to one knee, not so much out of desire but necessity. Was his jaw going numb?

The question felt hazy, and he had to concentrate to keep it from slipping away.

"Jacob?"

She fingered his torn sleeve with her free hand.

"It's nothing."

Her fingers came out red. She curled them around his forearm, shook. "Do you feel anything?"

"Yeah, pissed off."

The thrashing had stopped; the thudding footsteps had faded.

With his gun tipped skyward, Jacob rested an elbow on his upraised knee. "He's gone."

"Back to the farm?"

"No, that way." He gestured with the barrel. "Into the woods."

"I'll go…"

"No, you'll stay, and for once, listen."

He should have saved his breath. Using her teeth to pull off her glove, she tore at the sleeve of his jacket.

"The wound's not deep, but that won't stop the poison from taking effect." Grabbing his jaw, she stared into his eyes. "Is your vision clear or cloudy?"

"Clear." More or less. "It's curare, Romana. I know how it works. He shot a dart into the trunk of a Scotch pine…"

"I saw it. I pulled it out." Concern mixed with exasperation to soften her tone. "I was behind you, Jacob. You just run faster than I do in the snow."

Jacob spotted the blip of motion as she did. It came from the rear of a freestanding maple. Two guns whipped up. Romana edged sideways into the shadow of a more gnarly specimen.

Breathing had become a definite challenge. "Drop the weapon," Jacob called. "Romana's got you covered from the side."

The movement stopped. The silhouette quivered, then

slowly bent. A thunk on the snow told Jacob the weapon had been tossed as ordered.

"Come out and let us see you," Romana instructed.

Jacob watched the shadows. He heard the snow again underfoot. Then suddenly a light flared and a burst of motion transformed the silhouette into a man. In one quick move, he scooped up his weapon and launched it in the direction of Jacob's head.

HE PUFFED AND PANTED all the way back to his vehicle. Between being nicked by Jacob Knight's bullet and almost blown off the planet by a crazy woman with a shotgun, it was all he could do to start the engine and swerve onto the road.

His blood boiled. Hot bile rose in his throat. Rage all but blinded him. And he knew why.

He'd failed. He'd failed when, without realizing it, he'd wanted to finish it tonight.

Patience had never been his strong suit. He'd learned it over the years, just as he'd learned how to calculate, but there were times when it simply dissolved. Right now, he needed to take back control, calm himself and think things through with clear, cold logic. For Belinda's sake.

He'd done some part of it right. The dart gun on the passenger seat was proof of that. Why, then, was he still so furious that his hands were plastered to the steering wheel?

It wasn't until he felt the wet trickle on his forearm that he understood. Knight had wounded him. He'd drawn blood. Wounded animals lashed out. Wounded humans with a score to settle did so even more.

He breathed in and out, in and out. Pain was going to mark their deaths. More pain than they could possibly imagine.

To hell with Christmas and all the peripherals. The next chance he got—pow!

"CALEBAS CURARE. BRITISH explorers called it gourd curare when they were in South America. The most toxic formulas were found in this particular family, and there's enough of it in your system that Dr. McGee wants to call in a toxicologist to do a full workup on your blood."

Romana did her best to slow Jacob down, but it was a losing battle.

Features set, he simply caught hold of her restraining hand and pulled her along with him through the double Emergency doors.

"Jacob," she tried again. "My heart's still in my throat from watching that ax fly across the snow at you."

"It missed me by three yards, Romana."

She had to trot to keep pace with his long stride. "It missed you by half a foot, and only because the man throwing it realized at the last second that you were one of the good guys."

Although Romana still wasn't entirely convinced that the tree farmer's middle son—the one who, according to his mother, possessed a hair-trigger temper—had truly intended to miss his target.

"The farmer's wife saw Critch run through the yard with his dart gun. She grabbed her rifle and went after him. She fired into the air three times, which is incredibly courageous considering she's five years older than your downstairs neighbor." Romana dug her heels into the snowy pavement. "Jacob, stop acting like a lone wolf and listen to me. You have little to no sensation in your left arm, and McGee said your lungs have to be constricted."

"If I'm walking, I must be breathing. Do me a favor, Romana—go back inside and wait for O'Keefe."

"While you do what? Tear off into the night and possibly

straight into another dart? You can't keep presenting yourself as a target. It won't get Fitz back, and it won't help us catch Critch."

Jacob dragged the keys to his borrowed Pathfinder from the pocket of his jeans. "He got the curare from somewhere, Romana."

"Yes, South America, where he lived for several years as a child."

"And where he hasn't been for more than six years."

"You're being heroic, Knight. I hate that quality in a man."

"So you'd rather what? Sit back, do nothing and let him come to us? Again?"

"I didn't say that." She struggled for patience. "Fitz was right. We should go to the Christmas party tomorrow. Think of the people who'll be there. Cops who were around when Critch was arrested, James Barret, who I still think might have Fitz, people who knew Belinda and several who also knew her husband. Dr. Gorman's being honored, so key members of the forensics team will also be coming. We can talk…"

"You talk." Turning, he gripped her arms. "Start with O'Keefe. If he doesn't get my message, tell him I'm meeting an old friend whose name isn't Critch."

The objection on Romana's tongue died. "What is his name?"

Cupping her face, he gave her a kiss that, under different circumstances, would have made her head spin.

"He's someone I've known for years. A man with an expensive habit to support, and more than one secret he wants to keep."

THE ALLEY STANK OF URINE, human and animal. Jacob's eyes moved from side to side as he entered the narrow darkness, but nothing stirred except a tabby cat that wound itself around a trash can.

Lights shone from dirty, half-covered windows high above. The snow was coated with city grime, and the only nontraffic sound came from a tinny stereo in one of the upper apartments.

"An old woman on eight plays that same song all night long. Same song, same singer. Must be lost in a 1950s time warp."

The rusty voice contrasted with Bing's dulcet tone as he crooned about a white Christmas.

Too many cigarettes, too much whiskey and likely too jaded now to care, Gary Canter emerged from the dark, spit into the snow and showed a set of dingy teeth.

"Well, well, well, if it isn't my old nemesis, Detective Knight. I hear you wrapped up the Parker case all by your lonesome last night. How does it feel to be top of the heap in Captain Harris's eyes? He's a hard one to please, old Harris, yet he gives you free reign to investigate your cases while the demoted grinders like me spend the bulk of our time cozying up to street dealers and prostitutes."

Jacob waited, hands in his pockets, watching his counterpart's features curl into their usual disdainful mask. He noted the lines on a face that was too thin to be healthy and wondered about the condition of the body under it.

"Your clothes are hanging, Canter." He held the other man's gaze. "And the sole of your left boot is coming off."

"Observant as always." Canter pulled a pack of cigarettes from his pants, hesitated, then offered Jacob one. When Jacob shook him off, he chuckled. "No more vices, huh? You smoked like a chimney at the Academy."

"That was eighteen years ago."

"And six years ago, I covered your ass."

"Did you? I got the impression you wanted me to fry. Funny thing, perception."

Canter inhaled, savored and blew out a stream of smoke.

"If I'd wanted you charged and/or convicted, I'd have made it happen. Stubbs was a useless tit on that investigation." He inhaled again. "What is it you want, Knight? You pitched the word, I caught it, I'm here. Let's cut the crap and get to the meat."

"I need to know who deals in South American poisons."

"You want the short list? I can give you fifty names, maybe seventy-five. Most of them are illegal immigrants who go *poof* at the first sniff of a cop. Next question."

Jacob's laugh contained no humor. He looked away. "Why did you stint the Belinda Critch case?"

Canter shrugged. "Maybe I cut it short, but only a bit and mostly for your sake at first. You know things about me, Knight, about my lifestyle, my habits. Reasons don't matter in our world. You finger me and I'm gone, not just transferred from Homicide to Vice, but all the way gone, in disgrace."

"Who killed her?"

Canter stuck out his face. "I don't know. I told you, I thought it was you, that's why I skimped." He broke eye contact, shuffled his feet. "Changed my mind later on."

"Why?"

Canter swung away. He puffed for several seconds, then swung back. "Do you know how easy it is to make the slide from prescription to street drugs?"

"Yeah, I know how easy it is."

A smile crossed Canter's lips. "My God, is that compassion I hear? Or pity?" He kicked one of the trash cans, narrowly missing the tabby. "I don't want anyone's pity, not yours, or Harris's or your squeaky-clean partner's. How is O'Keefe, by the way? We don't cross paths too often these days."

"He's O'Keefe."

"Says it all, doesn't it? Must be hell to be such a drudge,

but at least his boat's steady. Except for the divorce. And a little thing I heard he had with Belinda Critch."

Jacob stared, and at length Canter deflated. "I know, I know, why did I stop thinking you'd killed her? I got a call after Christmas. I was hoping it'd be a tip, anything so we could put the case to bed and move on. There were other investigations going down, and I wanted in on them." Canter ran his tongue over his teeth, made a face as if he tasted something bad. "Probably wouldn't have worked out given that I was high on PK's most days, but a guy can dream, right?"

Jacob let his head fall back, and regarded the starless sky barely visible between the two buildings. "Who called you, Gary?"

"Someone who wanted the Critch case closed. If that meant destroying evidence, so be it."

"Did you destroy evidence?"

Canter took a long drag. "Didn't have to. There wasn't any. Killer cleaned up good, Knight. That's why I thought it might be you. We had zip for clues. The case was going cold before I even got the call. But, hey, a man in need, cop or not, can always use a little extra cash."

"You took the payoff."

"You don't sound surprised. But then you never were as squeaky clean as your partner." His features hardened. "Yes, I took the payoff. Why not? Like I said, the case was going nowhere. There was no evidence to destroy, so technically I didn't do anything wrong. Still, I found the offer rather intriguing. I figured we must have missed something, Stubbsy and me."

Jacob shifted his weight. His arm was burning now, from whatever McGee had shot into him to counteract the curare.

"Are you going to tell me who called you, or do we stand here all night while I guess?"

"You'd never guess."

"James Barret?"

Canter's eyebrows shot up. "Not bad, old friend. Care to tell me where that came from?"

"Romana found a watch."

"Huh." Canter studied him. "Well, that's cryptic." His sneer faded. "How is Romana? I always liked her. Word is Critch has it in for her, too."

"She stopped him from shooting me. Yeah, he has it in for her."

"I'm sorry to hear that."

Jacob regarded him steadily. The ache in his arm ran from shoulder to hand. The only thing worse was the throbbing in his head. "How much did your caller offer?"

"Enough to get me what I needed." Canter tossed his cigarette into the blackened snow. "I've paid for what I've done. I'm stuck in Vice until I retire, and that's a best-case scenario. We all have our skeletons, but you and me more than others." At Jacob's level look, he grinned. "Heard you and Romana have been tight lately. Maybe I'll see her tomorrow night, huh?"

Jacob recognized a weakness when he saw one. "Unless Critch gets to her first."

Canter's mouth compressed. "You hit low, Knight."

"Critch is getting close."

"I don't know about Critch. There's no word on the street. We all know he wants to off you, but where he's holed up..." He spread his fingers. "No clue. Have you talked to Hoag?"

"Talked to, worked out with, checked up on. There's no sign of contact between them yet."

"That Hoag's a slick one, but he's not stupid, only angry about Belinda." Canter's eyes sharpened. "You think Barret offed her?"

"It's looking that way. Still…" Jacob shrugged. "Appearances."

Canter's shoulders slumped. He started to walk, but halted five steps away and sucked in a long breath. "You never said a word, did you? You knew about my addiction—prescription and otherwise—but you didn't rat me out. I hated that you knew, hated that it worried me that you knew. Part of me wanted you to be guilty. The other part…I don't know. But I like Romana. She called me sir, and she meant it. I can't help you with Critch, but word's out about Romana's cousin going missing. You might want to look in Barret's direction for her."

With a nod, Jacob started off in the opposite direction. Canter's hand clamping onto his bad arm brought his head up and swiftly around.

"Lose the daggers, Knight. There's one more thing you should know. You were only half-right before. It was a Barret who called me six years ago. But it wasn't James Barret."

Chapter Twelve

"Romana?" Patrick North, bundled up and ready to leave the hospital, did a frowning double-take in the entranceway. "Why are you here?"

Romana walked back and forth near the double doors, swinging her arms to warm them. "I'm waiting for O'Keefe. He must have taken the polar route."

"Maybe he was a taxi driver before he became a cop."

A laugh escaped. "Why, Patrick, was that a joke? I'm proud of you."

"Wait until I've had a few drinks tomorrow night. I'll be the life of the party. Except—I'm worried about Fitz. She asked me to go with her. They're honoring Dr. Gorman."

"I know."

"Too bad he won't hear the accolades. He'll sleep through them like he slept through most of his later autopsies."

"Must have been some trick. Asleep holding a scalpel."

"It was a Pavlov's dog thing. Gorman saw a corpse and went through the motions. Eventually, we just started sitting him in the corner and carrying on by ourselves. It was our secret. I don't think he ever clued in."

A picture of Belinda's silver watch appeared in

Romana's head. "'May our secrets live on,'" she recalled. "'Forever.'"

"Please?"

"It's an inscription. On a watch." As a stream of exiting visitors swished through the doors, Romana halted. "You said you overheard Belinda telling someone that Jacob wanted her dead. Do you have any idea who was on the other end of the phone?"

"I thought maybe a woman, but only because I figure women talk to women more than they talk to men."

"Belinda talked to you, and you're a man."

"Talked to, yes, but didn't confide in. Sure, she'd tell me about men she knew who wanted her, but not usually their names. She'd say things like, 'this guy came on to me' or 'this cop's been after me to go out with him.'"

"This cop?" Intrigued now, Romana caught his lapel and eased him out of the doorway. "Did she actually say, 'this cop'?"

"Yes, a few times."

"Did you get a sense of who 'this cop' was?"

"I assumed she meant Knight."

"Why would you assume that?"

"Because she knew him, and she let everyone know she knew him."

Romana wanted to get this absolutely straight. "So sometimes she'd say Jacob Knight, and other times she'd say 'this cop.' Is that right?"

"I guess so. I never thought about it possibly being two different people." He gave his head a perplexed shake. "Are you saying that some other cop might have killed her? Because I heard her say Jacob Knight—and she used his name—wanted her dead."

Romana's mind raced. "He wouldn't get her a restraining order."

"He wouldn't—what?" Perplexity became outright confusion. "Okay, I'm lost. Belinda asked Knight for a restraining order? Against who?"

"Answer died with her, Patrick."

"Really lost now. How does Belinda asking Knight for a restraining order change what I heard her say on the phone? Or does it?"

"Jacob wouldn't give her what she wanted, so in her mind, maybe he wanted her to die."

"Ah-h-h." Comprehension dawned. "Because whoever she wanted to keep at bay had threatened her life. Knight knew that, but still wouldn't cooperate."

"It's a wild theory," Romana acknowledged, but she let it build. "So now we have 'this cop' who might not be Jacob and a statement you overheard that could be construed in more than one way."

Patrick hunched his shoulders against the wind that gusted under the overhang. "I'm glad I'm a doctor and not a cop. My head hurts just thinking about where you're going with this." Relief blossomed as he looked past her. "Thank God, O'Keefe's here. You can bounce your wild theories off him. Let me know if you hear from Fitz."

O'Keefe raised a hand to Patrick in parting. "Sorry I took so long, Romana. Plumbing problem in my basement. Where's Jacob? And what kind of a wild theory was Patrick talking about? Does it involve Critch?"

"Doesn't everything?" She scraped her fingernail over his tie. "You have a red stain, Detective."

Grinning, he buttoned his coat. "I stopped for a chili dog. Three minutes at the drive-through. Come on, into my car.

We'll discuss wild theories and how to get red sauce out of polyester."

Romana set a forestalling hand on his arm. "Jacob went to meet someone, Mick. He left you a message about it. It's someone he's known for years with an expensive habit to support. He had that determined-cop gleam he gets in his eyes when he knows he's in for a challenge."

"Poison darts weren't enough, huh?"

"No, they just pissed him off. And scared the hell out of me. Dr. McGee says a direct hit could have killed him."

"Or you."

"That's not the point, is it? The brakes failing felt like a warning, like he was playing with us. Hurting Jacob's neighbor, taking Fitz, that's torment. Tonight was an attack."

O'Keefe unlocked the door of his serviceable Escort. "You're not exactly easing my mind here, Romana."

"I know, and I'm sorry. I'm piecing it together, trying to get inside Critch's head, trying to see if he even has a plan."

"Oh, I'd say he has one. Could be it's been modified a time or two, but ultimately he'll know how he wants it to play out."

"Not exactly easing my mind here, O'Keefe."

He chuckled at the sarcasm. "Let's do it this way. You tell me about your wild theory, and I'll tell you about Jacob's post-Academy days, with his veteran partner and an overeager rookie who now has an expensive habit to support. One homicide turned vice cop named Gary Canter."

MIDNIGHT CAME AND WENT. Belinda's murderer came and went. Fitz shivered in the dark and the cold, but the fact that she was alive to shiver spelled hope to her.

Twice now she'd cooked meals for her captor, but always with one hand shackled to the leg of a heavy table. Like a dog in the backyard, she had a long lead, but chained, could go no farther than the kitchen. And so far the key to the cuff on her wrist had eluded her.

But tomorrow was another day, and it would bring another chance. Her lucky third chance, she prayed.

"Help me, Ro," she whispered out the tiny window in front of her. "I swear I'll never steal again. Just help me make my Christmas miracle happen."

And with her cousin's voice urging her on, she began to plot.

ROMANA WAS DOODLING A PICTURE of Warren Critch's face when the door to Denny Leech's apartment opened and a bandaged head with long white hair and a pink ball cap poked out.

"Thought I heard something." She surveyed the lobby before drawing a baseball bat from behind her back. "I'm glad it's you, dear."

Romana stayed where she was, on the upper step outside the elevator. "I'm waiting for Jacob. His captain told me he checked in at 1:00 a.m. and said he was going home for a while. How's your head?"

"Too tough to crack, but I wish I'd thought about ripping off that ski mask."

Romana doodled a mustache onto Critch's face. "What did he say when he knocked on your door?"

She snorted. "Claimed he was a courier with a package from my daughter in Columbus. I checked my security monitor, but it was all wiggly lines and fuzz, so, stupid me, I opened the door and, whoops, he grabbed me."

Romana heard a sound at the entrance and glanced up. Jacob came in, pocketing his keys. He seemed more surprised to see the two women talking than he was by Romana's actual presence.

"Suspicious of everyone and everything, this one." Denny beamed at him. "But he's a cutie, and I'd give my painting arm to be thirty again."

With a wink, she picked up her bat and disappeared back into her apartment.

"You live in a building of night owls, Jacob." Romana doodled a dart with mistletoe leaves plunged into the center of Critch's forehead. "Your upstairs neighbor invited me to join him for coffee and a hands-on demonstration of his spa tub. And the one on the mezzanine level has been in and out of his place twice with a suitcase. He's either re-creating a scene from *Rear Window* or he takes very short business trips. I've been here only forty minutes."

"He makes jewelry. His suitcase is his sample case."

She smiled, closed her notepad. "Jewelry samples at 1:40 a.m.? Like I said, *Rear Window*."

She couldn't read his expression as he walked toward her, but his smoky-green eyes elicited a shiver of anticipation.

"It isn't that I'm not glad to see you, Romana, but why are you here?"

She stood, set a hand on the railing. "You have my Christmas tree. And Fitz's."

"You weren't home, so I dropped them off at Fitz's place."

Her eyes danced. "I'd say I was sorry I missed you, but here we are, so I guess it's all the same in the end. How was your meeting?"

He kept coming, hadn't broken eye contact yet. "What meeting?"

Her long coat swirled around her ankles as she descended the stairs. "I talked to O'Keefe."

"Probably made his night."

"He told me about you and your first partner. He also mentioned another rookie and a vehicle pursuit that got out of hand."

"O'Keefe does like his stories."

"Yes, he does. At the wheel in this one was Sergeant Harry Plant. Next to him was his rookie partner, Officer Gary Canter. Police vehicle overturned. Plant was DOA. Canter almost lost his right leg. He was in rehab for months. A second patrol apprehended the runners. Veteran officer Roy Cleary, rookie officer Jacob Knight. Officers Cleary and Knight received commendations for their backup effort, which resulted in the arrest and conviction of a dealer with warrants in five states.

"Rookie officers Canter and Knight worked hard and eventually wound up in the homicide division, but, unlike Knight, Canter took a bit of a backslide. In and out of rehab, and not because of his leg, at least not directly because of it." Close enough now to touch, she ran light fingers over the top of his jeans. "That was about it for the story, except O'Keefe says that painkillers are just as addictive as street drugs, and Canter's had a hard time weaning himself off them."

"There was nerve damage," Jacob told her. Those mesmerizing eyes locked on hers. "Canter preferred painkillers to pain. Sometimes it affected his ability to function."

"I'm sorry to hear that, Jacob, truly sorry. Gary Canter was nice to me when I was a rookie myself." She teased him with her hands. "So why did you come home? Dull shift or the aftereffects of curare poisoning?"

"I have some time owing. Mick told me he took you back to your place, but you weren't there when I stopped by, and I couldn't see you visiting your brothers at one in the morning."

She grinned. "I have friends, you know. Maybe I had a sudden urge for a girls' night."

"If you had, you'd have gotten it going before one in the morning."

"Your point." She looked up at him, directly into those smoky green eyes. "Are you going to kiss me, Detective, or do I have to undress you right here in the…"

He hauled her into his arms so fast, she missed the movement—lost her train of thought, obviously, and her breath along with it.

If she'd been worried about any residual effects from the curare, that thought scattered as well. Poison restricted, it inhibited, but Jacob showed no sign of either. The bulge in his jeans proved that, and invited Romana to explore.

He kept his mouth on hers, changed the angle of his lips, but didn't stop kissing her. She went airborne for a moment when he scooped her up, but she settled herself against him quite easily. He hit the elevator call button with his elbow, and only dragged his mouth from hers when her breath gave a small hitch.

"What?"

"Gun in my ribs." Capturing his chin, she brought his head back around. "Relax, Jacob. I'm not made of glass. You swept me off my feet, literally. It's so…"

"Romantic?"

"You made that sound like a bad word."

"My inflection must be off. I meant to sound horny."

"Oh, well, you don't need words to convey that message." Swinging her legs, she bumped her hip against the front of his jeans. Her tongue slid along the side of his jaw. "I feel so 'You Tarzan, me Jane' right now. Push the button for your treehouse elevator again."

The heat that flared between them amazed her. The fiery ball of it erupted in her head, melting everything inside and snaking down low into her belly.

He held her against him while she ran her hands over his shoulders and chest. His mouth fed on hers. His tongue was hot and wet, and she met it with an eagerness she couldn't recall feeling before.

She heard the swish of a door, the grind of an engine, the clunk of metal cables. Then another swish and the music of the city washed over her.

She smelled paint and clay and a hint of spice. The night moved from shadow to pearled light around her. Red, to gold, to green.

When he set her down, her boot heels echoed on a bare wood floor. For the sake of her balance, to say nothing of her whirling thoughts, she dragged her mouth free.

"Heart's going to explode," she breathed. "Honest to God, I can't get air when you kiss me. Did you take lessons as a kid?"

His lips moved into a vague smile. "Jungle training. I took a hostel trip to Africa after high school. Got lost, got found, got out."

Got laid as well, she imagined, but whatever he'd done, wherever he'd done it, it had certainly worked. Her limbs felt weak and wobbly, her skin burned and her mouth tingled as if she'd been shot with electricity. And what had it been—five minutes since he got there?

The light continued to slide from red to gold to green. The play of it danced across his narrow, watchful features.

She wanted him to smile again, just a little, to lighten the load that seemed to weigh so heavily on him. She wanted even more to tear at his T-shirt and expose the hard, smooth flesh beneath it.

With a hand on her arm, he urged her forward. "Are you sure you want this to happen?"

She pressed her lower body against his erection. "If I

didn't, I wouldn't have come. This isn't a new thing between us. It's an old spark that never quite had a chance to ignite."

He halted his mouth a tantalizing inch from hers. "You don't know anything about my past."

Desire shot through her in sharp little bolts. Need cramped between her legs. She felt the insistent throb of him and wanted it inside her. Deep inside. Where all that wonderful heat could explode into liquid fire. Maybe she should rip off his shirt at that.

This time, it was Romana who captured his mouth while her hands worked at the snap of his jeans. "I know what I need to know. I promise, I'm not made of glass or anything so fragile it shatters at the mere suggestion of imperfection. It's cold outside, it's hot in here. There's danger in both places, but this is the danger I choose."

Finally, she won that smile. Jacob threaded his fingers through her hair, held it off her face as he stared into her eyes and murmured, "I hope you've chosen well."

Romana reveled in the alternating Christmas hues that streamed through the window. It was the only light source in the room and it worked. It enhanced.

She heard carolers far in the distance. Also fitting. Chestnuts roasting, fire burning, Jack Frost outside, Jacob hot and hungry for her inside—it was everything she needed right now. Well, that and to get the stubborn fly of his jeans undone.

With his mouth devouring hers, he stripped away her coat and scarf. Her clingy black top went next, then her jeans, her oldest and snuggest-fitting pair.

"Boots and black lace lingerie. I like it." While her fingers continued to work the zipper, he swept her back up into his arms and somehow managed to set his mouth on her breast.

"Ah-h-h…" Desire spiked through her, and she marveled

that her heart didn't stop dead in her chest. But when he lifted his head, she simply pulled it back down. "God, don't stop."

Her bare legs swung over his arm. She started to wriggle free as he approached the dark shape that had to be his bed.

She wanted him under her, not the other way around. He was still fully clothed—although she'd managed to get rid of his jacket. It was her turn to savor, to pull off his T-shirt and jeans and see that smoothly muscled body of his naked and ready for her.

Anticipation gleamed side by side with the hunger in Jacob's eyes. "Not a chance, Romana." He deposited her on the mattress. "I want to look at you."

She hooked a booted leg around his hip and tugged him with her. "Look all you want, Knight, but I expect the same privilege."

Amusement won out. Righting himself, he held his arms to the sides. "Go for it, then. I figure I've got about ten seconds of self-restraint left."

Thankfully, the zipper worked this time. She dragged off boots, jeans and black boxers, then caught back a breath.

"Okay…hah…" Shoving at his shoulders, she straddled him on the mattress. "That's ten. Now kiss me again, and make me crazy."

It surprised and touched her that he took his time, that he laid her gently on the sheets and began to stroke her as if she were a priceless musical instrument. He ran his hands over the silky flesh of her stomach, then lower until his fingers slipped under the strip of black lace between her legs.

She gripped his arms, dug her fingernails into his skin. She arched her body up into him, arched her head on the pillow.

Her body hummed, even her skin felt alive. And alight. God, it felt as though fireflies were whizzing around inside her, sparking everything they hit.

He bent his head, and through the lace of her bra, drew her nipple into his mouth. She bowed up to meet him, wanted quite badly to remove the barrier between his tongue and her breast, but couldn't form the words.

Threads of thought were all she had left. She took him in her hands and, even with only half of her brain functioning, managed to see his eyes go dark. And darker.

It wasn't about power, but there was something incredibly arousing in realizing she had as much of it as he did.

Sensation rocked her from surface to fiery center. Hunger turned to need as his fingers moved inside her. The room and the night spiraled away. There was only Jacob now and the erotic things he was doing to her. With her.

He was beautiful, truly beautiful to behold. She had enough of her wits remaining to acknowledge that. Smooth flesh over sleek muscle and bone. Romana wrapped her legs around him, stared up into his eyes and knew, simply knew, this was right. It was good.

She held on to him, felt his hand leave her and his body rise up. The black lace vanished. He moved between her legs, bent to kiss her once more.

He drew the moment out, like a long, lovely note of music. Unwilling to wait another second, Romana closed her fingers around him and took him inside.

"Not going to live through this," she murmured, then bit her lip around a sound that might have been a scream. She was wet and ready, and she matched his rhythm perfectly.

Something danced in her head as he drove himself inside her. A word, a feeling, pure wild sensation—she didn't know or care. He filled her up, that was all that mattered. His hands and mouth touched and tortured her. But it was a delicious torture.

He surged against her and she swore, just for a moment,

that her bones dissolved. And still she reached upward toward that exquisite peak.

Her nails bit into his shoulders. She squeezed her legs tighter, caught back a quick breath—then hovered, like a child on a roller coaster. Heart pumping, adrenaline flowing, flushed and breathless, waiting for the headlong rush.

It came in a burst of heat and a flash of light. The plunge through colored darkness that was her climax. And Jacob's.

"Okay… Ah… That's it." She shook the hair from her face, felt the dampness of his skin against hers. "I can't breathe. Can't move. Might never think again."

Jacob dropped his forehead onto hers. "It's all about nature, isn't it? Souls meeting, connecting, remembering."

She managed a smile. "I gotta tell you, Knight, that's a way more profound thought than I can form right now."

"Spectacular sex must make me profound."

"Only spectacular?" She blew at his hair, slid her arms around his neck and nipped his bottom lip. "Guess I'm losing my touch. I expected at least earth-shattering or maybe mind-numbing."

"Believe me, Romana, I'm numb and shattered."

"Me, too." Her eyes twinkled and a laugh bubbled up. "But believe it or not, I'm also hungry."

He couldn't even lift his head to stare at her. "You're joking. You want food?"

She teased him with her lips and eyes, feathered her fingers over his buttocks. "I didn't say I wanted food, I said I was hungry." Using her free leg and both of her hands, she switched their positions. "But this time, Detective Knight, I get to feed first."

Chapter Thirteen

It was close to 3:00 a.m. by the time Jacob remembered, barely, to check in with the desk sergeant. Tying up loose ends was what he told her. Tying himself in emotional knots would have been closer to the truth.

If he loved Romana, and he might, he wasn't ready to admit it yet. Not to her and certainly not to himself.

"Your father loves me, honey," his mother used to whisper. "He loves you, too, he does. He just doesn't always show it right. He has such a difficult job…"

Did that mean all police officers hit their wives? Even as a child, Jacob had had his doubts.

He hadn't wanted to become a cop—no way, anything but. And yet there he'd stood after two short years of college, reading the forms, filling them out, wondering what kind of perverted inner demon was driving him to do this.

Eighteen years later, he still hadn't figured it out.

He'd survived the training, done the job, climbed the ladder. There was more waiting for him, a great deal more if he wanted it. Harris had been trying to push him to the next rung for the past two years.

To the same rank his father had achieved before he'd lost it.

The clock chimed twice in the square below. That would make it three-thirty. He should be out there now, following leads, talking to informants, picking apart airtight alibis. Instead, he was sitting in an ancient armchair with his feet propped up on a wine crate, drinking merlot, staring at the city lights and trying very hard not to think about the woman curled up in the bed behind him.

They'd had sex, they hadn't made love. He couldn't accept anything so vast yet. The word overwhelmed him. As for the feeling, well…

He drank more merlot, heard a whisper of sound and set his head on the back of the chair. "I thought you were asleep."

"I was. Now I'm awake."

She stayed on the bed, and it took every scrap of Jacob's restraint not to turn around. Seeing Romana naked had fired a need inside that he hadn't realized existed. And the firing had been nothing more than a point of commencement.

He raised the bottle. "I have wine."

"Yes, I see that."

She didn't sound angry, but then she wouldn't be. Curious maybe, a little guarded and certainly intrigued, but not upset.

Reluctant amusement tugged on his lips. "You're going to use silence to make me talk, aren't you?"

When the bed creaked, desire turned lethal. "Actually," she said, "I'm hoping the wine will do that for me." He caught the deliberate shrug in her tone. "Or we could have more sex. Your choice." Her fingers slid through his hair. "You can talk to me or not, just feed my female vanity and make me believe you want me. Again."

Okay, he wasn't dead, he wasn't drunk and he sure as hell wasn't made of stone.

Whipping a hand around, he tumbled her into his lap.

He wore only his jeans. She wore nothing but skin, and miles of dark, silky hair.

Brushing it from her face, he let his gaze roam over her features. "I want you, you know I do. I've shown you twice already."

"Guess that makes me a glutton, then." She bit his earlobe. "Whatever it makes me, show me again."

She might be a glutton, he reflected, capturing her mouth in a hot, wicked kiss, but only for punishment. He just prayed he wouldn't be the one meting it out.

When he raised his head, she sighed. "You're so sure you're going to hurt me, aren't you, when I've already gone way past believing that's possible."

His lashes fell to shield his eyes. "How do you know…"

She stopped him with a kiss. "Later, okay? I want you, and I think," she wriggled against him, "you want me." Her eyes sparkled in the soft glow from the street. "Third time's lucky, Detective Knight."

"O'KEEFE DIDN'T SAY A WORD." Romana held up her right hand. "I swear. All he talked about was you and Canter as rookie officers—bet you were cute in uniform—and how much he misses his daughter."

Jacob shook the last drops of wine into her glass. "So you're telepathic, then?"

"I wish, but, no, not that either." Reaching over, she tapped a finger to his mouth and stage-whispered, "You talk in your sleep."

He stared for several incredulous seconds. "Are you serious?"

She sat back, dipped that same finger in her wine. "For once, I am. You mumbled things about—well, about your father, I guess. And your mother. I'm sure about her. You loved her."

"I sure as hell didn't love him."

"Grew not to love him would be my take."

"Same thing in the end."

He looked out the window. Broody, unapproachable—maybe it was time she said something, pried just a little.

Wearing only his T-shirt, she curled her legs on the rug in front of him and set an arm on the wine crate. "You look out, Jacob, at other people and their lives. But how often do you look in? You're not your father. You're not your mother or your grandparents or some barbaric ancestor. You're you. You're what you've made of yourself. Everyone, and I mean everyone, in my family, including Grandma Grey, swears I'm the reincarnation of her mother."

"The one with the winter-lake eyes?"

"That's her. But you know what? I'm not her, and no one's going to convince me I am."

"You don't believe in reincarnation?"

"I'm open to the possibility. But in the case of my great-grandmother Rostov, she was alive when I was born. So it wouldn't be reincarnation so much as spiritual possession, and, whether by a good spirit or an evil one, I absolutely will not buy into that. I am who I am, you are who you are, and I'm really, truly sorry for what you must have gone through as a child."

A muscle ticked in his jaw. He glanced into his wineglass, then back up at her. "I could have killed her. It's possible."

He wasn't talking about his mother. Romana's heart gave a tiny stutter that settled the second she felt it. "You can't account for your whereabouts at the time of Belinda Critch's death, is that right?"

"I was on duty. It was one of my first night shifts."

"What part of the night don't you remember?"

"About half of it. O'Keefe and I were partners back then,

but as you know, partners don't spend every minute of their shift together."

"You separated." She rolled the stem of her glass between her fingers and thumb. "When? What time?"

"Close to midnight. O'Keefe had personal business to take care of. Problems with his wife. He went home. I went looking for Durphey—an informant."

"I've heard the name. Did you find him?"

"Yeah, I found him, around 1:00 a.m."

"The medical examiner pinpointed Belinda's death between 1:00 and 4:00 a.m. How long were you with Durphey?"

"Ninety minutes."

Amusement sparked. "That long? With someone who smells like a sewer and drools when he speaks?"

"The drooling's an act. Keeps people at arm's length."

"The sewer smell would do that no problem. He must have had some valuable information to impart."

"He did. We spent most of those ninety minutes in a dockside warehouse, searching for an outgoing shipment."

"Of drugs?"

"Homicide division," he reminded her.

"You were searching for a corpse?"

"Two. Drug related. They weren't there."

"So you split at the warehouse?"

"He left, I stayed, searched a bit longer. I remember lighting a cigarette, looking at the moon, then—nothing."

"Well, okay, hmm. So from, say, 2:30 to 4:00 a.m. you don't know where you were or what you did. When did you—" she rocked her hand back and forth "—wake up, so to speak?"

"Dawn." His features darkened as his mind traveled back. "It was starting to snow. I woke up in my car—literally woke up, so I must have been asleep."

"Where were you?" When he didn't answer, Romana tapped his leg. "Where, Jacob?"

"Three houses away from O'Keefe's place, parked by the curb."

"Did you go inside?"

"I used my cell to call first. There was no answer, so I went to McDonald's and had breakfast. I heard about Belinda after I checked in with Harris. O'Keefe was in the captain's office when I got to the station. They said Critch was freaking in his holding cell, accusing me of killing his wife. He kept screaming that I'd done it and they should have let him shoot me when he had the chance."

"*They* meaning me."

"And so began the Christmas card parade."

Romana's brow knit. "That's right, the cards. I'd almost forgotten about those. Carefully worded portents of doom. Until the last one. Well—or actually no, the one before it was quite vicious as well."

The ghost of a smile appeared. "Prison guards get complacent after a while. Critch was a model prisoner. They'd have stopped checking his outgoing mail after the first few years. He'd have known that and reacted accordingly."

With an elbow propped on the wine crate, Romana slid her fingers through her hair. "So, going back to the morning after, no one could vouch for you except an informant whose testimony wouldn't have been worth anything anyway. You didn't see O'Keefe after the two of you separated, or you wouldn't have woken up in your car. Critch was behind bars at the time, so he didn't kill her. Where was Barret?"

"At home, asleep, he said."

"And Shera?"

"Couldn't alibi him because she was in Columbus at her

sister's place, working out the details for an upcoming family reunion. Allegedly."

Romana opened her mouth, but at his last word, closed it again. "What do you mean? Was Shera in Columbus or not?"

"Her sister says she was."

Romana tipped her head for a better view of his shadowed face. "And you think what? That her sister's covering for her?"

"It's possible."

"Most things are, but why this particular thing? Come on, what do you know that you're not sharing?"

"A tip I got tonight."

"From Canter?"

Again that ghost of a smile. "Source isn't important. I talked to Shera Barret's sister earlier tonight. She lives in Cincinnati now. She admitted that Shera went to bed with a migraine at 6:00 p.m. the night before Belinda Critch died. She didn't come out of her bedroom the next morning, and her sister, knowing what migraines are like, didn't disturb her. She went to work as usual and came home to a note Shera had left on the nightstand. It said she had to go back to Cincinnati, and she'd call soon."

"Did she call?"

"The sister doesn't know. She left on a buying trip to Mexico that evening. When she got back after Christmas, she was in the middle of a business war and never thought to ask Shera for an explanation."

"Well, that's convenient. Doesn't mean Shera had anything to do with Belinda's death, but it sounds like the opportunity was there." A shrewd eyebrow went up. "Was it? Did your tipster say?"

"Yeah, he said." Jacob's gaze slid to the window. "Five days after Christmas, the investigating officer received a phone call and the offer of a substantial amount of money if he'd be willing to make the case go away. Whether the call was intended to protect her husband or the caller herself, he didn't know. But it was made by Shera Barret."

ROMANA KNEW THERE WAS MORE to the Gary Canter story than Jacob was telling, but since it didn't appear to relate to the Belinda Critch investigation, she didn't press for details. He'd tell her what he wanted to when he wanted to. It was Jacob's custom to hold back and hers not to push. Which might, she reflected, be the reason she hadn't been the most effective officer on the Cincinnati force.

In any case, the night had been incredible. So had the sex. Better than incredible—it had overwhelmed and, if she was honest, been more of a revelation than she was prepared to handle right now.

Her marriage had left holes in her self-esteem, had burst bubbles of hope and allowed doubt to creep in and take root. Even Grandma Grey's unwavering support hadn't managed to offset all the damage. And reflecting on cause and effect hadn't been high on Romana's to-do list. Until now.

"Really missing you, Fitz," she said to the ceiling of her condo. "Please be safe. Please, let me find a way to find you."

She wished she could go out and search tonight, but it was almost eight o'clock and the police/forensics party would be getting underway in a few minutes. Rushton Hall had been rented and seasonally decked out. It wasn't a black tie affair, but that wouldn't stop the partygoers from dressing up in their holiday finest, especially the females, who tended to wear uniforms or lab coats on a daily basis.

The intercom buzzed at 8:02. *Not bad, Knight,* she thought, and added an extra dab of perfume to her wrist.

"A woman with a dachshund let me in. I was checking out the utility room when the elevator door opened." He closed the gap between them, his eyes steady on hers. "You look gorgeous tonight, Professor Grey."

Her lashes veiled her eyes as she cocked her head. "Back at 'cha, Detective Knight." A tiny tapping sound behind her brought a sigh. "Envelope came unstuck, didn't it?"

Catching her chin, Jacob gave her a quick kiss. "Gun," he said and, drawing his own, went to retrieve the fallen message.

"The envelope's white instead of red this time," Romana noted. "And the printing's different. It's—neater."

Jacob lifted the flap, removed the plain white card inside. Tilting it down with her gun barrel, Romana read,

I give you this gift, Romana Grey:
Warren Critch is not your only foe.
Fear more the person who did the deed.
Fear more still the madness in control…

The phone rang before she reached the security monitor. She picked up en route.

"It's me." Jacob's voice reached her over a static-filled line. "I'm stuck in traffic."

"And here I was complimenting you on your prompt arrival." She switched on the security monitor. "How long?"

"Twenty minutes. We'll be fashionably late."

"It never hurts to be—" Romana stared at the image on screen "—late." Icy fingers of dread skated down her spine. "Damn."

"What is it?"

"Nothing. Well, something, but you don't need to use your siren. Someone buzzed me just as you phoned."

"And?"

"There's no one in the lobby. All I see is an envelope taped to the wall. It might have my name on it." She finished the sentence with a sigh. "You're using the siren, aren't you?"

"Five minutes," he told her. "Don't leave your apartment."

SHE HELD OUT FOR THREE of those minutes, but when she heard old Mr. Hastings across the hall preparing to leave for his Saturday night poker game, she rushed out to intercept him.

"Oh, my, don't you look lovely, young Romanov." His blue eyes twinkled, and he tapped a gnarled finger to his cheek. "Give us a peck for luck. I've got sixteen grand and seven great-grandchildren to buy for this year."

"I'll do better than that." She gave him two quick kisses, hooked her arm through his. "I'll walk you down."

"Appreciate it. Cane gets tangled in my feet. Where are you off to tonight? Wedding?"

An eyebrow winged up. "In a black spaghetti-strap dress?"

"My great-granddaughter wears black everywhere she goes. Says it's the in thing. I say she looks like Morticia."

"Goth," Romana said and hoped the elevator would take its time arriving. "How old is she?"

"Thirteen."

"It's probably a look more than a mindset at that age." The door swished open, and with a subtle shift, she positioned herself in front of him.

Nothing and no one leaped out.

"So far, so good."

"Beg pardon?"

She smiled, loaded him in and managed to hit all the floor buttons while he steadied himself. "Your Tennessee roots are showing, Mr. Hastings. Cincinnatians say, 'Please.'"

"I say that when I ask someone to pass the salt." He swiveled his head back and forth as the door opened on the floor below. "Huh. Don't see anyone."

Romana glanced at the lighted panel. Would Critch be waiting in the lobby or, having delivered his message, would he have vanished into the darkness?

"You sure do look pretty tonight. You know, you should be married with children and far too busy to be helping an eighty-nine-year-old man to the curb."

He was ninety-seven by the lowest building estimate, and if Critch tried to hurt him, he wouldn't be walking upright for a very long time.

Three more floors, three more open doors, no more passengers.

"Must be a malfunction in the panel," Mr. Hastings decided. "I'll have a chat with the electrician."

Beside him, Romana watched the numbers. When the doors opened to an empty lobby, she breathed out and helped the old man over the ledge. Even so, he stumbled slightly. His

cane whacked the wall, and fell to the floor with a clatter. Which was probably why she missed the footsteps.

But she spied the shadow in her peripheral vision.

Tightening her grip on Mr. Hastings's arm, she whipped the gun she'd had hidden behind her back up and out to the side.

"One more step, Critch," she warned softly, "and you're a dead man."

Jacob believed her. Totally. He might have been able to disarm her since she was propping up an ancient man in a plaid overcoat, but he didn't want to test her.

Fortunately, he didn't have to. The moment she realized her mistake, she lowered the gun.

"You owe me five years, Knight."

He held his hands out to the sides, palms up. "I just came around the corner. You're the one with the gun."

She turned a dazzling smile on the old man. "Is your ride here, Mr. Hastings?"

He flapped a hand at the curb, couldn't seem to take his eyes off her. "I never knew you were armed, young Romanov, and I was a corpsman in World War Two. Could've used you back then for sure. You didn't even look at him, yet you pointed that gun of yours right between his eyes. Didn't she, young man?"

"Right between," Jacob agreed. He noticed the envelope taped to the wall across from the security monitor. There was no doorman in evidence tonight, so either the entrance lock had failed or someone had let Critch into the building.

Romana propelled the old man forward by his elbow. "Your taxi's waiting, Mr. Hastings. Win lots of gift mon—

She waited until the taxi door slammed before wh— confront Jacob.

"You scared the hell out of me. How did you ge—

Chapter Fourteen

"You have no idea who left the card." O'Keefe walked in measured lines within the confines of the party hall cloakroom. "Did you search the building?"

"Jacob did." Romana gave one of her spaghetti straps a twist to straighten it. "I knocked on doors for an hour with no luck."

"It had to be Belinda's murderer."

"Warning me to fear him more than Warren Critch? Calling him—or herself mad? Would you do that if you were a killer?"

"If I wanted my share of the attention and was, in fact, mad, I might."

"It could have come from Shera Barret."

"I know about the bribery attempt, Romana. Jacob filled me in earlier. You believe that James Barret murdered Belinda, and now Shera Barret is warning you to watch your step around him?"

"Or you could flip-flop that and theorize that Shera killed Belinda and James is warning me. Either scenario works."

"Not so much when you factor in the phone call to Canter and the attempted bribery."

"It still fits, Mick." Jacob came in, shaking snow from his hair. Romana wanted to sigh. He looked positively edible in a long black coat and European-cut black suit. His too-long hair and vaguely haunted features added a poetic air that had her fanning her face as she motioned them forward.

"We can hash this out later, gentlemen. Party's in full swing, and we need to make the rounds. Is anyone not here?" she asked O'Keefe.

"Only Fitz."

The pang that shot through her hurt more than any bullet. O'Keefe winced.

"Sorry. Not what I meant to say at all."

Jacob caught her hand, brought her fingers to his lips. "Let's dance."

Mingling would have been more productive, but Romana needed a moment to rebalance her emotions. And, while dancing with Jacob had its dangerous points, it was certainly no hardship.

They swayed to a Rod Stewart song, something nostalgic and quite lovely, under a canopy of darkness liberally sprinkled with silver fairy lights.

A fifteen-foot traditional tree took pride of place at one end of the hall. Other, more sculptural trees dotted the perimeter. Garland swagged out from a star-shaped center point, and everything from the linen-covered tables to the black-velvet chairs seemed to glitter.

Romana estimated that there were over two hundred people in attendance. Jacob guessed closer to three. Whatever the count, it would be a skeleton police crew, at best, minding the city that night.

Her ankle-length chiffon-over-silk dress floated as she danced. Her silver shoes had stiletto heels and were really more strap than substance. A pair of Grandma Grey's drop diamonds swung from her earlobes, and her own slim diamond bracelet slid up and down her arm whenever she moved.

Jacob fingered one of the earrings. "You really do look beautiful, but then I could say that about you any day or night."

"And I'd be okay with it." She kissed the corner of his mouth. "Any day or night."

"You did have that gun pointed right between my eyes, you know."

"Apparently, some points of training stick."

He eased her away from the center of the floor. "Why does the old man call you Romanov?"

"Because that's how his wife heard it when I introduced myself to her. She passed the mistake on to him. Two months later, she died. I've never had the heart to correct him." She gave his hand a light squeeze. "There's Patrick."

Jacob followed her gaze. "He's dancing with the new dispatcher."

Another pang forked through her heart. "She has red hair."

Jacob used his body to block the pair. "We don't have to be here."

"Yes, we do. But thank you." She saw a hand come down on his shoulder and offered a pleasant, "Hello, James."

Barret's practiced smile didn't waver under Jacob's sharp look. "You can't bring the best to the ball and not share, Detective. Shera's at the punch bowl if you're up for a challenge. But I should warn you, my wife's in a bit of a temper this evening."

Romana gave Jacob a barely perceptible headshake and James Barret her full attention as she drew him away.

"And so we dance again, Mr. Barret. I hear you were in Cleveland for a few days."

"We'll descend into business talk if I answer that question. I prefer a more festive topic. I trust the police are still tracking Warren Critch. Has there been any progress in the case?"

That was his idea of a festive topic? Interesting. "Not yet," she replied. "Although it's not so much a case as a manhunt."

"Somehow that sounds even more dangerous."

"Only for Jacob and me. The public's in no real danger." She hoped. "Tell me, exactly how well did you know Belinda Critch?"

"It always returns to business in the end."

"Did it ever leave?"

Although his smile remained, the gleam in his eyes became a diamond-hard glitter. "I met Belinda for the first time in Gilhoolie's Pub."

"Yes, I know that part. Let's fast-forward to the inscribed silver watch you gave her, date unknown."

"Ah, yes. I'd forgotten about the watch."

"When did you give it to her?"

"I don't remember."

Romana affixed what Fitz called her killer smile. "Try. Close will do. Was it shortly after Ben Brown's death?"

He studied her through half-closed eyes. "Should I be contacting my lawyer?"

To keep him amenable, she went with her heart. "You must know by now that Fitz is missing. I found the watch in her room."

He laughed and both gleam and smile returned full-force. "Bless her sticky little fingers. The woman's an artiste. Fine, then, yes, I did give Belinda the watch, shortly after my partner's funeral. She assisted in the autopsy, and at my request made certain that the procedure kept moving."

"You mean she put a rush on it."

"Yes."

"Why?"

"Because I needed Ben's money for a business transaction

into which I was about to enter. He would have backed me if he'd lived, but dying the way he did threw a very large, very awkward monkey wrench into the works."

"So you were thanking Belinda for getting her part of the job done quickly."

"Quickly and efficiently. There was no impropriety, on her part or mine."

"Then the secrets you referred to on the inside of the watch had nothing to do with your partner's death?"

He gnawed on his inner lip, regarded her with grudging admiration. "I think maybe you should have been a lawyer."

"Never know, I might get around to it. What secrets did you and Belinda share, James?"

"Off the record?"

"I'm not on the force anymore."

"Jacob Knight is. I repeat, off the record, and not to be passed on to my wife. Deal?"

"Deal."

"Belinda and I had an affair while I was engaged to Shera. It wasn't serious, and it didn't last. If she'd chosen to be vindictive, she could have gone to Shera and created all manner of problems. But she didn't. She walked away with no fuss and with no demands made. It was our secret, and we kept it. We remained friends after that—another surprise since I hadn't expected friendship from her. Marrying Warren didn't settle her in the least, but I do believe she loved him in her own way. I'm convinced she never wanted to see him hurt."

"And yet she had one affair after another."

"Meaningless flings. Strokes to an ego in serious need of repair. She came from a bad home. Drug-addicted mother, alcoholic father. Mother divorced, then remarried—another alcoholic, unfortunately. They had very little money between them and even less to give Belinda or her brother. As she got older, Belinda found she liked things. She discovered she could use her body to get them. It isn't a new story, Romana. Men were toys to her. With the possible exception of Warren Critch."

"What made him special?"

"What makes anyone special? A feeling."

Since she couldn't refute that, Romana let silence reign until the song played out.

When it did, James gave his shirt cuffs a habitual tug and squared his shoulders. "Time to brave the lioness. Remember, off the record. Now enjoy the rest of the evening."

"I guess that means no more dances," she said to his back. "Fitz would call me a fool."

"For what?" a man's cool voice inquired.

She accepted a glass of champagne from a passing server before swinging around. "Why, hello there, stranger. The last time I saw you, you were limping off to a change room. Bruises healed?"

Dylan regarded her without a trace of amusement. "Your cop partner's got a female cobra coiled around him. You think I have bruises, wait until Shera Barret goes in for the kill."

Romana smiled, unperturbed. "Cobras don't coil around their prey. Boa constrictors do, but then they're not venomous."

Dylan drank deeply from his glass of beer. "Did they give lessons on snake anatomy after I left the Academy?"

"No, that came from Mrs. Farrell, my high school science teacher." She took a provocative step toward him. "Speaking of science teachers, have you heard any more from your brother-in-law?"

He narrowed his eyes. "Are we at odds for some reason? As I recall, it was your friend Knight who had me in a choke-hold at the gym, not vice versa."

"Critch cut Jacob's brake line, then came after us at a Christmas tree farm with poison darts. He also took Fitz." She wavered a little. "Maybe."

Dylan's forehead furrowed. "Warren took Fitz? Why?"

Romana's laugh contained no humor. "Well, gee, Dylan, let me think. Possibly to get to me?"

He waved a hand in front of her face. "Hey, not Warren here, okay? Fitz has no part in this. It doesn't make sense that he'd take her."

"Meaning you really haven't had any contact with him?"

"Pretty sure I've been saying that all along."

"Then help me. Tell me who you think might have wanted Belinda dead. Besides Jacob."

"There is no 'besides Jacob.'"

"She wanted him to get her a restraining order. That was what their lunch entailed."

"So he says." He drank again, then scoffed. "A restraining order against who?"

"Excellent question. Been asked a thousand times with no answer so far. Was she frightened of anyone that you know of?"

"Men didn't frighten Belinda."

"Did women? One particular woman?"

"Fitz tended to annoy her. And I don't think she was crazy about female cops who resemble Ava Gardner."

Romana started to speak, but stopped. "Belinda thought I looked like Ava Gardner?"

"She wouldn't have given Connor a second glance otherwise."

Determined to remain unruffled, Romana sipped her champagne. "Didn't see that one coming. Good shot, Dylan. A bit low, but nothing I didn't already know." Her eyes fastened on his. "Did Shera Barret frighten Belinda?"

He blinked, clearly mystified. "Did they even know each other?"

"For a man who loved his sister, you don't know much about her."

"I know there wasn't a man in her life she cared about," he countered. "Except me and, later, Warren. Belinda did what she had to do to get the things she wanted. I understood that, and her. You see a female viper. I see a desperate little girl."

"And a boy who wanted to protect her."

"Belinda wasn't perfect, okay, she was simply like the rest of us. Screwed up and searching for something or someone who could make her happy."

"Apparently Warren didn't quite do that."

"He did in as much as anyone could." Dylan finished his beer. "Believe what you want to, Belinda wasn't the evil woman people make her out to be."

"I never thought of her as evil, but I wouldn't use the word *nice,* either. Screwed up I can accept because, as you say, who isn't, but one lunch followed by a phone call…" She trailed off, eyed him with consideration. "What do you know about that phone call?"

"What phone call?"

"The one Belinda placed after her lunch with Jacob. The one Patrick overheard."

"Sorry, no idea what you're talking about."

"And if you did, would you tell me?"

"Might. Might not."

Exasperation won out. "Honest to God, Dylan, you have such a pissy attitude. Innocent until proven guilty—remember that one?"

"I must have washed out before the Academy instructors got to it."

"Why can't you admit that you and Critch just might be wrong?"

"Because Belinda's dead, and Knight, the only man we know of who argued with her before she died, isn't." He ground his teeth, struggled for control. "Okay, look, I'm worked up. I'm sorry. I don't condone Warren's actions. We're not Third World here. Slashing brake lines, shooting poison darts…" He broke off. "What was in the darts?"

"Curare."

"Anyway, I agree Warren's going too far. He's not thinking, Romana. He's functioning on pure hatred."

"Yes, we kind of figured that." Watching him choke his empty glass while he searched for a server brought a head-shake. "Bar's over there." She paused, frowned at his suddenly shocked expression. "What is it?" Twisting her head, she saw Jacob talking to his captain and O'Keefe dancing with the red-haired dispatcher. "What are you…"

She spied him on her second scan of the crowd, a man wearing the black pants and a white jacket of a server. He had a full gray mustache and his equally gray hair was pulled back in a stubby ponytail. Glasses partially hid his eyes, but his face said it all. If Dylan was startled, the server was positively stricken.

Except he wasn't a server, and both Dylan and Romana knew it.

"Oh, man…" Dylan breathed, not moving. "He's lost it."

Romana's lungs burned, the crowd noise vanished, and time seemed to freeze—as she stared across the floor and straight into the eyes of Warren Critch.

"YOU'RE SURE IT WAS HIM?" O'Keefe endeavored to hold Romana back. "You couldn't be mistaken?"

"If I'm wrong, so was Dylan." Romana slapped at his re-straining hands. "Let go, Mick. He's not after me. He took off as soon as he realized I'd seen him."

O'Keefe trailed her through the increasingly curious crowd. "Which direction did he take?"

"Kitchen." She spotted Jacob near the door and made his back her goal. Until she crashed into a man so frail she had to grab both of his arms to keep him from pitching onto the floor.

"Dr. Gorman, I'm so sorry."

Long, clawlike fingers closed on her dress. He gave an owlish series of blinks before finally locating her face.

"Did someone die?" He patted the pockets of his dinner jacket.

"No." Jacob vanished through the door, and, resigned, Romana stilled the old man's thin hands. "Everyone's fine. O'Keefe?" she said through her teeth.

"Following. Gray hair and mustache, right?"

"Unless he ditches them."

"Dylan?"

"With Jacob. Go."

Dr. Gorman's mouth opened and closed like a codfish. "All this fuss and bother, and no one's dead? Officer Grey, isn't it?"

"Yes it is. I'm flattered you remember me." And more than a little surprised.

"I remember your rapscallion husband well enough." His lips compressed to a disapproving line. "Made a mockery of my department. Caught him signing my name to an incoming shipment of supplies once. Another time, he falsified a report that said a live man was dead. And signed my name—again. Or was that Belinda?"

Romana's gaze slid from the kitchen door to his wrinkled face. "Belinda signed your name on a report?"

He drew back as if slapped. "Did I say that? Oh, no, she wouldn't do that, not in her condition."

"Condition?" The skin on Romana's neck prickled. "What condition was that, Dr. Gorman?"

"The usual one," he replied with mounting impatience.

"Belinda was pregnant?"

"Never told me she was, but even I can tell blue from pink."

"Pink." Romana stared. "The test strip turned pink?"

"Three times, she said. She was holding the third one in her hand when I saw her outside the washroom. Pink." He blinked again, appeared to lose his train of thought. "Must mean she was going to have a girl."

Pink and blue strips of thought streaked through Romana's head. They moved so fast she couldn't hold on to them. But through the stream, one grisly fact emerged.

If Belinda Critch had, in fact, been pregnant when she died, she'd taken that secret to the grave.

Chapter Fifteen

At the head of the alley, Jacob slowed. He looked left and right, listened for several seconds, then shook his head. "He's gone."

Two other officers joined him. The female of the pair gave a thumbs-down. "I'd have done better in my regulation shoes, but with or without them, that guy's fast and slippery. Did Harris call it in?"

"He was on the phone when we left." Jacob combed the alley one last time, then motioned to the other two. "Go back to the hall and talk to the caterers. One of them might have seen him skulking around."

"I can't believe he'd take a risk like that." Still bent over, Dylan wiped a bead of sweat from his upper lip. "That was a suicide mission, infiltrating a police party. And for what?"

"Not the canapés, that's for sure." Pulling out his cell phone, Jacob punched in the captain's number. When he ended the call, Dylan stared in disbelief.

"You actually think he'd want to hurt all those people? Those cops?"

"Doesn't matter what I think. The hall needs to be evacuated and searched."

"Merry Christmas, everyone."

"Can you walk?"

Disdain marred Dylan's features. "Yes, I can walk. But I can't run ten blocks flat out and not be winded. Neither can Warren."

"Unless he's been working out."

"Well, that wouldn't be the Warren Critch I knew, but then he backed down from Romana six years ago, and he's sure as hell done an about-face in that regard." Dylan swept an arm around the network of snow-encrusted alleys. "We missed him, Knight. He jumped into a Dumpster or scuttled up a fire escape. I still think you're out in left field, though, thinking he'd blow up a roomful of cops. Assuming he even knows how to construct a bomb."

"Internet's full of information, Hoag."

"And you figure, wherever he's holed up, that Warren's online? Man, what is it with you and Romana? He doesn't want to make a statement to the world—'Hey, look at me! I'm a raving lunatic who likes to kill people.' He wants you and Romana to pay for what he seriously believes you did."

"And then?"

Dylan popped apart his fingers. "Like I said before, *poof.* So long U.S. of A., hello Amazon hideaway. You won't catch him once he's out of the country."

"Probably true." Jacob took a final look around. "But he's a long way from out right now. And I'm a long way from finished searching for him."

WARREN CRITCH STUMBLED INTO his basement room, slammed the door, locked it and backed across the floor to the window. He snaked a hand under the blinds to make sure he'd locked them, too, then dropped onto a hard chair and fought for calm.

No fists banged on his door. No knuckles tapped on his windows. The panic of flight began to subside. He'd be fine, just had to get through a few more days, then he'd be high above the clouds, soaring off to his new life.

He shouldn't have gone to the party tonight. Cops were adept at seeing through disguises. Better to have saved this one for his escape.

But the voice in his head had been pushing him hard lately. It pushed him even now.

Still struggling for composure, he stripped away the gray mustache and wig, peeled the sideburns from his cheeks and ordered himself to empty his mind. Keep it blank. Keep control.

Then he looked down at the table and spied the sprig of mistletoe.

"Romana, slow down." Jacob set his hands on her shoulders to keep her in place. "Start again, and go through it slowly. Pretend I'm just learning to speak English."

She made a frustrated sound but stopped talking and sucked in a deep breath.

It was Sunday afternoon, and they were in Jacob's apartment above the theater. Snow had been falling since dawn from clouds more forbidding than his captain's face when they'd discovered two pipe bombs buried inside a pair of trash cans at Rushton Hall.

He and Harris had been on the streets ever since.

Finding Romana waiting for him when he'd arrived home had been a welcome sight at first. Then he'd looked closer and realized she'd been ready to deck him.

"Fifteen hours," she repeated now. "You've been on the hunt and virtually incommunicado, for more than half a day."

"Romana, I'm here. I'm listening."

She glared at him, then gave in and sighed. "You look too damn good. I can't think when I'm this tired."

He tipped up her chin. "Did you get any sleep last night?"

"No, but I ate, which is probably more than you did. Did O'Keefe ever catch up with you?"

"No, why?"

"Because I told him what I discovered, and if you'd seen him, he would have told you, and I wouldn't have to go through it all again. Which I will." She held up a forestalling hand. "I just need one more minute, okay? You can't spend fifteen hours being annoyed and not feel like kicking something when you're done."

He covered a flicker of amusement. "Are you done, then?"

"Yes." She *whooshed* out one last breath. "Yes. Okay, I'll keep it simple. Point number one, Belinda and James Barret did in fact have an affair. It was one of the secrets he referred to in the inscription on the watch he gave her. Point number two, he gave her the watch because she rushed his partner's autopsy through to its conclusion." At his doubtful stare, she smiled. "I know. Thought of it myself. We can verify the legitimacy of the results later and should, because, point number three, Dr. Gorman claims that Connor, and possibly Belinda as well, faked his signature on some of the medical shipment and autopsy reports."

Jacob rubbed his thumbs in circles on her shoulders. "You realize if that last thing gets out, your ex's crimes are going to hit the gossip fan all over again."

"Doesn't matter. I want Fitz back. A bit of emotional discomfort will be nothing if we can make that happen. Which brings me to point number four. The pink strip."

It took Jacob a moment to clue in. When he did, his insides turned to liquid. "Pink—as in pregnant?"

"Yes, pregnant, but no, not me, so you can wipe that shocked look off your face and let me finish. Except that now

I just want to laugh, and that's totally inappropriate, so I must be even more tired than I realized."

"Second that." Jacob dropped his forehead onto hers. "Okay, whose strip turned…" His head came up. "Belinda's?"

"So says Dr. Gorman. Now I'll admit, he has lapses, and he's the only person I know who can nod off in the middle of a party hall evacuation, but he was very definite about it, Jacob. He said he found Belinda outside the women's washroom holding a pink strip and staring at it as if she'd never seen the color before."

Something clicked in Jacob's head. He glanced around the apartment. "I have the police report."

"Here?" She bunched the front of his T-shirt in excited fists. "You have it here?"

"Somewhere."

"Figures."

It took twenty minutes to unearth the folder, and in the end it was Romana who thought to look in the fridge.

"Six brothers, sixth sense." She handed it to him. "I need coffee. You read, I'll brew."

"No, don't." He caught her wrist before she could move. "Get your coat and boots."

"You want to go out for coffee?"

"I want to go to the forensics lab."

She used her forefinger to lower the folder. "Let me guess, there's no mention of a pregnancy."

He slapped the file closed. "There's no autopsy report."

He went through the papers three times. They were all in order. All false, but they'd work. The people who created these things were among the best in the business.

Warren Critch would be a ghost after today. From the ashes

of his life would emerge one Willem Cortez, scientist of no particular note, traveling to Venezuela to study the feathered fauna of the Amazon rain forest.

Oh, yes, everything was in order—with one very large exception. Romana Grey and Jacob Knight were still alive.

He stripped mistletoe leaves from a long sprig and let them fall willy-nilly onto the pictures in front of him. With a crimson paint pen, he drew in pools of blood. As a morbid amusement, he made droplets spurt from the holes in their chests.

The order remained the same. Romana would die first, Jacob second. One bullet apiece, fired from a gun exactly like the one that should have killed Jacob six years ago.

He squeezed the pen hard between his fingers, felt laughter surge into his throat. He couldn't stop it, couldn't hope to contain it. It emerged in a watery blast…

That sounded dangerously close to a sob.

"GOOD MORNING, DETEC—TIVE."

The morgue attendant Jacob jostled past stared after him in confusion.

"He hasn't eaten today," Romana explained. She raised her voice. "Left, Jacob, turn left for Path Lab Records."

The automatic door clanged shut before she could get inside and, being carded, merely blinked red at her when she turned the handle.

"Always the gentleman." Setting her elbow high on the frame, she crossed her feet at the ankles, knocked and waited. When the door opened, he pulled her inside, turned her to the right and said simply, "Find the *C*s."

It was all on computer, of course, but the original hand-signed reports were methodically boxed and filed. As Romana swept her gaze over row upon row of metal containers, a chill rippled across her skin. Were there really this many dead people in the city's cemeteries?

"God, it's a creepy world down here."

Jacob brushed past her, his eyes on the upper shelves. "It's a quieter one than the world up there."

"Nothing morbid about that thought." She skimmed a finger over the labeled fronts. "You need to spend a few hours playing air hockey with my nephews. You'll crave silence when you're done, but it won't be the silence of death."

"You're assuming I'm good with kids."

She smiled, kept skimming. "You would be. It's all down to exposure and practice. And not minding jam fingers in your hair… *CRIS* to *CRIV.* It's here."

Jacob levered the box down so she could leaf through the files. She paused partway. "Mary Cristleman? I went to high school with her. My God, she died five years ago."

"Romana…"

"I can read, flick and have a memory at the same time." She continued to page forward. "Here it is. Critch, Belinda." Extracting the folder, she opened it and scanned. "Okay, well, Dr. Gorman signed it—or so it would seem."

"We'll take it to the police lab for verification. Is there anything down here you know for sure Gorman signed?"

"Unfortunately, yes." She pressed the folder into his stomach. "Connor's termination papers. I was here when Gorman pink-slipped him. The forms will be in the human resources section."

Fifteen minutes later, and in possession of both files, they returned to Jacob's vehicle and headed for the station. Romana held the signatures up side by side in front of her. "They look identical to me, or close enough in terms of pressure points and loops that I can't see a difference."

"What, are you a handwriting expert now, Professor Grey?"

"No, just observant. If one was a carbon copy of the other, I'd be suspicious, but these are both similar and different enough to be genuine."

"Sounds like you've done a little forgery in your life."

Her smile was completely false. "High school physics was a tough subject, and Grandma Grey frowned on anything less than an A."

"You doctored your report cards?"

"You don't need to look so shocked. I didn't touch the originals. I made new ones, and made Grandma Grey very happy. On the down side, I never understood the significance of the ripple tank."

"Water moves outward in mathematically aligned waves. End of lesson." He squinted through the windshield at the blowing snow. "What's the time difference between Connor's termination and Belinda's death?"

"I knew you were going to ask that." She straightened the files on her lap. "Six months. Belinda died first."

"Who was the assist on the autopsy?"

"I hate you."

His lips moved, and he reached a hand toward the folder. "Who, Romana?"

Could you hate a man and love him at the same time? Right now it seemed entirely possible.

"You know you're only postponing the inevitable, don't you?"

"I know. Still tired here." But she made herself reopen the file. "Oh." Surprise washed through her. "Not Connor. That's good." She frowned. "I think."

"Patrick?"

"Well, I see a *P* and an *N* and a bunch of squiggly things in between, so I'd guess Patrick."

"Okay, let's run with that for a minute."

"Snow's getting heavier, Knight. I'll run, you watch the road." Bracing a foot on the dash, she studied the signatures. "Let's say Gorman had begun signing reports without actually reading them—age, apathy, routine. Patrick does the autopsy, Gorman takes a nap. Gorman wakes up, signs off. Second scenario, Gorman does the autopsy, forgets about the pink strip and misses the pregnancy."

"While Patrick is doing what?"

"Well, being upset about Belinda, I imagine." Leaning over, she set a hand on his chest. "Think with your heart, Detective."

"Any other scenario?"

"Barret—Mr. or Mrs.—pays one or both doctors—more likely Patrick—to overlook certain details."

The trace of a smile appeared. "That's thinking with your heart."

"Heart, wallet, how do we know where Patrick's priorities lie? But I'll go with the heart for now, because unrequited love has to sting just a little."

"You're getting muddled, aren't you?"

"Very." A cell phone rang, and Romana glanced around. "You or me?"

A female voice emerged from the dashboard speaker. "Phone's yours. Radio's mine."

She pulled out her cell, read the screen and covered her ear while Jacob fielded the incoming police call beside her. "O'Keefe, hi… Sorry, what? There's a lot of interference."

"Where are you?" he shouted from the other end.

She wiped steam from the window. "On Main, a few blocks north of Fountain Square, I think. I can't read the street signs."

"Well tell Jacob to hang a right and get over to Hyde Park."

"Mick, we've got Belinda's autopsy report…"

But he cut her off. "One of our patrols responded to a call about an injured woman. It's Fitz, Romana. Your cousin's been found. She's alive."

Chapter Sixteen

Romana swore time stopped while they worked their way across the river, but in reality, it probably took less than fifteen minutes to reach their destination.

Jacob's radio call from the station had carried the same message. An injured woman matching Fitz's description had been discovered in the back of a bakery truck on the edge of Hyde Park.

Romana spied the truck's outline through the snow. It was a large cube van with a happy-faced loaf of bread wearing a seasonal Santa hat painted on the side. She bolted from her seat almost before Jacob stopped.

"Let her go," he called to the patrol officers.

"Fitz?" Romana hoisted herself into the back, knelt beside the rookie in attendance. "How bad?"

"I think she has a concussion. Her shoulder's been cut, and she's suffering from exposure. She lost a fair amount of blood, which is probably why she's so pale. Her pulse is thready, but regular. Sorry, that's the best I can do. Paramedics should be here soon. Traffic's a bitch with all this snow."

Romana touched Fitz's cheek. It felt dangerously cold.

The van's springs gave slightly as Jacob and a second

officer climbed in. Jacob crouched beside her. "How is she?"

"Unconscious, but alive."

"She was carrying a knife, sir," the rookie said.

"Boning knife," the older one elaborated. "Blood all over it, and her. The driver's having kittens. Swears he didn't know she was here until he started to unload the flat to our left. My guess is, she was running, saw the truck, hopped in and hid. Must've passed out afterward. I've got the route, but the guy's made about thirty stops since this morning, so there's no telling how long she's been here. He covered her up and called it in as soon as he found her. I recognized her from the picture you and O'Keefe circulated."

Blood had seeped through the gray wool blanket, but Romana thought it might be coming from Fitz's clothes as she and they warmed up.

The older man gave the blanket a tug. "You can look if you like. She's already been moved. The driver couldn't get to her where she was holed up."

Jacob glanced at the flats. "Where was that?"

"Show you."

Jacob set a hand on Romana's nape and his mouth next to her ear. "She's strong, Romana. She'll make it."

"I know." As carefully as she could, Romana drew the blanket back.

"She's not wearing much," the rookie noted. "But at least the sweatshirt's big. Comes down way over her hips and hands."

"Yes it does." Fingering the fabric, Romana reached under Fitz's good shoulder and eased the blanket completely free.

The rookie officer shifted his weight. "Shouldn't you leave her covered?"

But Romana was diverted by the printing on the front of the sweatshirt. "University…" Careful not to disturb Fitz, she worked the blanket back a bit farther until the final word was exposed. "Oh, damn. Jacob?"

"What is it?" He appeared behind her.

"This isn't Fitz's sweatshirt. It's huge, plus she hates college logos. She thinks they're snotty."

"Are you sure?"

"Absolutely. She didn't go to college, and if she had, she wouldn't have gone to one in Houston." Romana's eyes sparked with the memory of a recent conversation. "But I might know a man who did."

Jacob made no attempt to stop her from coming with him. He knew he should have, but truthfully, he wanted her where he could see her. Plus she'd had excellent aim with groin kicks. More than one Academy instructor who'd cockily told her to go for it had wound up writhing on the gym floor.

He cast her a sideways look as he maneuvered his SUV through the icy streets of Eden Park toward Patrick North's home. "He might not have gone to college in Texas, Romana."

She tucked her hair behind her ears, pulled on her hat. "He told me about his family in Houston when I talked to him in the park. Is O'Keefe meeting us there?"

"If he can. The snow's causing accidents all over the city."

"Don't you just love December?" She rapped her fists on her knees. "Patrick loved Belinda, he told me that. Love spawns jealousy, which can spawn hatred and rage." Her brow knit. "He never struck me as a rager. Can you hide a thing like that?"

"Some people can. Left or right?"

She double-checked the address. "Turn toward the river."

And lose the siren, he decided, switching it off. "Ten minutes," he promised and linked his fingers with hers. "Don't worry, we'll get him."

"One way or another," she agreed. Then her eyes went wide and she sucked in a sharp breath.

He glimpsed it in his peripheral vision, a blue minivan sliding through the intersection at a forty-five-degree angle, out of control on the ice and heading directly for Romana's side of the vehicle.

THE DOORBELL RANG. AND RANG. And rang. Patrick would have shot the thing, but he didn't want to alert his neighbors to anything suspicious.

He tossed clothes in a suitcase. He'd lost too much time after Fitz had blindsided him. He thought he might have stabbed her. There'd been blood on the kitchen floor when he'd woken up, but was it hers or his? God knew, she'd succeeded in sticking him more than once.

Nothing life threatening, though. He'd deal with his wounds and worry about recovering once he was out of the city.

If only the damn doorbell would shut up.

He peeked through the upstairs window. There were no cars at the curb, no police lights flashing. Maybe it was the busybody woman next door, bringing him the fruitcake she'd insisted on delivering.

Okay, she could be trouble. Her brother was a retired State Trooper. Not good, and not worth the risk of ignoring. He dragged on a bathrobe, checked for blood in the mirror and went downstairs.

To his annoyance, the peephole showed a man. He started to turn away, but stopped, spun and shoved his eye back up to the hole.

Sweat coated his palms. No way. Not him, too. First Fitz had shown up—although she hadn't actually figured out the truth so much as blundered in and caught him off guard—and now a second person.

This man *had* figured it out, though. *Look at his face.* Features set, mouth grim. He knew. He knew, and he wasn't about to go away. Not with Patrick's car sitting in the driveway and half the house lights burning.

Be calm, he ordered himself, then panicked and ran for his gun. Magazine snapped in place, hands steady, robe belted tight, he inhaled, turned the knob and opened the door.

The visitor kept his right hand in his coat pocket. Patrick kept his in his robe. Who'd be the faster draw, he wondered?

The man startled him by shouldering roughly past. "I need to talk to you, North. About Belinda."

He withdrew his empty right hand. Patrick's lashes fell slightly, but he kept his finger on the hidden trigger.

"I'm in a bit of a hurry, actually."

"This won't take long."

Bullets never did. But they made noise, and the busybody's grandson was outside shoveling her driveway.

Patrick nodded forward. "Kitchen's at the back of the house."

His visitor grunted. "I'm starting to think maybe Jacob Knight didn't murder Belinda, after all."

"Really." Patrick motioned again. "Kitchen, straight ahead. I'm right behind you."

"We don't need to sit for this."

Muscles taut as piano wire, Patrick pulled his gun. "I think we do, Warren. Turn, walk and don't try to be clever." He twitched his injured left arm, pictured Fitz's face as she'd launched herself at him. His lips thinned. "Just trust me when I tell you I'm in one hell of a crappy mood right now."

"WE'RE ONLY GUESSING, ROMANA. Maybe North's guilty, maybe he isn't." Catching her chin, Jacob gave her a hard kiss. "Stay behind me, and don't offer him a target."

Romana's knees were still wobbly from the near miss at the intersection. Even twenty minutes later and recreating the incident in her head, she didn't know how Jacob had avoided a collision with the minivan, because all the driver had done was cover his face and plow his foot down hard on the brakes.

Looking up and around, Jacob murmured, "I don't see any lights. He could be gone."

Romana pictured Fitz's blood on the too-large college sweatshirt she'd been wearing. University of Houston. Patrick had been born in Houston. He'd admitted to being in love with Belinda. He'd also said she hadn't loved him back.

The door swung inward when Jacob tried the knob. "On three," he told her.

Romana angled her gun skyward and waited through the count.

No sound came from inside, only the sickly creak of hinges as the door rocked in the gusting wind.

Jacob swung into the foyer, made a half circle with his gun. Still nothing moved, and no sound emerged.

Was it a trap? Romana wished for light, but knew it was better this way. While darkness might hide Patrick, it also concealed their presence.

The college logo flashed like a neon sign in her head. Her conversation in the park echoed and overlapped. A sensation akin to hysteria tickled her chest. She could deal with that, but with the memory of Fitz, bloody and pale as death, not so much.

Five feet into the foyer, Romana detected a soft scrape. When she tapped Jacob's arm, he nodded.

"Back there."

She made out a doorway, black and imposing, twenty feet ahead, possibly a portal to death. But only if Patrick was lying in wait. On the other hand, if the knife Fitz had been clutching had hit its mark, the portal might simply lead them to a corpse.

"I smell food," she whispered. "Old grease, chili spices, green peppers."

"Blood," Jacob added.

"I was trying not to notice that."

"I know. Ready?"

"As I'll ever be." She double-handed her gun. When he kicked the door and hit the switch, she mirrored his swing across the threshold—and felt her stomach roll. "God, I hope some of this is chili sauce."

Jacob straightened. "Probably most of it is." He held out a hand to hold her back. "Cover me, okay? I want to see what's behind the table."

She took note of a long chain with a pair of handcuffs fastened to the end. The cuffs, a sleek, glossy black, were covered with spikes and looked totally kinky.

When Jacob swore, she forgot the cuffs and snapped her gun down. "Something?"

"It's Critch."

Shock led the emotional parade, with disbelief close on its heels. "Critch? Here? In Patrick's house? Why?" Then she shook herself and skirted the table leg. "Is he alive?"

"Barely."

Jacob shoved his gun into his waistband. Romana kept hers out as she reached into her pocket for her cell phone.

"Ambulance is coming," she said, a minute later. "Was he shot or stabbed?"

"Shot in the stomach."

Within the shadows to their left, a sudden flurry of footsteps erupted. A split second later, a round of bullets discharged. Before Jacob shoved her head down, Romana spied
Patrick's bone-white face framed by a door in the corner.

It had to be the basement door. She smelled the mold and
mildew of a damp cellar. He must have run down there when
they'd come in.

He stumbled toward the front of the house, firing blindly.
His teeth were bared in a grimace, and the ratty bathrobe he
wore had come untied. The belt dragged along behind him.
Twin smears of blood stained his T-shirt with other, smaller
spatters circling them.

"Stay with Critch," Jacob told her.

"Jacob, I'm not going to sit and—" but he was gone before
she finished "—do nothing," she said to the air in his wake.

She started to stand and would have gone after him if
Critch's fingers hadn't clamped like steel talons around her
wrist. She let out a quick hiss of surprise before he yanked
her back down—with far more strength than she would have
anticipated.

"It was North," he managed to whisper. "North killed her."

"Yes, I know." Romana pried ineffectively on his fingers.
"Critch, you're not helping here. Jacob's gone after Patrick
alone. If anything happens…" She set her teeth, rephrased.
"He needs backup."

The faintest of smiles played on Critch's lips. "Not Knight.
Damn good cop alone. He let me catch him—in the alley—
just stood there and let me point my gun at him. Didn't fight
back, only spoke a few words. That had to mean I was right,
didn't it?"

Romana considered striking his hand with the butt end of
her gun, but she couldn't bring herself to do it. "Let go." Even

using her fingernails, she couldn't pry her wrist free. "I don't care how good a cop Jacob is, Patrick's unstable, and that makes him doubly dangerous."

"Tell me about it." A wet laugh gurgled up. She glanced at the door, then back down at his sweat-pearled face. "Damn you." Snatching a wad of paper napkins from the table, she pressed them to his stomach. "Why are you here?"

"Came to talk. North worked with Belinda. Thought he might know something."

"About what?"

"I was so sure." Critch's eyelids fluttered. "So damn sure Knight did it. Had to be him. Had to be…"

She kept a firm pressure on his stomach. "Didn't you ever think it might be someone else?"

He stared up at the ceiling now instead of at her. "Not at first. But after a while, it didn't seem so cut-and-dried anymore. You spend time alone. You want it one way, but you start to doubt. Seeds blow around, get into your head. Mine were slow to take root, but time passed and…" He faded out.

"Critch!" Romana used a seat cushion to elevate his head. "Stay with me here. Did you have any idea what you were walking into tonight?"

He gave another burbling laugh. "Hell, no. Thought he might know something is all. People talk to coworkers. Pulled a gun before I even asked the question. No need for talk after that."

"Did he tell you he murdered her?"

"Think so. Doesn't matter. Truth's out now."

"It would have been nice if you'd gone looking for it a bit sooner." She slapped his cheeks lightly to keep him conscious. "Come on, Critch. You're tougher than a little bullet."

But his eyes rolled back in his head, and his jaw went lax.

Outside, sirens wailed, both police and ambulance. Blood saturated the napkins and Critch's breathing grew shallow.

Romana bent closer. "Critch, can you hear me?"

"Really cold," he rasped.

"The paramedics are almost here. Just hang on, okay? Two more minutes."

"You should want me dead."

Did she? In spite of everything, Romana couldn't wish for that. "You loved Belinda," she said. "Love isn't always logical. Mostly isn't logical," she amended and battled a shudder when she envisioned Jacob chasing down an injured killer. "Maybe a lot of us would snap under similar circumstances."

Boots and wheels clattered into the foyer. "Back here," she called to the rescue team. "Straight ahead, in the kitchen."

Removing the sodden wad of napkins from Critch's stomach, she pushed upright and reached for her gun. "You'll be fine, Warren. Just keep breathing."

The paramedics rolled a stretcher through the door. Romana backed up to make room. But Critch's body gave a violent jerk, and once again, he snared her wrist.

"Critch, I have to move."

"You don't know," he whispered. "The cards. I wasn't sure at first, but every year, cards, threats."

"Yes, I know. We got the Christmas cards, all six of them."

"I didn't want to see, or care. Really didn't."

"You need to give us space," the paramedic growled. He looked big, mean and menacing.

"Trying to." She twisted on her wrist. "It's like he's got hooks on his fingers."

Mean and Menacing offered an unexpected grin as he hunkered down beside her. "They get strong sometimes when they think they might be heading for the tunnel. Maybe they figure holding on to someone will keep them from being sucked in."

"Either that or they want company on the journey. Critch." She tugged harder. "Critch, these people can't help you unless I'm out of the way."

The eyes that rolled back in his skull popped open to stare into hers. His breath rattled out. With his other hand, he made a grab for her coat. "Listen to me, Romana. The cards... I only sent four."

Chapter Seventeen

If there was a blood trail, Jacob couldn't find it in the snow and the dark, but he heard the occasional bang as Patrick clambered over a fence or careened into an unlit Christmas display.

North knew the area. Jacob had to rely on instinct.

He heard the ambulance a short distance away, police cruisers perhaps a mile behind. Their wails rose and fell at the whim of a frigid northerly wind.

He suspected North was circling. Where to? Back to his car? To Romana?

Using the boulevard trees as cover, Jacob squinted through the snow. His hands were numb from the cold, but otherwise he was dressed for this. North wasn't. Combine that with blood loss, and he should be tripping over the guy's frozen body any time now.

He picked up movement ahead and worked himself around the trunk of the tree. No doubt about it, they'd wound a path back to ground zero.

Another movement caught his eye. Checking left and right, he ran for the next tree. And the next.

An outline took shape. Something thudded at the rear of North's garage, but Jacob remained focused on his quarry.

The outline darted sideways at the noise. Jacob followed. When the man slipped, he had him. He brought his gun down and shouted. "Toss the gun, North. Hands in my sight."

The hands went up as ordered. Slowly, the outline turned. Jacob's arms dropped and, with a curse, he closed the gap.

"Well, goddammit, O'Keefe. Where did you come from?"

O'Keefe lowered his arms. "Man, I thought you were going to shoot. I was right behind the paramedics."

Jacob scoped the area. "Where's Romana?"

"I didn't see her. I heard someone breathing hard before I went inside, so I followed the sound. Lost it after a few minutes. Have you been tailing me?"

"Did you flatten a wooden Frosty six or seven houses ago?"

"I flattened something fat and hard."

"Then I've been tailing you."

"Any idea where he went?"

Jacob started across the street. "Not to his car. It's boxed in by yours."

"Score one for me." O'Keefe blew into his free hand. "If North's out in this, he'll be a Popsicle in ten minutes."

"He's probably holed up in a neighbor's garage." Or his own, Jacob reflected.

However, a quick inspection of the structure revealed no sign of Patrick and no place he could conceal himself inside.

O'Keefe returned to his car to contact the captain. Jacob set his sights on the house. His biggest priority at the moment was to find Romana.

Wind buffeted him as he jogged toward the front porch. When he reached it, he saw a stout, wooly bear gesturing at a taller, calmer silhouette who was endeavoring to quiet it.

Sentence fragments reached him. Jacob took the stairs two at a time.

"I know what I heard," the female bear insisted. "And where the shots came from. I called the police straight away."

Shoving his gun into the top of his jeans, Jacob opened his jacket and showed her the badge clipped to his belt loop.

The relief on Romana's face was a palpable thing, but whether it was the result of seeing him safe or at being interrupted, he wasn't sure.

Go with the heart, he decided.

"Are you a neighbor?" he asked the woman.

A round, lined face peered up at him. She pointed with a mittened hand. "I live over there. Heard gunshots, thought Patrick might have been hurt by a burglar. Unless he's working, he's not usually out and about at night."

"Keeps to himself, does he?" Jacob asked while Romana leaned on the railing and took what was probably a well-deserved rest.

"I've tried to be neighborly." The woman sniffed. "Offered to bring him a homemade fruitcake. He said he'd take it. No 'thank you,' just a flat, he'd take it. I told my husband I thought he was a strange one. Spends half the nights he's home up on the third floor doing heaven knows what. Attic light shines right in our bedroom window. We had to buy blackout blinds so we could sleep. My husband figures Patrick being a doctor and all, he might be going over patient files. I have to remind him that the man's a doctor for dead people, and you can't bring that kind of work home with you. Not unless you're a ghoul."

Romana arched meaningful eyebrows at Jacob and glanced upward. He nodded, took the woman by her wooly upper arms and shuffled her gently toward the stairs.

"Do me a favor, Mrs…"

"Brenner. Kate Brenner. My husband's Peter Brenner, of Brenner's Plumbing and Electric."

"Mrs. Brenner," Jacob interrupted before she could rev up. "I need you to go back to your house and watch for anyone or anything suspicious. If you see Patrick North, call my cell phone." He dug a card from his back pocket.

"Where'll you be?" she demanded.

"Locking up Mr. North's place."

"So that wasn't him went out of here on a stretcher?"

Jacob looked at Romana.

She smiled and shrugged. "Hey, I'm just an unpaid by-stander with no information to impart. Except that the guy on the stretcher was alive when he left here."

"Go home, Mrs. Brenner," Jacob repeated. "This is a police matter. We'll deal with it."

She wanted to object but the expression on his face stopped her. With his card crumpled in her fist, she toddled down the stairs, across the snowy yard and out of sight.

"Thanks for the help, Professor." Jacob started toward her, his eyes dark and focused. "What cat stole your tongue all of a sudden?"

The last word pretty much died when, with a lightning-quick move, she reached out, snatched up the sides of his jacket and yanked his mouth onto hers.

THE KISS WAS GREAT, exactly what Romana needed to blow the negative energy out of her system. Jacob was safe. Finally, she could function without the oppressive weight of fear crushing her thoughts.

It hardly surprised her that Patrick had escaped—if you could call being on the run wearing nothing but a bathrobe, T-shirt and jeans an escape. The temperature had to be below twenty degrees by now, so unless he knew of a refuge nearby, he wouldn't be running for long.

With O'Keefe still making calls in his car, she and Jacob mounted the stairs to the attic.

Romana didn't know what she expected to find there, but it wasn't the sight that greeted her when they opened the door.

"Oh…wow!" She held the snow-dampened hair from her eyes, pivoted slowly in the center of Patrick's attic. "This is—well, sick."

He'd pinned photographs of Belinda, scores of them, to the walls. Many were life sized. All of them were lewd.

Looking up, Romana spied a larger-than-life shot of an impossibly contorted Belinda Critch peering down at her from the ceiling. "My God, how did she get into that position?"

"She was double-jointed."

With her gaze fastened to the ceiling, she traced the serpentine coil of Belinda's body with a curious finger. "That's more than double-jointed, Jacob, that's a woman with no bones." She continued to stare, fascinated and repulsed at the same time. "Did you know she could do that?"

A smile that looked suspiciously like a tease appeared as Jacob sifted through snapshots on a rickety table. "I knew she was flexible…."

"Okay, people." O'Keefe pushed through the door. "I just got off the phone with Harris and… Holy—whoa. What's all this?" His jaw dropped. "Man, oh, man, this guy is one sick puppy."

"Tell us about it," Romana murmured.

His phone rang, and still shaking his head, he stepped onto the landing to answer it.

Romana studied a montage of nude body parts. "Handcuffs with spikes," she noted, and ran her finger over the shiny chain. Her stomach pitched. "You don't think he—no, he wouldn't. Would he?"

"Hurt Fitz?" Jacob came up behind her, rubbed her arms

through her coat and kissed her hair. "I doubt it. He was obsessed with Belinda. They're together in at least half of these shots, so obviously they had an affair."

"Unless he's a computer whiz, and he created the photos. His own virtual reality."

"Always a possibility."

She pressed herself into him, absorbed his warmth and strength. "I knew he loved her, knew it but didn't take it any further than that. So was it Patrick who frightened Belinda to the point that she wanted a restraining order?"

"Answer's probably yes." O'Keefe came back through the door, pocketing his phone. He shook his head one last time at the photographic wallpaper. "Man, oh man, what some minds can do. That was Harris. Patrick North's been picked up. He hailed a taxi three blocks from here."

"The driver let him get in?" Romana was incredulous. "I'd have gunned it in the opposite direction."

"The guy's been driving for thirty years, probably seen it all. He got a message through to headquarters. Two patrols intercepted his car. North's being transported to a well-guarded hospital room. Apparently, he's decided that everyone in the world knows he murdered Belinda. First Fitz showed up on his doorstep, then after she got away, Critch appeared. Finally, you two descended on him."

"Critch said he had no idea Patrick and Belinda were involved," Romana recalled. "He came to find out if Belinda had mentioned being afraid of or worried about someone other than Jacob. He said that lately he'd been starting to wonder if he might not be wrong about who killed her."

Wrapping his forearm lightly around her neck, Jacob leaned over to ask, "Did he define *lately?* This is Sunday night, Romana. Twenty-four hours ago, he showed up disguised as a caterer at a Christmas party and left two pipe bombs behind when he took off."

"Hey, we didn't get into time frames, and I have to tell you, he threw me totally when he admitted that maybe he'd been wrong about you. Of all the things I expected him to say, that was pretty much at the bottom of the list. Except..." Another memory slipped in and brought her eyebrows together. "He mentioned the Christmas cards. Not once but a couple times."

Making a final sweep of the walls, Jacob motioned to O'Keefe and ushered Romana from the room. "Don't tell me he apologized for sending them."

A knot of dread unfurled in Romana's stomach. "No, he didn't do that." She brought her head around to meet Jacob's eyes. "But before he passed out, he told me he sent only four of the six we received."

"HE WAS JERKING YOUR CHAIN," O'Keefe maintained while they sealed the doors and windows of Patrick's house. "You're believing him too easily, Romana. The guy's barely clinging to life. He was probably hallucinating, floating somewhere between fantasy and reality."

He hadn't been floating when he'd grabbed her wrist, of that Romana was certain. But had he been telling the truth?

That was the question that haunted her—at least it did until they reached the hospital.

Jacob waited in the corridor while she visited her cousin. When she emerged, he pushed off from the wall. "Give me some good news."

"Okay. Her dad's with her now. She hasn't regained consciousness yet, but her pulse rate and blood count are both up."

"How's her shoulder?"

"The stab wound's deep, but so far it doesn't appear any nerves were severed." Because he looked as exhausted as she felt, Romana hooked her arms around his neck and gave him a nice long kiss. "It's all good, Detective. Fitz is going to be fine, and the clouds that were hanging over that gorgeous head of yours are gone. Soon everyone will know what I've known all along. You didn't kill Belinda Critch."

"You knew that all along, huh?"

"Yup." She kissed him again. "And deep in your heart, so did you. Okay, you might wonder why you woke up in your car near O'Keefe's place, but that's no different than a drunk waking up in a jail cell the morning after."

His lips quirked against hers. "Somehow, the comparison doesn't fill me with positive thoughts."

"Give me twenty-four hours of sex, sleep and food, and I'll do better. Getting back to the up side of this story, Patrick's in custody and Critch is—well, hanging on at this point, but he's strong and judging from his past performance, cantankerous enough that he'll want to pull through so he can make sure Patrick pays for killing Belinda. Like I said, all good—with that one small niggle about the cards."

"Romana?"

The voice that hailed her had Romana dropping her forehead onto Jacob's shoulder. "Doesn't anyone stay home anymore?" She raised her head, but didn't turn. "Hello, James."

"How's Fitz?"

"Improving. Her father's with her now."

"You see, darling, I told you we didn't have to rush over here." A bleary-eyed Shera Barret twirled a strand of Romana's hair around her index finger and smiled just a little too widely. "I knew teacher would have it all under control."

Her husband ignored her and spoke to Jacob. "Is it true what I was told about North? He murdered Belinda?"

"Apparently. His statement's being taken now."

"All tied up in a pretty red bow," Shera mocked. Romana caught the strong smell of gin on her breath. "Isn't it wonderful how things work out? Now the handsome detective can get on with his life while the rest of us eat worms, or whatever that stupid expression is."

She probably meant that Patrick's arrest would open a whole new can of worms. Part of that being, Romana assumed, the bribe she'd offered to Gary Canter.

Poor Shera, she loved her husband and wanted him to love her back. But she had absolutely no idea if he did or not.

"Critch is the one I feel sorry for," Shera slurred while James made a futile attempt to shuttle her away. "Married to someone who treated him like that. One affair after another. But as we know," she tapped the side of her nose, "that's how it goes sometimes, right? You love someone enough, you'd do anything to protect him—her—that person."

James forced a smile, gave his wife a firm shove. "We'll offer Fitz's father our best wishes, then be off."

It didn't surprise Romana that Shera fought him. But the crack of her palm across his cheek made everyone blink.

"Stop pulling me along, James. I'm not one of your empty-headed playmates." She jerked free. Tears of frustration and anger welled up. "I love you, you jackass, have since before we got married. But did you ever take the time to notice? Oh." She set a woozy hand on her mouth, drew back and seemed to lose her focus. "I think I'm going to be sick."

Romana located a distant washroom sign and sighed. "Do you want me to come with you?"

"Thank you," James answered for her.

"I'll get some coffee," Jacob offered.

Romana sent him a dry look as Shera stumbled against her arm. "You're a big help, Detective."

"Coffee's to keep us awake, Romana." He brought her fingers to his lips. "Dinner's on me." His eyes caught and held hers. "So's dessert."

Okay, well now she wanted to hurry Shera up.

Nudging the door open, she pointed her toward an empty stall. But Shera, being Shera, balked at the prospect of throwing up in a public restroom.

"It's gross in here." The hand she'd pressed to her mouth fell to her throat in disgust. "The floor's wet. I can't go in there."

"You're a very picky drunk, Shera."

"Not picky." Her eyes filled again. "Don't want to be here. Wouldn't be if we hadn't been having cocktails with James's friend the mayor. It's very hush-hush, you know—Critch being shot, Patrick North being captured. Gotta keep it under wraps until all the wrinkles are ironed out. Make sure the city house is in order, then make the grand announcement. It's all about politics, flash and glitter. Gonna clear a cop's name—goody for the police department. Not bad for the mayor's office, either. But it has to be done so the credit for both clearing and capture translates to votes. I repeat, hush-hush. No one here in the hospital but us mice. No Warren Critch, no killer, no comment."

Romana waited her out, drummed her fingers on the sink. "So are you going to throw up or not? Because I have better things to do, Shera, than stand here and listen to you babble about political secrets, ploys and tactics."

"He's coming for Christmas dinner." Shera stuck out her tongue. "James insisted. We sent the invitations last week, got a flood of cards back saying yes. Mostly from men with ornamental wives."

Cards...

Word triggered question and sent Romana's mind spiraling back to Critch's final declaration.

"Four cards," she echoed, and felt a chill crawl down her spine.

Overhead, the lights flickered. Shera clutched Romana's arm. "What was that?"

"A stutter. Don't worry, the hospital has backup generators."

"Do you think James is seeing someone in Cleveland?"

"You need to ask him that question, not me."

"Did you ask your ex-husband? Is that why he's your ex?"

"We had other problems, Shera. Every marriage is different."

"Like Belinda Critch's marriage?" Shera swayed, gripped the sink. "Why would she want Patrick?"

"I'm not sure she did in the end." Romana indicated the door. "Can we leave now?"

Shera considered the possibility. "Maybe. Not sure yet. I've had four gin fizzes on an empty stomach."

"That's more gross than the wet floor."

The lights flickered again and made Shera groan. "Don't do this. I hate blackouts. Oh…" She teetered sideways, pressed a hand to her stomach. "Maybe I should check out that other stall before we wind up in the dark."

Lovely, Romana thought. She had the prospect of hot sex waiting for her right outside the door, plenty to celebrate—minus one disquieting question—and here she was in a hospital washroom with a woman whose stomach was taking exception to an overdose of gin fizzes.

Sometimes a situation just plain sucked.

THE LIGHTS DIMMED TWICE, but stayed on. Sensing that Shera would prolong the drama as long as possible, Jacob drained his coffee and backhanded Barret's shoulder.

"When Romana comes out, tell her I'm having a chat with Patrick North."

"If she comes out." Barret plucked a thread from his coat. "Shera can be difficult."

"Romana handles difficult better than anyone I know. Give them five minutes."

Which didn't give him a lot of time to talk to Patrick, because the moment Romana reappeared he wanted to get the hell out of here. Maybe they'd have dinner in a restaurant, or maybe they'd order in—after he made love to her about five times.

"Evening, Detective Knight." The guard on Patrick's door took a huge bite from his take-out burger.

Jacob scanned the corridor as the lights dimmed again. "Where do you put it all, Jefferson?"

"Call me Hollow Man." He cocked a thumb. "North's awake and pissed off. If you're searching for some inventive new ways to swear, he's your man."

"Should be interesting."

Patrick glared when Jacob entered. He wore sterile blue, and his arm was taped to his chest in an immobile sling.

"You know where you can go, Knight."

"Been there and back." He halted at the foot of the bed, left his hands in his jacket pockets. "Why did you kill her?"

Patrick's lip curled. "What, no good cop, bad cop routine?"

Jacob kept his eyes steady on the other man's face. "Captain says you made a full confession. Anything you tell me won't make much difference."

Patrick picked at his bandages. "The cops'll go through my house, won't they?"

"From cellar to attic. They'll talk to your neighbors, too." He added the soft sting. "And Fitz."

A disgusted sound emerged. "You knew her. You went out with her."

"Before she married Critch, yeah."

"She was a siren."

Not from Jacob's perspective, but people saw things differently. "Did you have an affair?"

Patrick launched a visual spear. "Of course we did, for five months. I loved her, and we were hot, like fire. She was going to leave Warren."

"Did she say that?"

"No, but I can read between the lines."

"What happened?"

"She didn't do it. For whatever reason, she came in to work one day and said it was over. We were done. I think he threatened her."

"Is that what she told you?"

"Well, hardly," Patrick scoffed. "She claimed she loved him, said she was tired of proving herself to herself. Warren loved her, she loved him, and we were done."

"So you killed her?"

Disdain twisted his mouth. "Not then, no. I told you, I loved her. I gave her space, let her think. I figured he must have brainwashed her. I thought if I didn't see her, she'd start to miss me. When she didn't, I got a little—well, steamed. I confronted her." The fingers of his good hand curled around his gown. "She laughed at me." He glowered at the bedsheets. "I don't like it when people do that. Mortician's son, mother who works in the morgue—kids figured maybe my name was really Igor."

"We were talking about you and Belinda, Patrick."

"It's my dime, Knight. I'll say what I want to."

The room lights went out completely, then snapped back on.

Patrick's eyes heated up. "Brainwashed or not, she laughed at me. Then she told me to leave." He smiled. "So I did."

"Just like that?"

"Exactly like that. I gave her another chance, of course, and another. But she kept saying she loved him. She wouldn't listen to reason, and it made me mad, so I threatened her."

"Did you have any idea that she was pregnant?"

"I—no, at least not until I did the autopsy."

"Which Gorman signed as his own work."

"He'd sign pretty much anything I gave him at that point. I didn't forge his signature like Hanson did, if that's what you're wondering." Patrick's brow furrowed. "I didn't expect her to be pregnant."

"Was it your child?"

"No idea. Maybe. She never said and she couldn't have told her husband because he never mentioned it…" Lost in thought, he scratched his fingernails over the bandages in the region of his heart. "I didn't mean to hurt her, but she said she had no feelings left for me, not even friendly ones." Red blotches stained his cheeks. "I knew she was lying, but I couldn't help myself. I used her own gun on her. It wasn't registered. She'd gotten it for protection when Warren wasn't home. One shot, and it was done.

"I thought I'd fall apart. I mean, I started to, but then I didn't. I put everything right. I do autopsies. I knew what had to be done. I cleaned the place, and I left. I thought maybe I'd screwed up somewhere. I kept waiting for the cops to come and arrest me. But they never did. And Stubbs and Canter only went through the motions."

"So where does Fitz come into this?"

Patrick made a dismissive motion. "I thought she knew the truth, thought she'd figured it out, when all she really wanted was to ask me some dumb question about James Barret and a watch. It sounded like she knew something, just like it did when Critch showed up tonight. But I'm told I was wrong about him, too."

He fell back against the pillow, stared blankly at the ceiling. "They called me Igor. Can you believe that?"

When he began to hum a Christmas song, Jacob decided it was time to leave. At the door, however, he turned his head and offered a quiet, "Why the mistletoe leaves?"

Patrick's lips moved, but he merely continued to sing.

That's when the lights went out.

Chapter Eighteen

"I won't be sick. I won't, I won't, I won't."

The bathroom lights flickered several times, prompting Romana to push off from the sink.

"Okay, that's it, Shera. We're leaving, or I am."

Shera angled her jaw in defiance. "I'm not going to see your cousin."

"Leaving, Shera, now."

She took the woman's hand, pulled. But the lights snapped off completely, and this time they didn't pop back on.

"Wonderful." Romana kept them both moving. "Night's just getting better and better."

"You said there were emergency generators."

"For the vital areas, not out-of-the-way bathrooms. Ouch." Shera kicked her heel. "You don't have to drape yourself all over me, okay? I won't abandon you."

"He always does."

"I'm not your husband." Romana located the wall, but not the door.

"I—oh!" Shera slipped, clutched at Romana's coat, then gave a yelp and went down.

"Shera?' Romana crouched, slashed a hand across the low shadows. "Where are you?"

A moan was her only answer.

The door opened behind her and a weak shaft of light filtered in. She saw Shera's face, saw her lips move, her eyelids flutter.

"Sher—ah-h-h…"

Romana emitted a painful gasp as someone's hand tangled in her hair and gave it a vicious yank. The hand—it had to be a man's—hauled her roughly to her feet, snapped her head back and her body up against his.

Yes, definitely a man…

She glimpsed a red suit and whiskers and saw a quick flash of teeth. Then his other hand came up, and an even greater pain sliced through her skull.

She heard a soft, icy chuckle as the washroom faded to black.

JACOB LEFT PATRICK'S ROOM at a jog. He wasn't sure why, but he knew he had to get to Romana.

He punched O'Keefe's number into his cell as he went. The service said O'Keefe was away from his phone.

The emergency lights came on, making the corridors navigable, but many of the patients were nervous and plucked at Jacob's jacket and jeans.

Barret wasn't where he'd left him. Had he taken Shera and left? Jacob glanced back. Could he have missed Romana along the way?

Not a chance. She was far too striking to be missed, especially tonight in her long red coat, black boots and scarf.

Outside the washroom, he looked around. No one paid any attention to him. Drawing his gun, he knocked, glanced around again, then pushed it open. "Romana?"

A groan emerged, followed by a weak, "James?"

Jacob swore as a pale hand came into the light. Holding

the door back, he crouched and helped Shera sit up. "Where's Romana?"

She swallowed, pushed at her hair. "Left with Santa Claus... Really strange."

His light shake of her shoulders belied the knot of fear building inside. "Where is she, Shera?"

"Told you," she mumbled. "Went with Santa Claus." She rubbed her forehead. "Carried her away... I think."

"Santa carried her out?"

"Think. Pretty sure. Might have hit her."

Terror spiked through him. He propped Shera against the door frame. "Orderly."

A young man rushed past. "I'm kinda busy."

Jacob set his sights on the exit. Where the hell was Barret?

He tried O'Keefe's number again on the stairs. Still away from the phone.

Santa Claus. The image took root in his head. Not a jolly version, but a vengeful one. If he hadn't known better, one with Critch's face.

But it wasn't Critch, and he wasn't sure who that left. Except...

Four cards. That's what Romana had told him, what Critch had said to her. He'd sent only four cards.

As he shoved through the fire door and into the lobby, the question that had been nagging Romana now became Jacob's.

If not Critch, who had sent the other two?

ROMANA AWOKE IN A CAR, with her wrists bound and her mouth covered. The tip of a Santa hat bobbed above her. She didn't make a sound, hardly moved, and yet he knew. At a stoplight, he turned and set a finger on his whisker-covered lips.

It was a taunt. With her mouth gagged, she couldn't scream,

and even if she could and did, her head would probably explode.

Slashes of pain attacked her every time the tires hit a rut. She knew she had to get past it, had to beat down her terror and think.

Whoever he was, he hadn't killed her in the hospital. Why? Where was he taking her, and again, why? He wasn't Critch, but he was wearing a disguise. He had a plan. Whatever it was, it couldn't involve fleeing to South America or any other country. He wanted to stay right here.

Did he want her to think he was Critch? Possibly. No, probably.

But Critch was in custody in the hospital, under police guard.

Pain shoved gleeful knives into her brain. The car began to move. More ice ruts, more knives.

What had Shera said? No one knew about Critch and North. Well, yes, some did, but mostly the news of Critch's capture and Patrick's arrest had been contained.

Different approach, then—who did know about it? James and Shera Barret, certainly, the doctors who treated both men, O'Keefe, Jacob and her.

Romana breathed carefully, ordered herself to hover above the pain. If monks could do it, so could she.

Okay, straying now. Focus. Critch. Who besides Warren, who didn't know about tonight's arrests, would have enough anger inside over Belinda's death to want revenge on her and Jacob?

Names glimmered to life, then fizzled out. Only one lit up and held.

Turning her head was agony, but she did it. With the movement, her scarf, which she'd thought was a gag, fell away from her mouth.

The Santa hat bobbed. White gloved fingers gripped the

steering wheel. She saw his face in her mind, had to swallow the fear in her throat before she could utter his name.

When her vocal cords finally cooperated, the best she could do was whisper a soft, "Dylan?"

"I'M TELLING YOU, JACOB, the word's not out yet," O'Keefe shouted at him on his static-filled cell phone. "Harris is keeping a lid on it for now. Mayor's orders."

"Someone's got her, Mick." Jacob shoved through the door to the underground lot where he'd parked. He dug for keys as he ran. "Shera Barret said he was wearing a Santa suit."

"Shera? Dammit, Jacob, her husband knows the mayor…"

But Jacob stopped him. "I ran into Barret in the lobby. It's not him. It has to be Hoag. Motive, means, opportunity—he's got it all. He's had it all from the start. And there's no reason to think he'd know what went down between Critch and North tonight."

O'Keefe went silent. Jacob yanked open his door, started the engine and peeled out. He didn't notice the red envelope on the passenger seat until it fell over. Swearing, he put his phone on speaker and hit the brakes.

"What?" O'Keefe demanded.

Jacob tore into the envelope and drew out the card. It was a drawing of a woman with a rough-cut photograph of Romana's face pasted to it. She was lying in the snow surrounded by mistletoe leaves. The bullet hole in her chest spurted blood. A red arrow indicated that he should open the card.

"What is it, Jacob?" O'Keefe shouted. "Can you hear me?"

"Yeah, I hear you." Eyes glued to the bloody scrawl, Jacob read the words. Then he tossed the card aside and hit the siren. He responded to O'Keefe's repeated demands with a grim, "I know where he took her."

"AND SO WE WAIT, ROMANA, at the scene of the crime."

The tip of Dylan's Santa hat stood straight up thanks to a wind that managed to blow in all directions at once.

Romana's teeth chattered so hard she could scarcely form words, let alone sentences.

"Scene of the crime," Dylan spat again. "Not where Belinda died, although that was one hell of a crime scene, but where Warren should have killed Knight. Where you stopped him from doing it. Where you aided and abetted Belinda's murderer, Officer Grey. The crime that predicated the crime that took my sister's life."

"Jacob didn't shoot her."

He'd tossed her down on a snow-covered trash can. For five long minutes, he'd been storming back and forth in front of her. Now his contempt spewed out in a bark of laughter. "Jacob didn't do it," he mimicked. "Jacob didn't do it. Say It Until You Believe—is that your motto? Man, you're going to wind up so dead."

Was there any point telling him about his brother-in-law?

Romana's lips felt numb. So did her wrists where the ropes dug in.

"Phone the hospital. Better yet, phone Jacob's captain. He'll tell you that both Warren Critch and Patrick North have been arrested and are under police guard."

"Lies. Total bull. You're trying to save yourself and that murdering lover of yours."

She willed her teeth not to clack together. "Critch told me he sent only four cards. He told me that, Dylan, while he was lying shot on the floor in Patrick North's house."

"He wrote four cards," Dylan corrected, "and sent them to me. I rewrote them, drove to Kentucky and mailed them to you. The last two were entirely my own."

"But don't you see, Critch stopped writing them because he suspected…"

"He didn't suspect anything. He wimped out. Prison broke him. Okay, fine, that happens, but it wasn't going to end because his balls up and deserted him." Whipping out a hand, Dylan grabbed the front of her coat and yanked her face up into his. "Tune in, Romana. You're going to die here. Don't let the last thought that ever runs through that pretty head of yours be one of stupid, blind denial."

Behind him, in the region of an ancient market wall, Romana sensed a movement. Didn't see it—even the best eyes couldn't hope to penetrate the curtain of swirling white flakes—but felt certain something within the white shifted position.

Jacob?

"You're right," she agreed before he could release her and turn. "I should have handled the situation differently. But it was my job to help him. That's what we were taught at the Academy, right? Always help an officer in trouble."

"You helped him, all right," he snarled into her face. "You got Warren to back down and made it possible for Knight to kill Belinda two days later. She phoned me after they had lunch. She told me Knight wanted her dead."

"She didn't mean that literally, Dylan. Jacob wouldn't get her a restraining order, so she got angry and…"

"We were a team, Belinda and me." He spoke through his teeth now. Fury and sorrow mingled. Fury won as he gave her a head-snapping shake. "She was all the family I had. I protected her, my beautiful baby sister."

Step-sister, Romana almost said, but held her tongue. Truthfully, it was the only part of this tragedy that had a touching aspect. Belinda had been family. And she'd been taken from him.

The shadow within the snow curtain moved again. Obviously Dylan expected Jacob to show up here. Just as obviously he hadn't expected him to do it so soon.

He shoved her away in disgust, but only executed a half turn.

Romana wriggled forward on the trash can lid. Dylan hadn't bound her ankles, only her wrists behind her back. If she could draw him close again…

Wind slapped at her cheeks and blew her hair around like wild streamers. Dylan paced, a caged animal once more. The movement behind the snow stopped.

"You did all of it, didn't you?" she said. "Critch hid out while you threatened us. Did he even know?"

Dylan cast her a scathing look as he passed. "Warren is a damned ostrich. He saw what he chose to see and did what I, his concerned brother-in-law, encouraged him to do. South America was his best option, better than endless years of parole. Trade a ball and chain for the freedom of his youth. Make a fresh start. Leave the past behind."

"You talked him into jumping parole?"

"And waiting for the false documents I would happily provide."

"He was suspicious of you."

"Oh, more than suspicious. I think he followed me the day I slipped the sixth card into your purse. He never said anything, but then why would he? It wasn't like he could turn me in. Okay, I impersonated him. I was only building on what he'd started. When that prison door clanged shut behind him six years ago, he wanted you and Jacob dead."

"But he mellowed."

"No, he melted. He went all soft and gooey. Didn't matter,

I was there to take up the slack. It'll all come out as it should when Knight gets here. You die, he dies, Warren escapes to South America and I go on—the grieving brother who wasn't stupid enough, despite what his Academy instructors believed, to let himself be followed or his tapped phone rat him out."

Romana caught a glimpse of Jacob then, in her peripheral vision. It had to be Jacob. She knew how he moved. She also knew that Dylan was pumped on adrenaline and not about to be taken down easily.

She wriggled forward a little more, knew she was close to the edge of the frozen can.

Keep talking, she told herself. Forget fear and pain. Think of Jacob. Think of something.

She pitched her voice low while still pretending to shout. "Aren't you worried that someone will see you here, Dylan?"

"What?"

"What?" she called back.

Pent-up frustration made his movements jerky. He swung toward her at the exact moment she gave her butt one last twist on the lid.

"What are you…?" he began, then growled as the can toppled sideways and sent her tumbling onto a snowy mound.

When he reached down to snatch her upright, she rolled onto her back and planted her foot squarely in his groin.

The world clicked into surreal mode after that. She knew Jacob flew through the white curtain—she saw the blur of black leather and denim, spied the gun in his hand.

"He's got three guns," she managed to shout. "And a knife."

Dylan's foot narrowly missed her head as he flailed. Using the heel of her boot, she spiked his calf.

In spite of everything, he got a hand inside his Santa suit

and drew a gun. The same gun Critch had held on Jacob seven years ago?

Jacob tackled him before he could take aim. The gun discharged. Dylan grunted like an animal. With one hand clutching his crotch, he grabbed a second gun from his waistband.

"Jacob!"

The only target Romana had was Dylan's butt. She used the toe of her boot to spear him, then ducked as the weapon flew out of his hand.

"It's over, Hoag." In an anchored crouch, Jacob held him at gunpoint. "Don't be stupid."

Desperate, Dylan scrambled back and grabbed Romana's ankle. Although she tried to kick free, he held fast.

"You won't do it, Knight." A third gun appeared and pointed at Romana's head. "But I will."

Romana squirmed and fought. Driving snow blinded her. She heard a shot. Then another. Dylan emitted one of his barking laughs. Her heart stuttered, almost stopped.

But she wasn't dead. So…

"Jacob!'"

Dylan's laugh became a gurgle. The hand on her ankle relaxed its grip. She kicked free and bumped herself upright. "Jacob?"

"Right here." He sounded winded as he dropped to his knees beside her.

"Are you…?" Without her hands, she couldn't check him for bullet holes. "Did he shoot you?"

"Shot at me. Missed." Still breathing hard, he pulled a knife from his pocket and sliced the ropes on her wrists.

She started to throw her arms around his neck, but dug her fingers into his shoulders instead. "Where is he?"

Jacob moved his head. Romana moved her eyes. The crumpled heap that was Dylan didn't move at all.

There was no need to ask. She saw the blood and knew.

"Oh, God." Dropping her head onto his shoulder, she let reaction set in.

While Dylan's blood turned the snow and two protruding sprigs of mistletoe beneath him red.

Chapter Nineteen

"You are so, so lucky, Romana."

By Tuesday morning, Fitz was sitting cross-legged in her hospital room, pigging out on Christmas candy and eager to hear every gory detail Romana could relate. Could remember. Because most of the rest of Sunday and a great deal of Monday were jumbled together in a wind-whipped haze.

"So Dylan's dead, right?" Fitz asked.

"As the proverbial doornail." Romana sighed. "I don't mean to sound cold, but he did everything in his power to kill Jacob and me, and he didn't seem to care who else might get hurt along the way."

"He had a mission," Fitz translated. "Avenge Belinda's death. Just like Warren Critch."

"Except that Critch's conviction wavered and Dylan's didn't." Leaning over her cousin's folded legs, Romana selected a chocolate cherry from the box. "Critch regained consciousness last night and gave a brief statement. He did follow Dylan when Dylan slipped me the sixth card, so he knew what was going on. I guess he couldn't live with it, because he tried to intervene. He left a note in the lobby of my building warning us about Dylan. It was too cryptic to make a whole lot of sense at the time, but in retrospect, I can see it."

"So Critch gave you that even though he didn't know who'd killed his wife. He only knew he didn't think it was Jacob Knight anymore."

"I think he also understood by then that grief had driven Dylan insane."

"That's sad, isn't it?"

"Once you get past the horror, it really is."

"What about Belinda being pregnant? Do you think Dylan knew?"

"I don't think anyone knew—except Dr. Gorman, and Belinda didn't mean to tell him. On a less somber note, I heard some gossip about your dad's employer."

"I'm all ears, Ro."

"You remember I told you that James was supposed to be in Cleveland about the time you went missing? Well, he did in fact go there—via Columbus. He was checking out rehab facilities for your father. He figures your dad deserves the best, and that's what he's going to get."

"No affair?"

"Not on that trip. Possibly not at all. But that's for James and Shera to hash out. Your job is to get better."

"I'll work on it, after I hear more gory details. All I have so far is that Dylan's dead. What's Critch's prognosis?"

"He's improving. The doctors are optimistic."

"Did he know about everything Dylan was doing?"

"Possibly—on some level." Romana summoned a half-hearted smile. "When worlds collide…"

"No kidding. So Dylan figured he could kill you and Jacob, send Critch off to South America with fake ID, and just carry on with his life as before. Everyone would think Critch had fulfilled his promise, and no one would ever see or hear from him again. Story over."

"That was the plan. Not sure how he thought he'd get out of that alley Sunday night, but, hey, insanity makes its own rules, right?"

"And Patrick?"

Romana's expression softened. "I'm really sorry about him, Fitz. He's, well—not well."

"Man, can I pick 'em or what?"

"Huh, I married Connor. No one can top that blunder."

Fitz snickered. "Ain't we a pair, cous'?"

"Mmm."

The snicker transformed into a sly smile. "So, have you and Jacob had sex yet? Was it great? Where's it going for you two?"

Laughing, Romana leaned forward and kissed her cheek. "None of your business." Then she smiled and added a teasing, "Yes, yes, and I don't know. However," she tapped Fitz's leg, "now that the dust's more or less settled, I think it's time I found out."

NIGHT FELL AS IT ALWAYS DID. The blizzard moved on. Only the cold remained—and a legion of last-minute Christmas shoppers.

O'Keefe had been badgering him for information nonstop since Sunday. Harris hadn't been much better. He'd seen Romana exactly twice since Dylan's death, and for no more than thirty minutes at a time.

Dropping his head onto the back of his chair, Jacob listened to the elevator door swish open and waited for O'Keefe's voice. He had one hour before Harris wanted him at headquarters, no doubt for another round of questioning.

He caught the scent of her skin first but didn't have time to react before her hair fell over his cheek.

"I believe, Detective, that the last words you spoke to me came in the form of a promise—one, to call me and, two, to hunt me down and make love to me until we were both unconscious." Her lips brushed his ear from behind. "My phone hasn't rung once today."

"Uh-huh, well, you might want to check your battery."

The tease in her voice strengthened. "Oh, good, you're in a funk. I love it when you go all dark and broody."

Something cinched inside him. He drank a mouthful of coffee, kept his eyes on the city lights. "You have no idea, Romana, what my father was like. What I could be like and not know it yet."

Undeterred, she circled his chair and made herself at home on his lap. "If you were half the monster you're afraid you are, you'd have shown signs of it long before now. You deal with your anger, I've seen you do it. And don't forget," she traced the outline of his lips with a light finger, "I have a wicked kick to the crotch in my repertoire."

Amusement kindled in spite of everything. "Have you ever not taken risks?"

"Grandma Grey says life would suck if we did that. Answer's no," she added with a twinkle. "On an up note, Fitz is fine. She's also totally unrepentant about her sticky-fingered past. She lifted the key to Patrick's handcuffs without him feeling a thing."

"So, as a cop, I'm supposed to applaud that?"

"In this case, absolutely." She touched her lips to his. "When do you have to report in?"

"Fifty minutes."

She shifted position on his lap. "Doesn't give us a whole lot of time, does it? You could call in sick. Harris would understand."

"Anyone who's met you would understand."

"There you go then, problem solved. Except…"

He wouldn't let her coax a smile out of him. Yet. "Except what?"

"You haven't done your Christmas tree."

"I've been a little busy."

"Me, too. And Fitz. So here's my plan." She kissed him twice, then caught his lower lip. "We'll take all three trees to Grandma Grey's and make our own mini tree farm there. Her ranch is huge. We're all going down for Christmas—my brothers and their families, Fitz and her father, my parents. And before you whip out the standard lame objection, I happen to know you don't have any plans."

"O'Keefe…"

"Playing poker with O'Keefe and three other single cops is no way to spend Christmas Day. New Year's Day, no problem, but Christmas is family, and you're getting one this year, like it or not. O'Keefe, too, if he wants to come."

Jacob quirked an eyebrow at her. "Are you going to run that spiel past Harris, or do I have to try and repeat whatever it was you just said?"

"The running's done. Harris has four kids. He understands Christmas very well. Now, think suitcases and snowballs because you're off the clock for the next fifteen days."

Dubious surprise shimmered through him. "You want me to spend two weeks on your grandmother's ranch?"

"Well, no." She played with the ends of his hair. "I thought after Christmas we could go skiing—if you ski. And if you don't, there are other activities we could pursue. Life's all about unexpected adventures and enjoying the journey. Did Mark Twain say that? Anyway, enjoyment is the point, and I think we should strive to achieve as much of it as possible, don't you?"

"I see why you teach."

"And I see why you're still a cop—a very hot, very sexy cop whom I'm going to jump after I ask him one more question."

"We'll see who jumps who, but shoot."

"Why did Patrick surround Belinda with mistletoe leaves?"

"Ah."

Her fingers worked at the buttons of his shirt. "Could you be a bit more specific?"

"Long or short version?"

She twisted on his lap and sent a bolt of desire through his entire body. "Short and simple's fine."

"He didn't put the leaves around her, she did."

"Okay, maybe a little less simple."

"When Patrick came to the house, Belinda was hanging mistletoe in the living room. They argued, she told him to leave. She said she had no feelings for him. To prove it, she stripped off the leaves and tossed the bare branch at him."

"There was no significance to it at all?"

"None."

"So Dylan was going to shoot us and sprinkle mistletoe leaves around our dead bodies, and he didn't even know why?"

"He made a false assumption." The light of anticipation gleamed as he unsnapped her jeans. "It happens. Are you sure you cleared this Christmas thing with Harris?"

"Yes, Detective. His orders were for you to enjoy yourself. He also mentioned a ladder and some rungs you're going to be climbing very soon, but that part went over my head."

"The rungs are in his dreams."

"Forget his dreams." She stopped her mouth a tempting inch away from his. "Think about mine. And yours. Think with your heart, Jacob."

"Already have," he told her. And, capturing her lips, let the last of his nightmares scatter in the night wind.

* * * * *

SPECIAL EDITION

Life, Love and Family

*These contemporary romances will strike a chord
with you as heroines juggle life
and relationships on their way to true love.*

New York Times *bestselling author Linda Lael Miller
brings you a BRAND-NEW contemporary story
featuring her fan-favorite McKettrick family.*

Meg McKettrick is surprised to be reunited with her
high school flame, Brad O'Ballivan. After enjoying a
career as a country-and-western singer, Brad aches for
a home and family...and seeing Meg again makes him
realize he still loves her. But their pride manages to
interfere with love...until an unexpected matchmaker
gets involved.

*Turn the page for a sneak preview of
THE McKETTRICK WAY
by Linda Lael Miller
On sale November 20
wherever books are sold.*

Brad shoved the truck into gear and drove to the bottom of the hill, where the road forked. Turn left, and he'd be home in five minutes. Turn right, and he was headed for Indian Rock.

He had no damn business going to Indian Rock.

He had nothing to say to Meg McKettrick, and if he never set eyes on the woman again, it would be two weeks too soon.

He turned right.

He couldn't have said why.

He just drove straight to the Dixie Dog Drive-In.

Back in the day, he and Meg used to meet at the Dixie Dog, by tacit agreement, when either of them had been away. It had been some kind of universe thing, purely intuitive.

Passing familiar landmarks, Brad told himself he ought to turn around. The old days were gone. Things had ended badly between him and Meg anyhow, and she wasn't going to be at the Dixie Dog.

He kept driving.

He rounded a bend, and there was the Dixie Dog. Its big neon sign, a giant hot dog, was all lit up and going through its corny sequence—first it was covered in red squiggles of light, meant to suggest ketchup, and then yellow, for mustard.

Brad pulled into one of the slots next to a speaker, rolled down the truck window and ordered.

A girl roller-skated out with the order about five minutes later.

When she wheeled up to the driver's window, smiling, her eyes went wide with recognition, and she dropped the tray with a clatter.

Silently Brad swore. Damn if he hadn't forgotten he was a famous country singer.

The girl, a skinny thing wearing too much eye makeup, immediately started to cry. "I'm sorry!" she sobbed, squatting to gather up the mess.

"It's okay," Brad answered quietly, leaning to look down at her, catching a glimpse of her plastic name tag. "It's okay, Mandy. No harm done."

"I'll get you another dog and a shake right away, Mr. O'Ballivan!"

"Mandy?"

She stared up at him pitifully, sniffling. Thanks to the copious tears, most of the goop on her eyes had slid south. "Yes?"

"When you go back inside, could you not mention seeing me?"

"But you're Brad O'Ballivan!"

"Yeah," he answered, suppressing a sigh. "I know."

She rolled a little closer. "You wouldn't happen to have a picture you could autograph for me, would you?"

"Not with me," Brad answered.

"You could sign this napkin, though," Mandy said. "It's only got a little chocolate on the corner."

Brad took the paper napkin and her order pen, and scrawled his name. Handed both items back through the window.

She turned and whizzed back toward the side entrance to the Dixie Dog.

Brad waited, marveling that he hadn't considered incidents like this one before he'd decided to come back home. In retrospect, it seemed shortsighted, to say the least, but the truth was, he'd expected to be—Brad O'Ballivan.

Presently Mandy skated back out again, and this time she managed to hold on to the tray.

"I didn't tell a soul!" she whispered. "But Heather and Darlene *both* asked me why my mascara was all smeared." Efficiently she hooked the tray onto the bottom edge of the window.

Brad extended payment, but Mandy shook her head.

"The boss said it's on the house, since I dumped your first order on the ground."

He smiled. "Okay, then. Thanks."

Mandy retreated, and Brad was just reaching for the food when a bright red Blazer whipped into the space beside his. The driver's door sprang open, crashing into the metal speaker, and somebody got out in a hurry.

Something quickened inside Brad.

And in the next moment Meg McKettrick was standing practically on his running board, her blue eyes blazing.

Brad grinned. "I guess you're not over me after all," he said.